MAIN LIBRARY
STO

ALLEN COUNTY PUBLIC LIBRARY

3 1833 00492 1414

S0-BWM-873

FICTION
KURLAND, MICHAEL.   2298371
STAR GRIFFIN

**DO NOT REMOVE
CARDS FROM POCKET**

ALLEN COUNTY PUBLIC LIBRARY

FORT WAYNE, INDIANA 46802

You may return this book to any agency, branch,
or bookmobile of the Allen County Public Library.

DEMCO

Star Griffin

Star Griffin

MICHAEL KURLAND

DOUBLEDAY & COMPANY, INC.

GARDEN CITY, NEW YORK

1987

All of the characters in this book
are fictitious, and any resemblance
to actual persons, living or dead,
is purely coincidental.

Allen County Public Library
Ft. Wayne, Indiana

Library of Congress Cataloging-in-Publication Data

Kurland, Michael.
Star Griffin.

I. Title.
PS3561.U647S7 1987   813'.54   86-19869
ISBN: 0-385-19395-5

Copyright © 1987 by Michael Kurland
All Rights Reserved
Printed in the United States of America
First Edition

This book is for Tony Sabatini,
who is truly a friend;
and for Varya DuCormier,
likewise.

2298371

I would like to thank Randall Garrett for his invaluable assistance in the plotting and writing of this book.

*But as a rule the ancient myths are not found to yield
A simple and consistent story, so that nobody need
Wonder if details of my recension cannot be reconciled
With those given by every poet and historian.*

Diodorus Siculus
Book IV, 44: 5, 6

Star Griffin

ONE

The evening ended with a bang.
With a bang.
With a triple bang.

Morning. Dawn up like silent thunder. The wall chirped incessantly, demanding attention. Peter ignored the wall. His hand reached out along the crumpled sheet, the tousled pillow, to find nothing. Nothing? His arm scythed the area. Nobody. No body. No human female body.

He opened his eyes. She wasn't there. The eyes focused on dull hotel-green walls and saw:

Item: one thin crack from left to right, fifteen or twenty centimeters long and straight as truth.

Item: three walls, flat and bilious green, without the slightest smudge or dust film.

Item: The chirping stopped. Had the wall decided to let him sleep? Had legal morning not yet come to the hotel's symbol-minded computer? Then why the chirp?

The green walls faded as his sleep-filmed eyes shuttered once more—
—and she returned. Essence of musk and flowers and short clouds of breath. Lips pursed, eyes shiny-moist, she came in morningdream. Like some gloriously multidimensional being, he became both horizontal and erect.

zzz-z-Z-ZZ-ZZZOOTT-T-t-ttt

His eyes snapped open again. Double goddamn. The telly. The blasted telly! Morning had arrived with its usual total disregard for one's own wishes in the matter, the telly-port had slid open with its inevitable ugly noise, and the double-goddamn telly was bright with cheery color. Half a wall full of clouds and sky, and the ultrabright, realer-than-real out-of-doors. Goddamn, goddamn, lewdly sing goddamn!

GOOD MORNING.

Blah!

THE NORTH THAILAND MERCANTILE UNIVERSAL CREDIT FACILITY, THE LARGEST BANK IN RATCHASIMA AND THE ONLY BANK IN THE SEMISPHERE WITH FULL-CREDIT REVERSIBILITY, BRINGS YOU "THIS MORNING!"

Double-blasted blah. Not the way to achieve consciousness, not the way at all. If they can send a man to the moons of Jupiter, to the craters of Mercury, they should be able to figure out a way to awaken one a little more gently. Whoever they were. He rolled over and buried his head in the nearest pillow.

"THIS MORNING" IS COMING TO YOU FROM LIMA, PERU, THIS MORNING, HALFWAY AROUND THE WORLD FROM RATCHASIMA.

They would have him believe he was in Ratchasima. And so he was. A good solid fact to ignore.

GOOD MORNING.

Now, that was unfair. The very male voice that had awakened him was gone. In its stead had come the essence of female voices; mellifluous and sweet and promising. A sister to last night. Last night— Slim and lithe, she had lain beside, beneath, above; her hands, her lips—

—TELL YOU OF THE EXCITEMENT HERE IN LIMA, WHERE IT IS EIGHT IN THE EVENING. THE BALLOON IS ABOUT TO GO UP!

They rose together on the mind-link cushion of bodysoul and melded parts, as link-by-link their fingers, arms, and shoulders, toes and knees and thighs; areas of sweat-slick, matted hairskin met cm^2 by cm^2 with glistening smooth-brown, silk-lean, and pairs of muscles tightened in desire.

JUDITH SAINT-JOAN PFEIFFER IS ON VACATION TODAY. THIS IS LYDIA FRAME, AND THIS IS "THIS MORNING."

SLOW PAN across an open field somewhere outside Lima, Peru. LYDIA FRAME can now be seen in the half-distance and, behind her and slightly to the left rises the massive minusbulk of *Montgolfier Revisited*, tugging at the anchored gondola below. The camera zooms in on the reverse teardrop of the balloon until it fills the whole screen.

IN JUST NINE MINUTES NOW, IF THE COUNTDOWN CONTINUES AS SCHEDULED, THE MOMENT OF LAUNCH WILL ARRIVE. THERE SHE IS, FOLK, FILLING YOUR HOME SCREEN NOW. ISN'T SHE BEAUTIFUL? WE'LL CONTINUE OUR COVERAGE OF THIS GREAT ANTI-HISTORIC EVENT IN A MOMENT—BUT FIRST A BRIEF SCENE OF A COMMERCIAL NATURE FROM THE NETWORK.

MUSIC OVER AS THE SCENE SHIFTS TO:

CLOSE-UP of an obviously masculine hand caressing the outside of an obviously feminine thigh. As the hand moves up, over the swell of the hip, along the side, and toward the breast, a VOICE comes over the music:

LOVELY TO TOUCH, LOVELY TO LOOK AT. HOW LOVELY TO BE *HER* AT THIS MOMENT. AND YOU *COULD* BE—FOR *HER* SKIN COULD BE *YOUR* SKIN.

FAST ZOOM IN UNTIL THE ENTIRE SCREEN IS FLESH-PINK, FOLLOWED BY FAST ZOOM OUT TO CLOSE-UP OF: an obviously feminine hand holding a tall cylindrical bottle. It is almost the same color as the hand, except for the bright red cap and the bright red label on the side, which says:

GENOGLO

GENOGLO SKIN CREAM IS NOT JUST FOR YOUR *FACE*; IT IS DESIGNED FOR YOUR WHOLE *BODY*, FOR EVERY SQUARE CENTIMETER OF YOUR SKIN, TO MAKE A LOVELIER *YOU*, A MORE *YOUTH*FUL YOU. THE SPECIALLY DESIGNED RNA MESSENGERS IN *GENOGLO* ARE SPECIFICALLY MATCHED TO YOUR OWN DNA CODE TO KEEP YOUR SKIN AS ALIVE AND YOUTHFUL NOW AS IT WAS AT

SEVENTEEN. MAKE AN APPOINTMENT WITH YOUR BEAUTY BIOCHEM TODAY, SO THAT YOU—AND *HE*—CAN ENJOY THE SKIN YOU DESERVE.

CLOSE-UP of an obviously masculine hand gently spreading smooth, creamy GENOGLO over the inside of an obviously feminine thigh.

Damn. He rolled over to the edge of the bed and groped around the catskin carpet. The remote must have slid, rolled, crawled, or oozed out of reach. He lay still, his nose jutting out over the side of the bed.

A LARGE NUMBER "4" appears in the center of the screen. Strong primary colors throb in and out of it in time with the human heartbeat. And over:

[Dynamic male VOICE through three powerfilters:]

SATWEB FOUR.
SATWEB FOUR—FOR TRUTH.
SATWEB FOUR—FOR HUMOR.
SATWEB FOUR—FOR ENTERTAINMENT.
SATWEB FOUR—FOR NEWS.
SEVENTY-THREE PERCENT OF THE HUMAN RACE, FROM THE FOUR POINTS COLONIES TO THE MOONS OF SATURN, KNOW IT'S SATWEB FOUR . . .
FOUR [echo]
FOUR [echo]
FOUR [echo]
FOUR [echo]
FOUR FOR TOTAL ENVIRONMENT.
SATWEB FOUR!

Go to black.

Blissful silence, praise the lord.

FRIENDS, ARE YOU SUFFERING FROM AN INCURABLE DISEASE?

Peter opened one incredulous eye. An unctuous face smarmed onto the screen and was staring at him.

WE DON'T CARE.

BEHIND THE FACE SUPER: a ticking pendulum.

THE SANDS OF TIME RUN OUT FOR ALL OF US, SOME SLOWLY AND SOME QUICKLY.

THE PENDULUM speeds up imperceptibly through this.

THIS IS SO NOW AS IT HAS ALWAYS BEEN. BUT, FOR THE FIRST TIME IN HUMAN HISTORY, THERE IS HOPE. HOPE FOR YOU, HOPE FOR ME, HOPE FOR ANY OF US WITH FOURTEEN DOLLARS, U.S., A MONTH. *[SUPER: VOICE:* THREE HUNDRED AND TWENTY BAHT A MONTH.]

THE TICKING can now be heard.

UNIVERSAL PARAMOUNT LIFE ASSURANCE GROUP OFFERS HOPE FOR EXTENDED LIFE—AND PERHAPS A GRASP AT IMMORTALITY—FOR BUT FOURTEEN DOLLARS, U.S., A MONTH. THE NEW FREEZE-A-BOD PROGRAM COSTS BUT FOURTEEN DOLLARS A MONTH FOR THE AVERAGE HUMAN OF THIRTY-FIVE YEARS IN GOOD HEALTH. TERMS WILL VARY WITH ACTUARIAL AND PHYSICAL CONDITIONS, OCCUPATION, HEREDITY, LOCAL ECOLOGY, TARGETABILITY, DEMONIC POSSESSION, AND OTHER SPECIAL RISK CONDITIONS.

THE TICKING is louder.

IS YOUR TIME RUNNING OUT?
IS YOUR CLOCK RUNNING DOWN?
OR WILL IT STOP—SHORT—NEVER TO RUN AGAIN BEFORE YOU HAVE MADE PROVISIONS FOR THE FUTURE? *YOUR* FUTURE?
ASSURE YOUR FUTURE NOW THROUGH ETERNITY.
WRITE TODAY TO FREEZE-A-BOD, HAMBURG, SIXTEEN, NINE-OH-THREE, BUD TWENTY-SIX, OR CALL FOUR-TWO-SIX-TWO, EIGHT MILLION.
FREEZE-A-BOD.

NO SALESMAN WILL CALL.
FREEZE-A-BOD.

FADE THROUGH TO: close-up shot of gasbag of Montgulfier Revisited.

HELLO AGAIN. LYDIA FRAME BACK WITH "THIS MORN-ING." FIVE MINUTES NOW UNTIL THE BALLOON GOES UP. THE CROWD IS BEGINNING TO FLOW RESTLESSLY. AMONG THE MANY DIGNITARIES HERE TODAY ARE THE PREXY OF PERU, THE KINGS OF SPAIN AND MEXICO, THE GOV. OF CALIFORNIA, AND MANY OTHER WELL-KNOWN ENTERTAINERS AND PUBLIC FIGURES. I SEE THAT BLIP-PING MAGNATE GILES ARES IS HERE WITH HIS LOVELY DAUGHTER LEDA. THAT'S THEM ON YOUR HOME SCREEN NOW. THE ONE ON THE LEFT IS LEDA. I'M NOT SURE WHO THE LADY ON DON GILES'S RIGHT IS. MY, SHE'S PRETTY, ISN'T SHE?

Peter opened both eyes. My right, he wondered, or stage right? Both ladies were beautiful.

Full night and empty bed, he told himself. Helluva thing. The trouble with *karava* was that it took an hour to turn one on, and twelve hours to fade away. Genuine imported mushroom wine. Essence of fine old fungus. Flavor of truffles and mead. She'd bought it herself, picking one brand carefully from the selection in the super-duper.

"It's really very nice, Mr. Peterlyon." Running the words together, proud that she could pronounce the strange English name properly, her lilting Thai tongue tripping a birdsong around the foreign syllables.

Two glasses of *karava* and much conversation. Two more and much less conversation. A third brace of *karava,* and no conversation whatsoever, only moans and cries of passion and the heat of two bodies.

And she was gone with the dawn, leaving only the empty *karava* bottle standing erect by the bed and lingering traces of sweetness and warmth. And it was tomorrow, and he had to get up.

LET'S JUST SEE IF THAT CAMERA IN THE GONDOLA IS WORKING PROPERLY.

SCENE SWITCHES TO INSIDE OF GONDOLA. WIDE-ANGLE LENS PICKS UP THREE WISE MEN OF GO-THAM AS THEY MAKE FINAL PREPARATIONS FOR THE ASCENT. The nearest, a fine-looking, portly man with a snow-white beard clipped straight across a foot below his chin, is painting a large circle surrounded by cabalistic signs in watercolor on his ample belly. He is garbed in knee-length riding boots, polo gloves, and nothing else. To his right, a young man sporting a handsome walrus mustache and dressed like an RFC flying ace, vintage 1917, is doing sit-ups on the cabin floor. Behind these two, sitting on a steel-frame cot, Napoleon Bonaparte stares fitfully at the camera eye. He is scratching his chest.

SCENE SWITCHES BACK TO FIELD. Three men with fire axes are running around the balloon, cutting the myriad ropes that anchor it to the field. They are being ineffectually chased by two men in the powder-red uniforms of the Hemispheric Police.

WELL, LADIES AND GENTLEMEN, IT LOOKS AS THOUGH THE BALLOON IS GOING TO GO UP THREE MINUTES EARLIER THAN PLANNED. AS YOU CAN SEE, A GROUP OF VANDALS HAVE LEAPT THE BARRICADE AND ARE SEVERING THE TIES THAT BIND. IT IS NOT CLEAR AT THIS TIME WHETHER THESE ARE INDEPENDENT VANDALS OR MEMBERS OF THE LEAGUE. WE ARE TRYING TO FIND THAT OUT FOR YOU NOW.

[With a sudden loud cracking sound, the balloon thrusts itself skyward.]

WOW. WASN'T THAT IMPRESSIVE? I HOPE NONE OF YOU MISSED THAT. THE BALLOON SEEMS TO HAVE PULLED ITSELF FREE OF THE LAST FEW MOORING LINES, AND IS STARTING ITS JOURNEY. [Lydia holds her ear.] WHAT? WHAT WAS THAT? JOLLY-O! LET'S SEE IF WE CAN GET IT IN CLOSE-UP.

The camera zooms in on the slowly rising balloon, then pans gradually down, past the gondola, to the dangling mooring lines.

YES—THERE IT IS! OR, I SHOULD SAY, THERE *HE* IS. YOU CAN JUST MAKE HIM OUT. [Camera jumps to close-up with telephoto lens.] THAT'S BETTER. HE SEEMS TO BE DANGLING FROM ONE OF THE ROPES. OH, EXCUSE ME— *LINES.* YES, HE IS. HE'S CAUGHT BY HIS LEFT FOOT, MY DIRECTOR TELLS ME. I THINK WE CAN SEE THAT. IT'S ONE OF THE VANDALS NOW GOING ALONG FOR THE RIDE. WHAT A SERENDIPITOUS EVENT! WHAT CLASS!

WE SEE the gondola from what seems to be a worm's-eye view. It seems to expand and contract rhythmically as the cameraman tries to keep his zoom lens focused on the rapidly ascending bulk of the *Montgolfier Revisited.*

SOMETHING SEEMS TO HAVE HAPPENED TO THE EQUIPMENT IN THE GONDOLA. WE ARE TRYING TO GET YOU A PICTURE FROM THE INSIDE OF THE *MONTGOLFIER REVISITED,* BUT WE ARE GETTING NO RESPONSE ON EITHER AUDIO OR VIDEO.

[The wind has caught the balloon now, and it begins to drift slowly toward the west, glowing like a mass of molten copper in the red-orange rays of a sun that is already below the horizon.]

IT'S GOING UP VERY FAST NOW. FROM HERE ON THE GROUND, IT LOOKS LIKE A SPARK OF ORANGE AGAINST A DARK BLUE SKY.

[SCENE FROM ANOTHER CAMERA: the balloon, looking like a spark of orange against a dark blue sky.] Then:
BACK TO CAMERA ONE: The balloon is easily visible, but the zoom lens has reached its fullest extent, and the *Montgolfier Revisited* is slowly dwindling in size. SUDDENLY IT SEEMS TO STOP AND JERK VIOLENTLY SIDEWAYS, THEN COLLAPSE IN ON ITSELF.

MY GOD! DID YOU SEE THAT? MY GOD! WHAT AN INCREDIBLE THING! IT POPPED! LIKE A—LIKE A BALLOON POPPING! I MEAN, LIKE SOMEBODY POPPED IT WITH A PIN. WITH A GIANT PIN! MY GOD!

THE GONDOLA is dropping now, trailing the shattered balloon above it. The cameraman frantically tries to back off his zoom lens as the gondola fills the screen.

THEN, with the unheard mouthings of Lydia Frame as a background, the gondola splits open, a great pod that scatters its passenger seeds in the air to fall upon the ground beneath.

INTERLUDE

A mob, a whirlpool, a jumble of bright and brilliant colors held static for the moment by the solemn words of the priest. The brocades, the velvets, the satins of wall hangings, altar cloths, and clothing were still during that short time. Even the small breeze through the open windows of the chapel died to nothing, as if to listen.

The twenty-four people before the altar were as statues, draped in cloth of gold, silver lamé, crimson velvet, and purple-and-blue brocade. The only motion was that of the priest's lips as he pronounced the rite with his right hand raised, palm outward.

"Do you solemnly give your pledge, individually and collectively, each to the others, and before this congregation here assembled, that, eschewing all vainglorious desire for offspring and avoiding the evils of procreation, you shall love, each the others, and all amongst you, physically, mentally, and emotionally, without regard to color, age, occupation, wealth, or sex, so long as this Group shall live?"

A slightly ragged chorus: *"We do so pledge."*

"Have you the rings? Please exchange them amongst you. Very good. Now, by the power vested in me by the Great One, by this congregation, and by the state of New Jersey, I now pronounce you men and wives."

A breath of silence. A shout of happiness! While the congregation sang a lively song of joy, the newlyweds helped each other off with their gaudy raiment and trooped out of the chapel to the soft greensward, to celebrate the Total Consummation of their marriage in the next few joyous hours.

TWO

The trip to Bangkok was smooth but eventful. Peter's compartment mate was a small elderly woman with a large umbrella and an even larger vacuum flask which she kept clutched tightly to her ample bosom.

"It's Alf, you see," she confided to Peter in that burst of camaraderie that comes upon some when engaged in anything as novel and adventurous as an hour-long trip on a commuter mono. " 'E's feeling poorly, so I'm taking 'is parts in to be fretted." She displayed the vacuum flask. " 'E's in 'ere."

"Sorry to hear that," Peter said, trying to display the proper amount of interest. His head hurt and he kept re-seeing the vivid, brief close-up of a naked man with a brightly painted belly screaming silently as he fell, and frantically pulling at his D-ring.

("We've lost him," Lydia, the telly lady, had commented sadly.)

"So was Alf," The woman said. "But then 'e's coming on twenty years, so what's the miss?"

"What, indeed," Peter murmured.

She would go on like that for hours—conceivably forever. Hers was a mind that was filled with words and small notions, incapable of producing ideas. The thought processes that generated intelligence had long ago been dried up and stultified—if, indeed, her brain had ever been capable of such processes at all. Like Alf's "parts," her brain was neatly done up in the vacuum of her mind, neatly preserved for all time, nicely protected against all external stimuli, save those that involved food, the telly, or her place in society. Across that interface no new thought could leap in either direction.

Her voice droned on.

Peter's mind was slowly becoming numb, except for one little pixie flame of awareness that stayed aside and watched the infection spread. The vacuum was being transferred to his own brain, his mind being sucked into emptiness by the interminable flow of words.

The isolated pixie flame noted a change in the endless drone and tried to analyze it.

"—and I told 'er as 'ow I'd rather be in Manchester, not but what Bangkok ain't got all the conveniences—shops and the like, you know —but I says to 'er, I says, 'It ain't like 'ome, what with the 'eat and all in the summer, even if it is nice and warm-like in the winter,' which I 'as to admit, it ain't at 'ome, but then even after fifteen years nearly—"

The woman's voice stopped abruptly, but oddly the droning sound continued.

"Gaww!" she said softly, her eyes widening to tarsier globes, staring past Peter's shoulder.

Peter turned to look.

Outside the monorail car, one wingtip only a few meters from the sealed window, was an American B-29 bomber, circa 1943. From tip to tail the pretty little thing measured just about one and a half meters.

There is a theory, which falls in and out of repute with a cyclic rate of about twenty years, that we live in an expanding universe. If so, the past is much smaller than the present.

Peter examined the visitation with interest. It was flying a perfectly even course, paralleling the mono's direction and speed. The gun turrets that blistered the skin had swiveled around until the tiny paired-matchstick machine guns were pointing at the safety glass.

Pingaping apingapinga pingaping.

Matchheads of flame spurted from the top turret, and a thin dotted line peppered across the window. The glass vibrated under the impact, giving off a low-pitched keening sound, but showing no sign of shattering. Nonetheless, Peter retreated into the far corner of the car.

"Tush!" the woman screamed. "Blighted tush! It's those ratty kids again."

The B-29 veered away from the window, to be replaced almost immediately by a Fokker triplane, which made no overt hostile act toward the mono car. Peter could make out the lens of the tiny telly remote that peeped out from the open cockpit of the Fokker.

"Indecent!" the woman yelped. She swung her umbrella at the spy plane, and looked surprised when the brolly bounced off the window.

The Fokker climbed out of sight. "Show 'em, right enough," she muttered.

Blap!

"Watzat?" the old woman yelped suspiciously, glaring at the ceiling.

Peter adjusted his tunic. "Expansion," he explained. "In the sunlight."

"I don't think Alf would like it." She placed the vacuum jug carefully in her lap.

CRABLAM! BLAM!

Something ripped through the ceiling and buried itself in the seat about six centimeters from Peter's hand.

The woman leaped up, screeching like a perturbed bat. The vacuum bottle in her lap spun into the air, arced out into the aisle, struck, bounced, struck again, and rolled.

"Alf! Omigodalf!" She scuttled to the floor and covered the large jug with her heavy body.

Two more cracking sounds, and the mono car reverberated sympathetically.

Peter squeezed the skypane control from opaque to transparent and looked up through the roof panel just in time to see two Junkers Ju 87 Stuka dive bombers come buzzing in from the front of the train. Just a flash, and they were gone.

CRABLAMBLAM! CRABLAM!

CRABLAMBLAMBLAM!

Peter winced. The silly bastards were bombing them. The planes are fast enough to keep up with the monorail, he thought. Airspeed, then, close to two hundred kilometers an hour, maybe more. The Stukas were coming in from the front, opposite the direction the mono was moving. Relative velocity nearly four hundred kay. The heavy little steel bombs they were dropping were coming in like bullets.

Damn stupid, he thought, dropping to the floor to get the steel back of the seat ahead between him and the incoming projectiles.

It sounded as if everyone in the goddamn world was screaming. He couldn't tell whether anyone had actually been hurt or not.

"Alf! Alf! Alf!" The sound of a sorrowing bitch barking after a loved one.

A Heinkel He 111H–3 snapped by almost too fast to be seen.

CRABABABAM!

More bloody goddamn bombs.

A Supermarine Spitfire, the most beautiful airplane ever built, floated lazily by the side window and stitched another row of tiny pockmarks in it.

To hell with the midget machine guns, he thought, it's the bloody baby bombs that are doing the damage. Do the stupid buggers behind the beam controls of those aircraft know what they're doing? Do they care? Does anybody care? Probably not.

The Spitfire was retreating, a tail and rudder cross on a flat-wing altar.

There was silence now. No screaming. Just a tight, expectant silence.

And there were no more planes, either. The sky was empty, except for the white-hot ball of the sun. Peter squeezed the skypane control back to opaque to cut out the glare.

Little streams of light came through the roof now. He examined the heavy plastic panel. It had neat round holes punched in it, each surrounded by tiny radial cracks where the little steel bombs had gone through. As he sat back down, his hand touched one of the projectiles and he picked it up. A chrome-steel bullet a little more than three centimeters long.

Peter dropped the object in his pocket and turned as he heard sobbing from across the compartment.

The ample lady with the nonstop tongue and vacuous mind was sitting on the floor with tears streaming down her cheeks and a joyously beatific smile on her face.

Clutched in her arms, snuggled to her vast bosom, whole and unharmed, was a bottle of Alf.

* * *

An hour and twelve minutes later, Peter enclosed himself in an I.V.C. Telecom privacy booth and tapped a number.

"Good day, sir," an overly cultured voice said flatly. "Griffin Universal here. How may we serve?" The screen cleared to reveal, not the speaker, but the company's device:

AZURE, a gryphon rampant, or, the head thereof
haloed by a spiral nebula argent.

"Mr. Parker, please," Peter said, speaking slowly and clearly. The voice was certainly a computer.

"Very good, sir. One second." The voice departed, leaving in its stead the muted strains of "Rule Britannia."

Peter fidgeted and examined the signs in the booth. There were four colorful notations in the lacy Thai script. The only thing in English was the stamping on the phone casing: I.V.C. WORLDWIDE WEB.

It was an unfortunate image. It made him nervous.

"Good day, sir. Griffin Universal. How may we serve?"

Machines have removed the drudge work from the shoulders of the human race.

"For the second time, please connect me with Mr. Parker." It credited one nothing to get angry at a machine.

"Very good, sir. One second." The dying strains of "Rule Britannia" were followed by "Deutchland Uber Alles," heavy on the brass.

"Good day, sir. . . ."

Peter cursed.

"—iffin Universal. How may we serve?"

"Get me Parker! Now! Emergency! Parker! Top Priority!"

"Very good, sir. One second."

The rampant gryphon wiped off the screen as if it had just been oiled, and was replaced by a precisely coiffed female head. "Good day, sir. May I tell Mr. Parker who is calling?"

(Company girl.)

"Peter Lyon."

"Yes, sir. Please hold for a second." The company blazon returned. The electronic orchestra segued into "Waltzing Matilda."

Peter wondered why secretaries and switchboard computers insisted on telling you to wait "a second" and then put you on hold for at least two minutes. Entropy, he decided.

Fifteen seconds later the screen blinked, and Parker's thin graying face, topped by thin graying hair, punctuated by fat blue eyes, was suddenly there.

"Well, Peter?"

A voice dry and gray as a lizard's skin.

"Some kind of disrupters hit the train, sir," Peter reported crisply. "Using model airplanes. Good detail work on the models. Came in ahead of us. Sprayed us with solid steel. No one killed or badly hurt, but the hippos held us up at the terminus. Wanted the whole story. It took a while. Want the details?"

"No. Any sign that they were after you specifically?"

"No, sir. Nothing I could lay a finger on. No way of knowing for sure. The only one that came close was a Heinkel 111, but it only made one pass; and only one out of four—or maybe five—bombs came anywhere near me."

"Good. Unlikely they could have spotted your face anyway; those microremotes don't have enough resolution, actually."

"Why would they want to be after me?" Peter asked.

"No reason. Did the Hemispheric Police ask you anything that seemed out of the ordinary? Perhaps something that might have been aimed at you specifically?"

"No. Not that I could tell. What sort of thing?" Peter had no idea what Parker was asking about, and it annoyed him. Griffin—or Parker, at least—had a habit of sending one out to do things with the bare minimum of information. There might be some reason why the police would be interested that they hadn't bothered to mention to him.

"Never mind. Don't worry about it, my boy. Now—" He glanced down at something below the level of the screen, then back up at Peter. "Now, there's no time to report back to the office. You must go immediately to the Amsialco Building—the big neo-Doric object on Anna Square—fourth floor, suite 401. Says Maritsu Merchandising Ltd. on the door. You will pick up a blue protect case from the young lady at the front desk upon presenting your Griffin credentials. You must go from there directly to the airport. You're booked on Royal Thai flight 231, which leaves in one hour and forty-"—he glanced to his left—"seven minutes. Everything has been arranged as usual. Any questions?"

"No, sir." From long experience Peter knew that there was no point in asking any question beginning with "Why—?"

"Excellent, my boy. Your contact is a man named Michael Wong Escobaga. He shall meet you at the airport when you land. The usual identification procedure. Now, get moving, my boy. Time is short."

"Yes, sir. Where will I be landing?"

"Oh yes. San Francisco. Hurry on!"

The goddamn griffin appeared on the screen.

Peter punched off and left the privacy booth. Management did not seem overly concerned about the adventures of labor. After him? Why would those midget mauraders have been after him? Oh well—hi, ho—move!

THREE

Miss Saralu Ngaxu was a haffenhaff.* Her father was an American of warm tan skin and coal-black idealism. His name, so far as could be ascertained, was William Blakely Exx. *His* father's name had been George X, and his mother—insofar as he could remember her—had been Mother X.

From the beginning, Bill had been a rebel. He did not care at all for his parents' Muslim religion, nor, as he put it, for "their middle-class black attitudes." After getting his degree at the University of the North Western Semisphere at Baton Rouge, he left home for Africa with nearly a quarter of a million dollars, American, which he had made by the illegal sale of various controlled substances—whatever was popular; he went with the flow—to his fellow students in Baton Rouge. He had eliminated the middleman, whenever possible, by using knowledge and friends acquired in the Chemistry Department, and a good deal of apparatus acquired in the same place and assembled in the basement of a house he had rented on Cotton Street.

He changed his name from X to Exx, and used his money to make a truly sizable fortune in Kenya during the Big Land Boom after the African War tapered out. He got out of the boom just before the new

* So spelled. See Dictionary of Central African English Slang, Second Edition. Timbuktu: Magnus House, 2092.

government clamped down and froze land values and put a supertax on the profits.

During that time, he had met and married a Bantu girl of reddish complexion and classic stature. She was six-foot-one, two inches taller than Bill, and, after two years, bore him a child. A daughter. She was named Sarah Lou Ngaxu.

("What's wrong with Sarah Lou, goddammit?" asked Bill.

"Not a damn thing, honey, but you'd better well know that I am most certainly not going to put up with a name like Exx!"

"What the hell's the matter with Exx? Good American name, Exx. Besides, a girl got to have her daddy's name."

"Not in this country, you illiterate uneducated son of a bitch.")

At sixteen, still a virgin and, as is the way with teenagers everywhere, thoroughly disillusioned with her middle-class parents, Sarah Lou had left home to Do Good. By a thoroughly legal and glacier-slick maneuver that even her daddy admired, she had left home with nearly fifty thousand dollars of Bill Exx's money.

Bill knew that the girl was going to waste it by trying to Help the Human Race, but he also knew she had a streak of him in her. And brains. "At sixteen," he told himself, "I'd have been lucky if I could have stole a hundred." And he laughed like hell.

Saralu, having changed the spelling of her name, went to the People's Federated Protectorate of South Africa. It was a poor country since the Events, and she didn't like the racial split. She felt—in spite of what her father had told her—that the White Man was as good as anybody else. She thoroughly approved of Minority Groups, and believed that they should Have Their Rights.

But she learned fast.

FOUR

Life is neither a cosmic accident nor a special favor visited upon the planet Earth. Given the proper conditions—and they are far from unique—the high-energy broth of compounds that make up the sea and atmosphere of a young planet will assuredly progress toward the chemical complexity that we know as organic matter. From there the bridge to true life is a long one, several billions of years, and only whatever gods there be can truly say when it is crossed.

From the DNA double-helix of the primogenital virus to the self-reproducing, chlorophyl-utilizing monocell is the important jump. After that point the further change is inevitable, barring catastrophe. The nitrogen–methane–ammonia atmosphere—to cite a specific example of most interest to us—will slowly shift to nitrogen–oxygen. Scavenger forms, using the oxygen freed by the chlorophyl cells as energy and the cells themselves as food, will arise. Both sorts of cells will specialize, group into cell colonies, and evolve into organisms. Call the first type *plants*, and the second *animals*.

The gravity-free, energy-rich environment of the sea is the home of these organisms for some time. One can speculate as to what force could drive an occasional life-form out of its hospitable sea and onto the jagged coastal rocks. Perhaps it was an inability to compete in the ocean depths, perhaps an accident of tide and wave, perhaps an adventurous soul, perhaps some inevitable process we know not of; but, at least on Earth, they did come.

The life force on our planet's land masses followed many divergent paths. Some prospered, some died out. Some found a convenient niche to sit out the millennia, while others evolved rapidly. But none remained the same. Life is change.

There were experiments. The large lizards almost made it, but they were blitzed in a cosmic accident. *C'est la vie.* A tiny lemur-like creature ancestored a host of bigger species that, for the most part, worked fairly well. They survived—and that is the test.

A group of these creatures switched from four-legged locomotion to two-, thus freeing the forepaws for fine manipulation and swinging through trees.

One of these, endowed with an overly large head, opposable digits, and a genetic tendency to mature late mentally—if at all—was almost as successful, in absolute terms, as the rat.

Homo sapiens prospered, gave up foraging in favor of controlled food production, and swinging through trees in favor of lower back pain; clustered in ever-larger groups, and bred uncontrollably. This is called *civilization,* and is, perhaps, the price of success.

* * *

Peter Lyon, when he thought of his ancestry at all, would picture his father, George, a statnet local news supervisor; or his mother, Edna, who crossbred maize for use in space stations; or perhaps his grandfather, Edward, who had owned a pub. He seldom approached closer to the lemur-ancestor of us all. But twenty million years of genetic connections have imposed patterns that five thousand years of civilization have not altered by as much as a molecule of one gene.

Peter strode across the plaza of the Amsialco Building, an American-designed glass-and-aluminum biscuit box twenty stories tall, fronted with immense pseudo-Greek columns, that glittered and glared in the tropic sun. The streets of Bangkok were fit only for the steaming of clams, but inside the biscuit box were gentle clam-cool draughts of filtered air.

Peter crossed the rich red-brown expanse of patterned teakstone flooring, heading for the elevator bank. People milled around him— mostly Thais with their small delicate faces. A sprinkling of Japanese— taller, heavier, with more determined expressions. Two Indians. No Afros. Three European types. Each moving in his separate orbit against the peach-colored synthetic marble background of the walls.

He entered the elevator, feeling like one more robot among the many, and said "Four" clearly into the grid. When he got out, he turned left to face:

MARITSU MERCHANDISING LIMITED
401–405 →

and, after twelve steps, to a glass panel door that read:

MARITSU MCHDSNG. LTD.
401

and pushed the door open and walked in.

The room was not large, but neither was it crowded. Walls pale cream, decorated with ancient Japanese ink sketches, stark against surrounding black borders. Four Yokomara chairs, three in front and one behind a Yokomara desk. Expensive. No partitions.

On the desk, a G.C.C. thoughtprocessor, the cables discreetly hidden. The screen was on, but there was no one in sight behind the desk.

In the far wall was one door:

DIVISION DIRECTOR
MOST PRIVATE

Peter glanced around at the empty room. Ceiling: bright red sound-absorbing plaques in a brick-on-brick pattern. Floor: thick pile of pale tan silon, clean as virgin snow.

"Hello?"

His voice was soaked up by the walls, ceiling, and floor.

"Anybody here?"

Soggy-dead silence.

He walked around the Yokomara desk. Looked behind it.

Nothing. Nobody.

He looked at the TP screen. Set for English characters. A half-written letter:

22 July 2119
Kruger Unterseewerke, I.G.
Sorgensstrasse 96
Köln, Deutchland
REPIXSAT 99 039 33409

Esteemed Herrnvolk /
Thank you for your bid on the construction of our proposed plant in two men with guns in their hands have just come in the door they do not think I have seen and they are walking tow

The rest of the screen was blank, empty.

Peter moved to the inner door and pushed it open, having no idea what he expected to find.

jesus

He turned away, facing the outer door again, his stomach churning.

jesus jumping god bloody mess splattered dead all dead

He held his hands over his mouth and suppressed the impulse to gag.

you've seen dead bodies before peterlyon. Hold back!

Control.

Control achieved. Deep breath. Don't puke. Don't gag. Another deep breath. Not going to be sick. No sick. Control.

Carefully take hands away from mouth. Don't turn. Not yet. In a minute. Have to in a minute, but not yet. Look at outer door.

Obvious what happened. Two thug types came in. Receptionist, working thoughtprocessor, pretended not to see them long enough to record start of message. Then they grabbed her and took her into the inner office, where they—

—not yet. Don't think about it yet. They did it. It was done. Why? Who would— Anyway, killers leave. Don't notice message on machine. Don't care.

Very well, Peter-my-boy. A smile twisted his lips as he heard his grandfather's voice. *We've evaded the main issue long enough. It's a dirty job, but somebody has to do it. Hop to!* It had been their private joke for anything from washing the dishes to sneaking off on a Sunday afternoon to watch the soccer matches. *It's a dirty job, but somebody has to do it.*

He turned again and looked into the inner office.

Something in him kept his eyes away from the girl—something cold, calculating, and logical. Something that knew it would work better this way. Both of them were in front of the inner office desk—man on right, woman on left.

The man was wearing ordinary business clothing. Well-made, good cut. Five great holes in his chest, three in his face. Blood all over the front of his body, still flowing gently into the great pool that had formed under the desk, fed by both corpses. Not too long ago, then.

Sniff the air. Nothing. And I, by God, have a good nose, whatever I may lack. Had the air-conditioning taken away any odor? Maybe. More likely, compressed gas guns had been used. Large bore. CO_2, Freon, or air. Easily concealed. Quick, deadly, almost silent.

His eyes went up suddenly to survey the rest of the room. It was much like the outer office, except that there was more equipment—a computer desk, a couple of comm consoles, and a bank of file cabinets against the right wall. The file cabinets were all closed, neat-looking.

Eyes back to the desktop.

There it was, the blue protect case. Wide open. Empty. Whatever he had been going to pick up was already gone. Someone—no, more than one—had thought it was worth killing for. And he didn't even know what it was.

Now was the time for the analytic mind. Facts. Clues. The Bangkok police, no better than any other local police in this international age, would have little time for this. Photograph, file, and forget. Round up the usual suspects. And the various worldwide police agencies interested themselves only in *important* crimes, like tax evasion and traffic in "bounce." Murder hardly matters any more.

Murder doesn't matter, doesn't matter, doesn't matter, murder doesn't matter any more.

Peter shook his head. Stop that! Examine the room. No, I've done that. Stop avoiding. Nothing for it now, examine the girl. Dead flesh—once living, recently living, felt dawn, saw sunset break—now dead. No reason to be squeamish, just another clue. Grist for the analytical mind to grind over and reach its unemotional conclusion. Look at the girl.

Go ahead, look at the girl!

Lying on the floor, long legs twisted under her, hands clenched into tiny fists to ward off inevitable doom. A small Thai girl. Sister to she of the lilting *peterlyon* voice.

And very dead. *Too small, too young, too soon to die. Too wet and crumpled, bullet-torn, skin-shredded, bone-broken, blood-soaked dead to be alive. Migod, I'm sick!*

There were two doors in the far wall. One proved to be a coat closet, but the other was a small wet bar. Peter emptied his stomach into the tiny sink and stood for a while staring at the running water. The water ran hot, and steam curled from around the edge of the faucet, damping his face and fogging the mirrored wall in front of him until he could no longer see himself in it. After a while he turned off the water and used some paper napkins to clean up the sink and surrounding area. He stopped short of compulsive scrubbing, but made sure that he had removed his fingerprints from everything he might have touched. Then he flushed the wad of napkins through the sink garbage eater and, neatly closing up the wet bar, turned back to the room.

The girl was still there; smooth, green crumpled dress, holed and blood-gore-stained by the bullet holes in chest, neck, and head. Neat, round holes they were, in a curved line, chest to head. She lay small, and very still.

Her *body* lay there. Just her body. *She* was gone. Metaphysically, and permanently gone. Remember, examine the body. For her. Find out for her. Nothing else to do. No one else to do it. For her. Force himself to look. Cold. Detached. Examine.

He knelt down by the body. Carefully placing his knee outside the gore, he knelt. Lovingly not-touching her, he examined the body.

Nothing more to see. Nothing in the hands, no pockets, damn little underwear. Just a body. Young girl. Plain green dress. She doesn't— didn't—need ornamentation. One pin. Curious pin. Talisman? Memento? Souvenir? Gift? Insignia? A gold reverse question mark with a horizontal bar through it, about three centimeters high. *Egyptian?* Peter wondered. *Indian? Not Thai, I think. Pretty.*

He unfastened the pin, touching the green dress with its hint of the body beneath as little as possible, and put it in his pocket. Then he stood and searched once more around the room with his eyes, willing each piece of furniture to give up its guilty secret and somehow accuse someone of ripping the life from two human beings.

Gently closing and removing the blue protect case, Peter wiped the doorknobs behind him as he left suite 401. He didn't remember the trip to the airport; his mind was occupied with speculation.

Whatever the protect case was to hold, they wanted. Whatever the protect case was to hold, they got. They couldn't have gotten it from Peter after he had the case. He was just a messenger boy, and wouldn't have the key. If anyone had taken it from him and tampered with it, they merely would have destroyed the contents. So they attacked at the vulnerable point. They must have known exactly what they wanted, and exactly what they were doing.

Someone in the company? No. No need then to kill. His only identification was the Griffin security badge. The protect case would have been turned over to anyone with a similar badge without question. And all the intercompany cases used the same pattern key, available at any office. What was in the case? What was important enough to kill two people for? How important was a human life? Not too important in these overcrowded days.

What was in the case? What sort of messenger boy was he? Carry this case or that parcel from here to there across the face of the planet. Find out if this company makes this or if these people are doing that or using these or buying those—without question, without thought, for five years. And now she was dead, two were dead, and why? He had no idea. He must find out. He would find out.

I shall find out. Who killed, and why, and what it is that I am doing. I shall find out.

His ticket and baggage were waiting at the airport, and he boarded the plane without further incident, without delay, and without noticing or caring. He was deep in the void of his own mind, leaving to his reflex and habit patterns the mundane tasks of motion and speech. Once seated on board the plane he suddenly felt incredibly tired. Inside of ten minutes he was in a deep sleep.

INTERLUDE

The digging and blasting had been going on for months. The people who worked in the area had gotten used to walking around the giant obstruction and holding their ears. Many of them were partially deaf already, one of the prices of Life in the Fast Lane in the Los Angeles–San Diego basin. The dirt trucks had carted away a cubic kilometer of dirt and the concrete trucks had driven in thousands of cubic meters of batter to pour over the waffle-iron grid of steel cable.

Then the hole was covered over and the street resurfaced and the obstruction removed. The only thing left as tangible result of the prolonged annoyance was a small gray cube with a gate in one side leading to a downflight of steps and the red-glow word SUBWAY over the gate.

The gate was carefully locked.

" 'Bout time they got a subway station out here in Sherman Oaks," One remarked. "We can sure use it. They've got two stops in Anaheim already."

"Well," Two said, peering through the gate, "they've got the station built, anyway. No telling how long they'll take to get a tunnel laid to it. The one in Venice took—what?—three years? Course it was always flooding."

During the course of the day, leaflets proclaiming the opening of the new station were given out at all businesses and passed out on the street. An uncommonly thoughtful act of the California Public Transportation Authority.

At 4:45 a man came by and unlocked and pulled back the gate. He unrolled two identical signs and taped one to each side of the door:

GRAND OPENING

THANK YOU FOR YOUR PATIENCE

WE WANTED TO DO IT RIGHT

ALL CONNEXIONS

and trotted down the stairs to prepare.

"About time," Three sniffed, trotting down the stairs.

" 'Exions?" Four wondered, following shortly after.

Then the dinner rush started.

Many people decided to try the new station that evening, since this was an overcrowded and underbused section of the West Coast megalopolis. A steady line of shoulders curved around the steps and down into the large man-made cave. Slowly, both large platforms filled up, until only the double ribbon of track between was empty. Then a green-glow sign suddenly lit above the still-crowded stairs:

EXPRESS → LOWER LEVEL

and a gate opened to another curved staircase, leading farther toward the Earth's core. The people streamed down, and soon both levels were full.

No train came.

They waited patiently, each a separate circle of humanity.

(Six—and only six—circles can be drawn tangent to a given circle of the same size without overlapping.)

They overlapped, and started getting nervous. The station was much too crowded for any of them to get out, or, indeed, do anything but wait.

There was a loud grinding noise. Many thought the train was finally coming. Only the ones in the rear could see that large concrete blocks had been dropped over the exit gates. Some of them started screaming, but the sound couldn't carry over the grinding noise.

Small vents in the ceiling opened, cascading tissue-paper leaflets on the packed crowd. Many people began screaming anew, and frantically brushed the leaflets aside, as though suspecting they contained a virulent poison. Others read them. Then they, too, began screaming.

> YOU ARE TRAPPED!
> In these circumstances it is permissible to yell,
> scream, or cry. You may even panic. There is no
> train. Shortly there will be no air. This absurd way
> to die is being brought to you by the League of
> Organized Vandals.
>
> ENJOY!

FIVE

Saralu Ngaxu sat at the desk in her office, certain that she was being watched.

Certain? What the hell good was certainty? Good enough to act on and to control one's behavior with. She had known for three years that she was being watched, but only in the last six months had she suspected why. Lately she had been calling herself a blotskull for not figuring it out earlier. One wall of her office, looking like fine old polished marble, was riddled with spy-eyes; *that* she knew. And some-one—she knew not who—was watching. Not always, not even regu-larly. But often. She could sense it. And the little detector in her shoulder pouch could sense it. It was on now.

She could not ignore it. She had to pretend at all times that it was not there, which made her ever aware of it.

Daddy Exx had always told her that she would have made one hell of an actress.

She pulled her mind away from that wall and focused upon the papers before her—white onionskin papers, glaring in the light from the north window.

There was something else strange going on at the orphanage. Why were they pulling out all those low-normal kids? Big hole in the curve. And who were they? They let the bright kids out for adoption. The stupid ones stayed for a long time. But the semi-stupid were taken away —to a high-class school. Which made no sense at all. Why would it want them? She was damn well going to find out. Somehow.

Meanwhile, ignore That Man Behind the Wall.

For some reason she was sure it was a man.

* * *

His name was William Jesse Harker, and he was known as "Big Bill," but even at six-feet-six he was only three inches taller than Saralu Ngaxu. He was old enough to be her father, but he never thought about that. It was his job to watch her—and watch her he did.

Like the other staff members of the orphanage, like most residents of the People's Federated Protectorate, she wore nothing but a minikilt in the summer. A subtle way of asserting their independence from the uptight Suid Afrikaaners, who had still not gotten used to the sixty-year-old change on their fortunes. Well, screw them; at least they hadn't been massacred.

The light from the window glinted off her smooth skin, making the highlights of her face and breasts copper-gold and dark bronze, while the shadows were dark chocolate and deep black.

She came into her office every afternoon promptly at two, and this afternoon Harker was at his post to watch. She walked in smoothly, her magnificent breasts and beautiful minikilted hips moving in an undulating sway as she approached her desk. From that moment on, William Jesse never took his eyes from her. He waited.

As always, Harker had to push the twinges of guilt away. He had never seen her do anything that his bosses would have disapproved of, but he had kept reporting that her behavior was "suspicious"—because if he had cleared her, he would no longer be assigned to watch her. And he needed to watch her. He *had* to watch her. Often.

At last. She picked up a sheaf of papers and turned the swivel chair so that it faced his wall. He switched from the overhead view to camera at waist level. Her eyes were on the sheaf of papers she was riffling through. Harker's eyes were on her.

Her left heel remained on the floor. Slowly she lifted her right heel as she leaned back in the chair. The right heel came to rest on the edge of the chair seat. The knee swung outward and down. Her thighs spread gently, slowly, as she made herself more comfortable. From the angle of the camera, it was as though her minikilt had vanished.

As always, Harker's eyes stared without moving. His left hand cautiously wiped moisture from his brow. His right hand was already at work.

INTERLUDE

"My antisodium propulsomotor will work on the atomic nucleides of the sodium atoms in the sodium chloride salt in seawater, releasing electrons of pure chlorine," the intense little man explained rapidly to the assembled newspersons and camerapersons, waving his arms about in choppy patterns as he spoke. "This is a totally new scientific principle, which I am planning to reveal to the rest of the scientific community as soon as I feel they are ready for it.

"The test model, along with my hydrogen–helium attractor, are installed in the Graveto-Propulso Excursion Trans-Solar Homo-Module."

He slapped the side of the huge plate-iron ball on the platform beside him, which rang with a hollow sound.

"I call it the *Space Ark.*

"The repulsion of the seawater will give it enough initial thrust to clear the Earth's gravity envelope, where the hydrogen–helium attractor will take over.

"The craft will travel at speeds far in excess of the one-gee shuttles, and yet, as the human body is largely hydrogen, the acceleration will be tolerable. It should reach one hundred and ten percent of the speed of light within three days. And then, having passed the light barrier, it will start accelerating. I have enough provisions for a month.

"Are there any questions?"

The reporters looked at each other. "Is this just a test trip, or are you going to explore for new planets?" one of them asked.

"Test?" The little man looked offended. "There is nothing to test. All my theories are sound. All my craftsmanship is meticulous. I hired only Japanese workers. No, my friends. I undertake this voyage in the spirit of Columbus crying because he had no new worlds to conquer; of Magellan setting out in the *Golden Hind.* This is but the prototype of a fleet of vast space arks that will ply the ether in the coming decades.

"My time is growing short. The launch window is approaching. I will answer all other questions upon my return. Splashdown will be at this very spot, exactly thirty days from today, Pacific Standard time."

With a final wave at the cameras, the little man climbed into his ball and closed the hatch. The waiting hoist lifted the *Space Ark* off the platform and over the edge. At a signal from inside, it released the catch.

The ball plunged into the Pacific Ocean and dropped swiftly out of sight.

The newsmen waited for half an hour, but the *Space Ark* never resurfaced. Then they phoned in the stories and tapes and ate the lunch that the little man had provided.

SIX

Michael Wong Escobaga was waiting for Peter by the baggage slot. Peter walked over in a daze, having been tranquilized to an almost hypnotic state by the twenty-hertz throb of the magjet and his own single-minded concentration on a time-frozen scene in a Bangkok office. Escobaga effortlessly brought him back to reality. Tall, fat, balding, sporting a mustache that a walrus would have been proud of and a bowler Lloyd George would not have acknowledged, he walked loudly where fools fear to tread. His presence acted as a bucket of water on Peter's closed-in nerves. Seltzer water.

"Welcome, my boy. Welcome to San Francisco," he bellowed, putting one arm around Peter's shoulders and the other around Peter's luggage and hauling both toward the nearest door. "Your guest abode while you're with us here in the City of Hills, Baghdad by the Bay, city of a thousand mystic delights—forty of them legal, home of the fabled four hundred and thirty-seven permutations; your guest abode, I say, awaits you. You are in the hands of Michael Wong Escobaga—myself!"

Peter pulled loose of Escobaga's embrace and shook his head. "This trip might have been pointless," he said. "Perhaps I shouldn't have bothered coming. I wasn't thinking too clearly. I should have called Parker. I'd better call him now, first thing."

"Second thing," Escobaga insisted, pulling Peter along. "First thing is to get you to the boatel, cleanse you, feed you, and—what?—rest you? No, sounds indecent. Well-designed language, English, but it has its blind spots. Whatever. What do you mean, you shouldn't have come? Here's the cable car."

Peter looked at the large plastic beach ball suspended from a gleaming silver monorail. "That?"

"I know it looks flimsy, but don't worry. It—"

"Not that. I thought the cable cars were like streetcars. You know, railroad tracks down the center of the street and like that."

"They were," Escobaga assured him. "They were. There's one still operating, if you want to see it. Goes from Fisherman's Wharf down to the bay. This is the new cable car. Really runs by cable, too. Moebus belt. Each car private. Just get in and state your destination clearly. Anywhere in the greater bay area. What do you mean, the trip might have been pointless? Here, let me take that suitcase. What's the problem?"

They got into the oversized beach ball and Escobaga muttered something into a panel by the door. Peter settled himself back into the seat cushion and looked around.

"View's better in a little while," Escobaga said. "Wait until we get near the Old City. Nothing like it. This thing goes fifty, a hundred meters in the air sometimes. What a view. Scares the crap out of you. Why shouldn't you have come?"

"Are these things private?" Peter asked.

"Pretty safe," Escobaga assured him. "First of all, they're random, so no one can plant a bug in a car with any assurance that it's the one you'll get into. Second, they wobble and curve too much for anyone to keep a beam steadily aimed. What's your problem?"

"Murder," Peter told him. "And robbery. Someone wanted the contents of this protect case enough to kill two people for it. At least, I guess that's what they were after; there didn't seem to be anything else missing from the office. When I got to the pickup point, this case was empty and two people were shot. A man and a girl. Dead. That's why I have to call Parker. What was supposed to be in the case? Do you know? It's empty now."

"Empty, huh? Two people killed. What a mess. The things people do." Escobaga whipped out a large square of polka-dotted cotton and wiped off his face. "Empty. Fancy that. Very fancy. So they took the contents and left the case, huh? Removed the papers and left the purse, did they? Scooped out the, ah, melon, and discarded the rind. Filched the meat and threw away the husk. They did that."

"All of that," Peter agreed.

Escobaga stuffed the pockmarked handkerchief deep into his jacket pocket and took a deep breath, as though he were testing the air. "Ha.

Hum. Ho. Ho, ho. Harrumph." He pushed forward, squatting on the very edge of his seat. "Let me take a look at the case."

"Here." Peter handed it over. "You don't need the key. I didn't set it because it's empty. At least, I think it's empty. Unless there's a secret compartment, or something. I brought it along just in case there's a secret compartment."

Escobaga paused in his examination of the blue case long enough to squint at Peter. "Did you? Did you do that?"

"Well—" Peter shook his head. "Not really. I just thought of that. I guess I'm trying to justify it to myself. I brought the case because I was supposed to bring the case. It never occurred to me to leave it behind. I guess it is a little silly, dragging an empty protect case halfway around the world."

"If it will make you feel any better," Escobaga offered, "we'll fill it up at the first opportunity. First thing, I'll get some secret-type papers and maybe a minimicrofiche or something, and we'll fill it up. Least I can do." He opened the case and peered inside. "They didn't damage it, whoever they were. They either found it open, or found the papers still outside it. Even the most skillful forced entry would have taken an hour or so, and some very specialized tools, and left some sign. And an unskillful entry would have destroyed the case and its contents. If it was closed, they probably would have just taken it with them and consulted an expert. Oh well, maybe we can hope for better luck next time."

"Better luck!" Peter started to stand up, but he had not allowed for the laws of physics. The cable car, now out of its slot and supported only by a slender rod to the overhead rail, went backward as Peter's weight went forward (action = reaction—eg., Newton) and the resultant vector threw him into Escobaga's paunchy lap.

"These things take practice, my boy," Escobaga assured him, pushing him back into his seat. "I *assume* that's not what you intended."

"How can you talk about luck?" Peter demanded. "Two people have been murdered. Shot to death and just left there on the floor. Just to get whatever was in this case. Surely the death of two people is more than just bad luck!"

"In this world? At this time?" Escobaga asked. "Don't be silly. Individual death is one of the least important things to consider in any situation. It's important to the person, ah, undergoing the transformation—at the moment it happens. After that nothing is important to him or can help him in any way, and our only debt is to the living. If you think an individual death is in any way important, you're fifty years and five billion people out of date. Very romantic, no doubt, and very decent, and all that sort of thing—but pointless. Perhaps even antisocial. A person who screams on a subway is a much greater nuisance than one who kills in an alley. You can get a good view of the Old City from right around this curve."

Peter maintained a sulky silence until they had reached the boatel. His cabin was at the far end of the pier, well out in the bay. It was small and immaculate, with a clear plastic floor that illuminated the myriad of tiny silvery fish that darted about beneath. After his shower, Peter lay prone on the double bed, chin over the edge, staring down at his microcosmic ocean. It soothed him and put his troubles in a different perspective. What, after all, would human problems seem like to a sardine? Think of everything that's troubling you right now; put it in terms that an intelligent fish could understand. Could it sympathize?

Michael Wong Escobaga came in without knocking, pushing a service cart ahead of him. "Clean and relaxed, are you, my boy? Ready for a night on the town? Not the whole town, you understand, just a select part. Selected by myself. I've brought you a little snack to settle your stomach before we get to the serious business of eating and drinking."

"Look at that, down there," Peter said, indicating the watery world below with a wave of his hand.

"Very impressive," Escobaga agreed. "Cost them a fortune to clean up the muck and put down that sand bottom. Have to pipe in oxygenated seawater, too, or the fish will drown."

"It's a miniature world," Peter said, "with all the troubles and joys of our own."

Escobaga peered doubtfully down through the transparent floor. "It's a fish-eat-fish world down there," he said finally, shaking his head.

"What are the nets for?" Peter asked. "Sharks?"

"Nets? Oh, you mean the wide-mesh gratings around the perimeter. Sharks of a sort—scuba divers."

"Excuse me?"

"Certainly. Oh—I see; an expression. When this boatel was opened, it quickly became a favorite rendezvous for rich lovers. Certain—shall we call them candid—photographers got the idea of swimming along

beneath the cabins and photographing interesting scenes from below.
A sort of worm's-, or fish's-, eye view of how the upper crust lives and
makes out."

"Why," Peter wondered, "would anybody want to watch anybody
else make love?"

"Oh, a wide variety of reasons. Some are so repressed that they can't
do it themselves; others watch for amusement or education. Sex can be
very educational. Some are interested in any activities of the rich.
Money can be very educational."

"We live in a strange world," Peter said.

"I could have told you that."

INTERLUDE

CARBON DATING AUTHENTICATES THOTH SCROLL
Tests Show Age of Mysterious Book
Special to the Zeitgeist *by Clu*

Scientists today announced that the mysterious so-called "Great Scroll
of Thoth," a lead-encased papyrus scroll found beneath the Pyramid of
Khufu when it was cleared away two years ago under the Greater Egyptian Urban Renewal Program, is so old that it contains only a miniscule
amount of carbon 14, the isotope used for dating dead, but once living,
objects. An international committee headed by eight prominent scientists declared that the scroll is "at least a hundred thousand years old."

The papyrus and the ink, said Dr. Panthumus, spokesman for the
committee, were tested separately and proved to be of about the same
age. "Considering the remarkable state of preservation of the scroll,"
Dr. Panthumus said, "these findings are truly astounding."

The text of the scroll, which proved to be in an archaic language
related to Hebrew, was first translated a year ago. An article published

in June in the *Journal of the Egyptian Egyptological Society* indicates that the text, which has not yet been officially released, shows that men of that distant era had solved the problem of faster-than-light travel and may have established colonies on planets circling distant stars.

This would put an entirely new interpretation on certain passages of the Old Testament, such as the assertion in Exodus that . . .

* * *

A tangled web you must conceive, if modern science you'd deceive.

The men who constructed the Great Scroll of Thoth had taken their time, and had done a superb job. The construct was perhaps a bit more recent than the distinguished scientists imagined.

RECIPE:

First, build a large terrarium, sealed and properly shielded. (A cavern a mile and a half below the surface, deep in the Pyrenees, had been chosen, and elaborate shielding had been erected around the apparatus.)

Place in the terrarium sand, gravel, and clay that has been baked free of all traces of carbon and nitrogen. Add the minimum necessary amounts of organic fertilizers. Flood the big tank with a mixture of pure oxygen (20 percent) and nitrogen taken from a fossil source, such as Andean sodium nitrate (80 percent). Add enough pure carbon dioxide from a fossil source (anthracite coal) to sustain plant life.

Introduce into this controlled environment plantings of the Nile sedge *(Cyperus papyrus)*, and cultivate this for several generations, removing the adult plants regularly, substituting mineral fertilizers for the elements they remove.

Analyze regularly for carbon 14.

The result, about the eighth or ninth generation, will be a plant that is essentially free of carbon 14, and therefore incapable of being dated by analysis for that isotope. Make papyrus from this plant.

The rest of the job, compared to the foregoing, is simple. Ink free from C-14 is ludicrously easy. Working out a "curiously advanced" cuneiform and a primal Hebraic to use with it is the sort of problem that imaginative archaeologists prefer to crossword puzzles.

Constructing the "Ancient Lead Capsule" in which the Scroll was supposedly enclosed for millennia, and burying it in a cleverly located spot beneath the Great Pyramid was no more than an adroit bit of slight-of-hand.

To a dedicated man with sufficient training, fooling a scientist is no problem. Scientific training prepares one to ask questions of the Universe, but does not teach one what to do when the answers are supplied by whimsical people. The Universe does not bend spoons.

SEVEN

Algol is divided into three parts, and the fourth is a planet called Belgium. The inhabitants of Belgium call the inner two stars, which circle each other every sixty-nine hours, Gaul and Goth; and the outer star, which is their sun, Frank.

The great blimp-shaped construct that was the gashopper *Gone With the Wind* reached slowdown point two weeks out from Earth. Since the interstitial drive was more efficient at speeding things up than slowing them down, a fact unexplainable by the relativistic mathematics used to invent the drive, that meant it was slightly less than three weeks out from Belgium.

Deep Spaceman Hillyard swam unconcernedly through the thick muck that currently permeated the ship's atmosphere and turned left at the inner corridor to the communications bay. He knocked at the door, which seemed to pulsate in and out under his hand, and entered. Just then the apparent atmosphere cleared, leaving only a residual green glow. Hillyard handed the pre-recorded message slug he was carrying to the communications officer and tossed its wrappings into a disposal net. "I don't follow this," he complained. "I thought these gashoppers were supposed to be a complete secret back on Earth. If that's so, then why are we sending a phony report back in the sounder torpedo? I mean, if they don't know we're here anyway, who's going to be listening?"

"Truth," Communications Officer Twhim said, blinking her long curved lashes up at him, "is like a roll of toilet paper; it's really all one long continuous strip, but if you punch through at any one point it seems to have many layers."

The ship began vibrating, and the walls seemed to twist. Neither Communications Officer Twhim nor Deep Spaceman Hillyard paid it any attention.

"This report is for the government, which knows we're here, but not much more," Twhim continued. "We have to make sure it doesn't know how well we're doing or precisely where 'here' is. Among other things, it thinks—and this report will confirm—that we're all dead. The common people, who are scarcely permitted to dream about such things, will never know anything about it."

Hillyard shook his head. "I still don't follow. What has the government got to do with it? We work for Griffin Universal, which is bigger than any government. This whole secrecy thing's a bunch of crap anyway. We've got colonies on a bunch of planets now, and no one on Earth outside of Griffin knows about it. What's the point? Why not just tell everyone? How could it hurt? They can't *do* anything about it."

"We already lost one of our ships—and one of our planets," she reminded him. "You know about that."

"Yes, ma'am, but that was some kind of freak accident. It couldn't happen again in a million years, the captain says. Besides, we're going to get that one back as soon as we solve the mathematics." Hillyard said that last with the assurance of one to whom mathematics was an unfathomable God. And if Griffin Universal could solve the mathematics, why then Griffin Universal deserved to be followed anywhere. "But I still think we could tell people about it," he said.

"They would get ambitious," Communications Officer Twhim offered. "And we might have to smite them for their ambitions. It's for their own good, you see." She fluttered her eyelashes. "It's *policy.*"

The interstitial maleffects cleared up completely, the green glow disappeared, the walls stopped moving, and the ship stopped vibrating.

Hillyard shrugged his massive shoulders and the muscles rippled beneath his shirt. "Whatever you say, ma'am," he told her complacently. "I only work here."

"We seem to be through whatever we were passing through," Communications Officer Twhim said, turning around. "There are some things about interstitial space that are not easy to get used to." She smiled. "I'm off in half an hour," she added, licking her lips with her moist tongue. "Come to my cabin and I'll explain it all to you, Hillyard. In detail. In copious detail."

"Yes, ma'am," Deep Spaceman Hillyard said, resigning himself to an evening's entertainments when he would have much rather stayed in his own cabin to work on his model of the *Enterprise*. The truly liberated woman can be a fearsome thing.

EIGHT

"Here you are, my boy," Escobaga said, handing Peter a large envelope, thick with enclosed paper.

Peter took it and weighed it gingerly in his hand. "What's in it?"

"Secret documents. Minimicrofiches. Classified information. All the very latest. For you to carry in that protect case. If they're looking for information, then why not give it them? Just stick that stuff in the case. No—not like that! Break the seal and remove the crap from the envelope first; it looks more authentic that way."

"What am I to do with it?" Peter asked, distributing the various artifacts from the envelope in as artistic a fashion as he could manage in the case.

"Carry it about with you. Everywhere you go, it goes. That way if someone kills you for what's in the case, they'll have something to show for their trouble."

"Good-o!" Peter said, looking sourly at the blue case. "You think that's probable?"

"We think whoever attacked that office in Bangkok did not get whatever he or they thought they were after. Therefore they may try again. If so, you are ordered to give up the case without much of a struggle. Do your best not to get killed or too seriously hurt. But try to look like a coward rather than someone under orders to let them succeed, otherwise they won't think the stuff they get is worth anything. Which it isn't."

"The milk of human kindness," Peter said, snapping the case closed, "flows sluggishly, if at all, through your veins."

"Ours is not to reason why," Escobaga pointed out.

"I don't like the rest of that quote," Peter said. "I never have. I'd hate to think that it applied to me."

"Don't blame me," Escobaga said. "This wasn't my idea. Although, come to think of it, you wouldn't have liked my idea any better. Come along; I have reserved a table and a brace of chairs for us at the Restaurante Balboa in Verne. The food is edible, the drink is potable, and the entertainment is watchable. More than that one cannot expect in this best of all possible worlds."

"Is this part of the job?" Peter asked. "Is there some specific reason why I should come with you? Because, if not, I'd just as soon call room service and spend the evening watching the telly. A couple of my favorite shows are on tonight."

"Have you ever been to Verne?"

"What's a Verne?"

"I thought so. Verne is a floating city forty kilometers off the coast. Surrounded by the deep Pacific and the bluest sky you've ever seen. It's a fishing and a fish farming center and an oil town and a free port and a gambling casino and a sport fishing and water sports resort. And it is bea-oo-ti-ful! And the Restaurante Balboa is probably the finest seafood restaurant in the world today. Okay? Tell your TV to put the programs you want to see on disk for you. You can view them later. Come along now."

When they were firmly settled in formfitting plush chairs on the hydrofoil, with the blue case resting carefully on Peter's knees, he tried again. "You do have something specific for me to be doing, I assume?"

"That is correct. Turn the page."

"Huh?"

"Yes-indeedy-do, we have something for you to do. The Griffin that knows all, sees all, and tells nobody nothing, our Mr. Parker, has a specific task for you, my boy."

"Is it a secret, or will I to be allowed to know?"

"Now now, my boy. Don't get testy. Meaning 'belligerently mascu-line,' related to 'testes.' From the Latin, you know." He pulled a sheet of onionskin parchment from his sleeve and handed it to Peter. "I have here a list of the establishments you are to explore. Hand-wrote at great expense. Hardly anybody does that stuff any more. Calligraphy, they called it."

*   *   *

The Restaurante Balboa was on top of the central spire of the com-pact floating city. It revolved slowly, making one revolution in slightly over an hour. It was supposed to be more exact, but nobody had ever been able to find the mistake. So during the course of dinner Peter had a shrimp cocktail, a Manhattan clam chowder, a very-locally grown Maine lobster, and a 360° view of the water.

"You've got to be kidding," he told Escobaga.

"It's hard to realize," Escobaga said thoughtfully, "that over two hundred thousand people live and work on this man-made buoyant object. It must be the world's largest houseboat."

"This list," Peter said, shaking the paper in Escobaga's face, "has to be a joke. You want me to investigate these groups? Ha ha. For what? And how would I know when I found it?"

"My boy," Escobaga said, taking the paper and peering closely at it, "don't personalize the situation to the extreme. It isn't *I* what wants you to investigate these groups. It is Griffin Universal, whom we call boss; lord of the manor and the manor of the lord. As represented by the exacting and secretive Mr. Parker. I symbolically tug at my fore-lock." He held the paper sideways and stared at it, and then edgewise, and then upside down. He looked baffled. "What, exactly, is your com-plaint about this list?"

"Well, it isn't the quality of the paper it's printed on." The room gave a slight lurch, and Peter caught the coffeepot before it turned over. "What was that?"

"Tsunami," Escobaga told him. "A big wave. Happens all the time. It's clear you've never been to sea before. Continue."

Waiters rushed about, clearing up spilled cups and glasses and dropped pottery, but none of the other patrons seemed unduly alarmed, except for one lady in the corner; but she had been screaming about something for the past ten minutes anyway. Peter looked around, then mentally shrugged. "Look!" he said, stabbing a finger at the list. "Read it!"

ORGANIZATIONS POTENTIALLY OF INTEREST
CLASS C
AREA 17 (SAN FRANCISCO)
ALPHABETICAL

AD ASTRA INC.

THE ATLANTEAN SOCIETY

THE BARSOOM INDENTS

THE BLACK HOLES

THE BROTHERHOOD OF THE VOID

FAR OUT UNLIMITED

THE KNIGHTS OF THE WHITE ROSE

THE KNIGHTS OF THE WHITE ROSE (reform)

THE LEAGUE OF LIGHT

THE MOVING VAN

NEUES VEREIN FÜR RAUMSCHIFFAHRT AUS
  CALIFORNIA

THE ORDER OF THE SECOND SANDWICH

SEEKERS OF THE TRUE MU

THE SOCIETY FOR TOTAL FREEDOM

THE SOCIETY OF THE PHOENIX

STARBRIGHT SISTERHOOD

THE UNIVERSAL MONARCHIST SOCIETY

WOMEN AGAINST MEN IN SPACE (WAMS)

"Fascinating," Escobaga said. "I read it. What's your complaint?"

Star Griffin

The waiter stopped in front of their table with two small stemmed glasses on his tray. "Compliments of the management, Mr. Escobaga," he said. "Fleur du Mer, an aperitif of the sea." The restaurant floor gave a sudden lurch and the sticky green liquid in the glasses splattered over Peter's face, as the two glasses flew over his head. The waiter fell, hitting his nose against the table before he could right himself. "Terribly sorry, sir," he said, trying to keep the incipient panic out of his voice. Blood from his nose dripped freely into Peter's coffee cup. "The floor jolted. It must be the tsunami. I shall replace the glasses."

"Don't bother," Peter said, dipping his napkin into his glass and dabbing at the sticky green mess on his face. "You have a nosebleed; go lie on your back with your head down."

"And send one of your compatriots with fresh cups of coffee," Escobaga added.

The waiter nodded and departed. Peter looked around for something stronger to clean his face with. "Here," Escobaga offered, "use my Scotch."

"Thank you," Peter said. "Look—here, for example: the Atlantean Society, or Seekers of the True Mu. What the hell is that? Or here: the League of Light. I'm to investigate these groups and see if there's anything wrong with them; anything unusual in their behavior. I am not given to know why I am doing this, or what, precisely, I am looking for. Just 'anything unusual.' But how could I tell?"

"How's that?"

"Well, how am I to know how the Black Holes are supposed to behave? Tell me what the Brotherhood of the *Void* does when it's at home, and I'll tell you when it's doing something funny. But my guess is that everything any of these groups does is going to look funny."

"I see what you mean," Escobaga granted. "It is an interesting problem. I will be fascinated to see how you handle it. Most fascinated." He choked slightly and clutched at the side of the table. "Fascinating." He looked slightly green.

"Thanks a lot for your kind advice," Peter said. "What's the matter?"

"If I didn't know better," Escobaga said from between clenched teeth, "I'd say I was getting seasick. I do get seasick. Easily. Urmph!"

"I thought this thing was securely moored," Peter said.

"Of course it is," Escobaga assured him. "I'm merely suffering a psychosomatic symptom, difficult to endure, brought on by my prime fear of rejection."

"The city is loose!" screamed a white-coated busboy, running haphazardly through the main dining room.

The headwaiter jumped up on a table. "Don't anybody panic!" he yelled. "Keep calm! We're sinking! Stay in your seats. Women and children first! Your money will be refunded. Help!" He dove off the table onto the carpet and did a breaststroke toward the door.

"What *is* happening?" Peter wondered. The other diners were clustered in little groups around the various tables, looking alarmed and clutching at each other, but none of them seemed to have the vaguest idea of what was happening or what to do about it.

ATTENTION, CITIZENS OF VERNE! ATTENTION, CITIZENS OF VERNE! ATTENTION! A T T E N T I O N !

Peter looked out. There was a small sky platform hovering above the artificial island with a large horn sticking out of the underside.

YOU MAY BE INTERESTED IN KNOWING WHAT IS HAPPENING. YOU HAVE BEEN SET ADRIFT. YOUR BALLAST TANKS HAVE BEEN PUNCTURED. YOU ARE SINKING. THE NORTH END WILL SINK FIRST, TIPPING YOU OVER. THAT IS WHAT IS HAPPENING. THIS EVENT IS HAPPENING TO *YOU*, LIVE, COURTESY OF THE LEAGUE OF ORGANIZED VANDALS. THANK YOU FOR YOUR INTEREST.

The platform bobbed once, in a sort of aerial curtsy, and sped away.

"Urmph!" Escobaga said, as the room suddenly listed to one side. "It's the old Chinese curse: May you live in interesting times. Interesting! This is fascinating!" He leaned over the side of the table and neatly threw up on the floor.

INTERLUDE

NEWSLETTER

OF THE OBJECTIVIST COUNCIL
Volume XIV, Number 4   June–July 2119

AN OPEN LETTER FROM BERTRAM FRAM: #160 in a series

MEMBERS and friends of Objectivism:

We are closer than ever to our great goal. In some ways this statement might seem a cop-out, since our goal lies in the future, and with every second that passes we approach the future at a steady pace. While reflecting sorrowfully that it is later than it ever was, one must establish the Objectivist Balance by noting that it is earlier than it will ever be.

But enough of that crap.

The question that faces Objectivists, as you must see from the news, is whether we shall reach the fort ahead of the wolves slathering to pull us down.

To look at the world Objectively, and see that Mankind is destroying itself, and realize that we, by intelligence, intent, interest, and intestinal fortitude, must save ourselves even if we cannot save the world; that is the primary Objectivist dilemma.

And this newsletter is the Objectivist Dialog, for those of us who have passed our prime and are engaged in conquering the second dilemma: what to do!

We, as individuals acting Objectively, must by group action leave this, the planet of our birth, for uncleared, untilled fields on other orbs.

The government will not admit the existence of a faster-than-light drive, which we have shown, by a clear process of inductive reasoning based on the deCampian model, *must* exist now. Why are they keeping this a secret at this time? They do not want us to leave. They are afraid of the mass reaction that will occur. They are afraid of losing control. The function of a government is to govern; they will not willingly lose the governed to the freedom of outer space! Even though the destruction of Mankind on this planet, and indeed throughout the whole Solar System, since the other colonies are dependent on Mother Earth, is threatened, they will cling on to their rank and privilege. They are committing suicide, but their corpses will have pretty uniforms.

EARTH'S 10 LARGEST CITIES APPROACH KHAN'S LIMIT

The news the stats won't print: According to official statistics of the Earth Census Bureau of the United Nations, as collected and analyzed by a private independent agency, the ten largest megalopolises on the planet will soon reach Khan's Limit of Compactability. According to the extension of Professor Gustave H. Khan's theory, formulated on information gathered during the popsplosions of Bombay and Tokyo by Khangroup researchers, when population reaches a density of point seven Khan units or above in a megaurban area, a self-propagating "chain reaction" starts an expanding population sink with a chaos center of killing, raping, looting, burning, drug-taking, public sex, and a myriad of other self-destructive, antisocial acts. By the time this burns out, as the examples of Bombay, Tokyo, Manchester, and Djakarta showed, there is little left.

The inner region of the City of New York, comprising the original four boroughs of Manhattan, Queens, Brooklyn, and the Bronx, are within or just outside of the theoretical limit now. (Staten Island, once an independent borough before the landfill and the creation of the free port, is still clearly under the limit.) The hemispheric authorities, who have consistently refused to acknowledge the relevance of the compactability equations, will not act to prevent the tragedy or even allow broadcast of the information over the statnet, the infoscreen, or public television. Private electronic bulletin boards and newsletters like this one are the only sources of honest, accurate information on this phenomena.

The mayor's secretary for the media, in a letter of reply to our query, stated that:

Unsupported scare news cannot be allowed free access to the public despite the First Amendment (as amended). No more could we allow a citizen, claiming the right of free speech, to yell "Fire" in a crowded shuttle. In our overcrowded cities a panic can be as dangerous as a bomb. You may appeal this decision within ten days.

The compactability equations predict a chaos center that will make a mass panic look like a ballet. Let us hope we are wrong, although Objectivist logic tells us we are right. But for the moment, we advise staying away from large population pools. Do not enter the urban crush of any city over forty million in population, as there may be a spark effect from the largest areas to the smaller.

OBJECTIVISTS KNOW—!!

BYSKB ACFDE OATDC QAVCP DOACT QWMKD CAVDH CPBBL MBAVC MDOEB BMMFI KMFRL CPBAQ VTDCQ BQBFO SDVPB HGMLS OHXMZ LIDAA IMXIM DMFSS HYIIQ UPYIM LQTXX

For further information, assistance, comfort, or courses in Objectivism, write:

Bureaucrat
The Objectivist Council
Box 2112/A-6
Orinda, California, N.A.
3-4/94563-6914-522

This letter is registered as polemic material with the Postmaster, Orinda, CA., N.A., 3-4/94563-1000-335, and can only be mailed to those whose written requests are on file in our current subscription book, which must be available for postal and public inspection. If you have received this letter without prior solicitation, and you object to its contents, you may report it to your local postmaster.

NINE

The holes in the north side of Verne prevented the floating city from sinking—they were too large. The North Face Ballast Tank Complex filled rapidly with water and sank, tilting the city to an angle of forty-eight degrees. This lifted the South Face Ballast Tank Complex high enough out of the Pacific so that the vandalized holes in it were above the waterline.

"I am relieved," Escobaga said, clinging to the railing of the tilted bar of the Restaurante Balboa. "I was beginning to think that the Organized Vandals were the only efficient organization left on Earth. It is comforting to know that even Vandalism has its screwups."

"I'm glad to know that you're feeling better," Peter said. He was perched on a table that was wedged firmly between a pillar and a water cooler, the rest of the tables having slid north to the glass wall. The lights had gone out, but the mechanism that rotated the room was still operating, so the tables would slowly climb into the east until, about every eight minutes, they would topple back down to the pole.

"I am feeling immortal," Escobaga explained, squeezing himself another whiskey. "And immortals don't get seasick. The prospect of imminent doom is past, and I am reassured that I will live forever, or at least until tomorrow—whichever comes first. These events are not to be regarded as mutually exclusive. Survivor's benefits will be paid. In case of hanky-panky, the life with the earliest postmark will be awarded the prize. The judges' decisions to be final in all cases. Prizewinners must agree to allow their images to be used as testimonials for the contest in whatever manner the conducting firm thinks appropriate."

"You're drunk," Peter decided. They were relatively alone in the restaurant, most of the other patrons and help having decided that one part of a sinking ship was preferable to another.

"Nonsense, my boy. That's a moral judgment, and therefore invalid. Sometimes the room really *is* spinning. You know what comes out of this faucet when I push the button? Mashed potatoes, that's what comes out. Hell of a note, I calls it. You know what all those groups have in common?"

Peter took a moment to realize that the last question was neither rhetorical nor redundant. "What groups?"

"The groups on that list I gave you. You're easily distracted, aren't you? You have to learn to keep your eye on the ball, your feet on the ground, and your nose to the grindstone, and not let yourself get rattled by these routine emergencies."

"What about them?"

"What about whom?"

"Those groups, you unrattleable paragon."

"Ah! Why didn't you ask me before?" Escobaga twisted around so that his back was braced by the side of the bar, took the soda water hose, and commenced squirting a high-pressure stream at the row of bottles still standing in front of the bar mirror. "They all have a common goal—a common desire. In a word, my lad, they are all after the same thing."

The spray of seltzer suddenly lost pressure, and a few last drops dribbled out of the nozzle. Escobaga stared sadly down at the chrome-plated fixture. "And so it goes."

"What thing?" Peter demanded. "Why do you all seem to have this conviction that the less I know, the better?"

"Working in the dark is very good training," Escobaga said, smiling up at Peter.

"Sure, for coal miners." Peter's table had begun to edge around the water cooler, and he grabbed for the pillar to stabilize himself. "What is this commonality? What thing are all of these groups after?"

"The stars, my boy," Escobaga said smugly. "Each of these groups, separately, is in search of the stars."

Peter sat back down on the pillar. "Don't stop there," he said. "What are you talking about?"

"I'm done talking," Escobaga said. "Talked too much already."

"Great!" Peter said.

INTERLUDE

The Grand KallaKak stood before the Portal of the Inner Lodge, as was prescribed in the Ancient Ceremony (1928; Revised 1989; Revised 2032), and beat symbolically on the hardwood door with his Enscribed Staff of Office in the Ritual Pattern: *Rump-titty-rump-titty-rump-rump-rump!*

"Porter," the Great Stamen of the Knights of the White Rose (Western Branch) exclaimed ritualistically, "ascertain who awaits without, and if it be a Christian and a Friend of the Order, bid him enter without cause."

The Porter stumped to the door and beat on its innards with his silver spoon. "Who awaits without?" he demanded.

The door was flung open. "It is I, the Grand KallaKak!"

"Who accompanies you?"

"Those who have been informed, and would join our Order as neophytes."

"Are they Christian men of good character?"

"They so are; I attest to it."

"Are they of White Blood, untainted?"

"They so are; I attest to it."

"Are they acquainted with the Good Works of this Order, and are they willing and eager to give themselves, heart and soul, body and mind, in speech and in deed, into the care and direction of the Great Stamen of the Knights of the White Rose (Western Branch), and obey such commands as he, or any of his Pistols may give?"

"As to that, I will allow the neophytes to speak for themselves."

The Grand KallaKak stood aside, and the twelve neophytes filed into the room. As each of them reached the First Position, he placed his hand on the Specially Abridged Bible that was mounted there, and murmured, "I so am" before continuing on to take his seat in the front row.

The Great Stamen held up his white-robed arms, and the assemblage grew quiet. "We have reached the planets," he intoned.

"We shall reach the stars!" the congregation replied.

"Who shall reach the stars?" the Great Stamen demanded.

"The White Race!" the congregation roared.

"So let it be," the Great Stamen agreed. Then he stepped forward and lifted his pointed hood, let it fall back around his shoulders, and donned the Golden Corolla of his office. "Brothers," he said, "tonight we are honored, indeed, in having as our guest speaker a man who I am sure you are all acquainted with, if not in the flesh, then, at least, in the printed and recorded word of—a man who, with little if not no vanity, has done more for our cause than a hundred preachers or a thousand cross-burners—a man who has spent a goodly portion of his millions on our holy cause—a man who I'm *proud* to declare is a White Man— Major John T. 'Jeb' Tucker. Let us hear it for Major Tucker!"

A tall, thin man with a hooked nose and several gold-capped teeth stepped forward and smiled. A buzzing noise ran around the room. Major Tucker looked startled for a moment, but the Great Stamen leaned over and whispered, "It's just our way of clapping for you. We ain't allowed to make too much noise in this here rented hall."

Major Tucker renewed his smile and leaned forward confidentially. "My greetings to each and every one of you," he said. "I come to bring you the Word, and the Word is good. And we must spread the Word and make it understood. And the Word is of God and the White Race." He lifted up his arms to the heavens and stared upward, through the dingy ceiling, to the Cosmos. . . .

TEN

The data screen was one square meter of glowing heliotrope emblazoned with brilliant chartreuse symbols, letters, and figures:

STAR: [beta] PERSEI A (ALGOL)
PRESENT DISTANCE FROM SOL: 114.21 LIGHT-YEARS
MASS: 4.30 SOLS
LUMINOSITY: 143 SOLS
RADIUS: 2,140 MEGAMETERS
SATELLITES:
  (1) STAR: [beta] PERSEI B
     DISTANCE FROM PRIMARY: 10,200 MEGAMETERS
     MASS: 0.86 SOLS
     LUMINOSITY: 0.79 SOLS
     RADIUS: 2,450 MEGAMETERS
     PERIOD OF ROTATION ABOUT PRIMARY:
                 69 HRS 0 MIN 19 SEC ± 0.9 SEC
     SATELLITES: NONE
  (2) STAR [beta] PERSEI C
     DISTANCE FROM PRIMARY: 430,000 MEGAME-
     TERS

*

*

*

*

FLICK—FLACK—FLICK—FLACK

A new set of symbols replaced the first, and Senator Pedro Dooley blinked inadvertently in time with the flicking. He had not had time to finish reading all the data on the screen, but he would be damned if he would let Pencannon know he was a slow reader. Instead he concentrated on the next set of data. It was concerned with the planets circling [beta] Persei C, and the senator found that he was not in the least interested.

The senator and the data screen gazed at each other with no trace of mutual comprehension. Had the computer's scanner been focused on the senator, it would have registered that he was 167.6 cm tall (Senator Dooley, an old-fashioned man, thought of himself as "five-feet-six"). Had the computer been programmed for historical correlation, it might have equated the senator's shoulder-length white hair and long, pointed, white beard with the ancient descriptions of King Edward the Confessor, but it had never heard of that saintly monarch.

Other correlations might have been made between the senator and the saint. Decent. Peace-loving. Politically charismatic. Kingly. Kind. Concerned about people. Seemingly naïve. And possessing a façade that projected just a soupçon of homely stupidity. The People really liked homely stupidity.

Senator Pedro Dooley was a Man of the People.

As with so many other political Men of the People, Dooley felt quite qualified in handling the People's affairs without bothering to inform the People. Which is why Griffin Universal felt quite secure in entrusting Senator Dooley with its version of the truth.

FLICK—FLACK—FLICK—FLACK—FLICK

The data screen turned heliotrope all over, except for a bright orange border, and stayed that way. Dooley turned to look at Pencannon.

"Is that all? I mean—everything?"

Pencannon's eyes opened a trifle wider in his otherwise expressionless face. "You can see any other data you'd like, Senator. Was there anything in particular you feel you should like to go over? Is there anything we can repeat for you? Is there anything you'd like explained?"

"It's not that," the senator said somewhat stiffly. "The data were quite adequate, I imagine. At least, so far. But I trust you didn't ask me here merely to show me a dozen screensful of undigested data."

Pencannon allowed a smile to come over his face. "My apologies,

Senator. I should have known you'd want to get to the meat of the thing quickly." His long fingers began moving over the control console.

"The data you are looking at is from the gashopper *From Here to Eternity*, which has been in orbit around Beta Persei C for three years now. It has located seven planets of Mars size or better, none apparently habitable or habited."

"Why do you call them 'gashoppers'?" Dooley interrupted.

"It's a slang expression. It has to do with their shape. Each ship is about two and a half kilometers long, shaped like an old-time dirigible, and full of a combination of rare gasses—except for a cylinder going down the middle that holds the—ah—experimental apparatus."

"How does it work?" Dooley asked.

"You've got me there, Senator," Pencannon said. He took a deep breath and continued with his spiel.

"The second gashopper, *Gone With the Wind*, under full automatic control, should have reached the null point—what we would call the turnover point if it were a constant-acceleration ion-drive ship—uh, should have reached the null point just about three hundred and forty hours ago. At that point, if all went well, the status of the test animals and plants aboard was recorded and sent back in an automatic sounding torpedo. That torpedo will arrive near Earth in a very few minutes now—uh"—he looked at the time readout on the console—"that is, between ten and forty-five minutes from now. It will orient itself, then beam a signal toward Earth. The deep-space radio telescope net will be watching for it, and we will immediately triangulate its position. Then we'll be able to beam a signal to it to empty its data crystals and—"

The door to the big room opened, and Pencannon turned his head to look. So did the senator.

Four men entered at the far end of the huge instrument-filled room and walked toward Pencannon and the senator. Their faces were all beaming with businesslike smiles.

"Not too late, I hope, Mr. Pencannon?" said the foremost of the newcomers.

"Not at all, Mr. Lettmore," Pencannon said. "Plenty of time. Gentlemen, may I present you to Senator Pedro Dooley. Senator, these are four of our directors. Mr. Lettmore, Mr. Darthwaite, Mr. Parker, and Mr. Landau."

Senator Dooley shook the hands and mouthed the words, but he didn't have to think about what he said; those phrases had been engraved on his mind for decades. Instead he was carefully listening to what was being told him and carefully observing the manner in which it was said. In the next thirty-two minutes Senator Pedro Dooley had formed a fairly accurate assessment of all five of the men from Griffin Universal.

He knew they were lying to him.

But he didn't know what about—or why.

It was shortly after he had reached that decision that the various detectors in the room came to life. A loudspeaker emitted a shrill

BREEP!

The torpedo from the *Gone With the Wind* was signaling from a point well inside the orbit of Jupiter. It had slowed down from its orgy of relativistic travel, but it was still moving right along. At the speed it was going it would be out of the Solar System again in twelve hours. The technicians busied themselves in the effort of draining it of all knowledge.

Senator Dooley settled down to watch the show, confident that it was, indeed, a show. And all he had to do was figure out why.

ELEVEN

"We're *so* glad you've come to see us," the woman behind the desk trilled. "How did you hear of us? Have you read our pamphlets?"

"Just a few," Peter confessed. "You see, a friend told me about your organization and—I thought—you see—" He managed to look nervous, shifting his blue protect case from hand to hand.

"I understand completely," she assured him. A skinny, too-pale woman in her late thirties with mouse-brown hair that she kept poking at, she was dressed in puffy pale blue—puffy at the shoulders, elbows, bustline, and waist. She looked like a slightly overdone turnover. "Here, take some of this reading material. Anything that looks new to you. Come to our outing Saturday—my gosh, that's tomorrow—and you can see what we're like. Then, if you like us and we get along with you, you can join on Monday."

"Isn't there any probationary period, or testing, or anything like that?"

"Hell no," the woman said, looking pleased that she had been so daring. "How could we call ourselves the Society for Total Freedom if we had membership restrictions?"

"I don't know," Peter admitted.

"We have to like you and you have to like us. Friendship—close, personal friendship—is what it's all about. Is there a woman you can take to the outing? We like our couples paired up sexually, you know. Every man should have a woman. Unless, of course, they happen to prefer other men. Total freedom is, after all, total freedom. Every person should have a partner, we like to put it."

"How often?" Peter inquired. He pictured the couples busy pairing up sexually. Someone faster or more impatient than the group average inquiring, "May I play through?" He grinned.

"I take it you don't currently have a woman?" the woman asked. "I will give you a list of names. They are all nice girls. Friendly, but nice. They could also act as guides and mentors."

"Thank you," Peter said. *Also?* he wondered.

The men called the women, Peter discovered. It wasn't merely the hangover of a time-honored custom, it was also that there were three times as many women in the organization as men. Peter chose names at random on the list. The first two were busy, "But thank you for calling and maybe some other time. You look like a nice man." The third thought it might be all right, but she wanted to meet him in person first because she didn't go out on blind dates, and seeing him on the phone wasn't the same as meeting him, after all. A half hour cup of coffee in a restaurant would be fine.

They met at Daisy-Bee Coffeehouse Number 27,956, "A Member of the Fastest-Growing Chain of Quality Food Dispensers in the North Western Semisphere—Sit Down, Let Our Helpful Waitresses Serve You." Her name was Shirley Vermont. She was small and slender, with pitch-black hair and glowing almond eyes and tiny hands that assumed positions while she spoke. A fine mechanical doll come to life, she was always in motion and, in motion, she was lovely. Her voice had a peculiar lilting quality, and a trace of accent that Peter couldn't place. It reminded him of the Orient, but was somehow totally different.

They sat in a corner booth and stared at each other for a time measured in heartbeats.

"I'm sorry," the waitress said. "This table is reserved for three or more."

Peter didn't bother pointing out that the place was empty except for them. "We're expecting a friend," he told her. "Any minute now."

The waitress sniffed. "Do you want to wait for your friend before I take your order?" she asked suspiciously.

"My friend is a member of the Grand Order of Bactrian Camel Drivers," Peter told her, "so we'd better order now."

Still suspicious, but puzzled, the waitress took their orders and went away.

"Did that mean anything?" Shirley asked.

"I hope not," Peter assured her. "Tell me what it's like, being totally free?"

"I don't really know yet. I've only been to a few meetings. So far, they seem to be just as hung up as I am."

Progress, Peter reflected, is when a girl admits to you that she has hang-ups. Step two is when she confides that she wants to get rid of them.

"I'm working on my hang-ups," Shirley said. "Trying to get rid of them. But it's hard to tell the difference, sometimes, between hang-ups and natural laws."

"I know what you mean," Peter said. "Fear of traveling on airplanes is a hang-up, but fear of stepping out of ten-story windows isn't. As far as sex goes, when society allows you to do anything you want, as long as it hurts no one else, how do you decide where to draw the line?"

Shirley looked appreciatively across the booth. "My mother would like you."

"Thank you," Peter said, wondering what her mother had to do with it. "Where are you from?"

"Brooklyn. You couldn't tell? Most people say they knew it the moment they saw me."

"I'm not such an expert. I like your accent, but I couldn't place it."

"Well, thank you. I thought it was all gone by now. I've been living here for a little over three years. But as long as you like it, I don't mind. I like yours, too. You're not from around here either. I can tell."

"That's right," Peter admitted. "I'm from Britain. London, actually. My parents are living in Sri Lanka at the moment, but I still have an apartment in Broxton. I seldom get to see it, because I travel a lot in my work, but it's there."

"You travel?" Shirley asked, her eyes wide. "I've always wanted to travel."

"It has its disillusioning moments," Peter said.

The waitress brought over two coffees. "I'll get your Danish in a minute," she told Shirley. "The cook is heating it by hand."

It was an interesting image. "What's wrong?" Peter asked. "Is the toaster broken?"

"Toaster? No. We're using self-heating Danishes, and the whole carton of cheese have been burning up when we open them. You rip the airtight liner off and in a couple of seconds it's too hot to hold, and a minute later it's a black, bubbly glob on the floor. You should have been here for breakfast this morning; it was a mess. So now we've gone back to the good old-fashioned microwave." She retreated back to the kitchen.

Peter took Shirley's hand. "It's these little crises that bring two people together. I feel that I know you much better now that the Danish has self-destructed."

"You have the right attitude," she said, patting his hand.

A large gaunt man wearing a giant's cast-off clothing came through the door. He paused, a study in suspended motion, for a long instant, then twitched decisively, shuffled to Peter's booth, and settled in across from Peter, driving Shirley into the corner. His hair was dirty blond, thin and long, falling well past his shoulders. His beard was patchy, as though he occasionally shaved small random sections of it. His eyes were deep blue, with prominent red veins running through the white, and sunk deep into their sockets. "Wel-come," he said.

"Would you please move to another booth, sir," Peter said clearly, in the manner one adopts with small children or drunken adults. "I'm afraid you're disturbing my wife."

The man continued staring at Peter, oblivious to his words. Shirley hunched in the corner, drawing herself as far away as she could. "Do something!" she demanded.

"Talk about your crises," Peter said, getting up. He took the man's arm. The man didn't notice, continuing to stare across at the spot Peter had just vacated. He was vibrating gently all over and making constant slight motions and then overcorrecting, as if his muscles were being operated by remote control from a great distance away.

"Pe-ter," he said to the empty space across the booth. "You are good to me. It is even. I am good to you. Pe-ter. Welcome. I see you, Pe-ter. You stretch across my time. Stretched tight, you are. You bounce. I bounce. The others fade or pop."

"Goddamn!" Peter said softly. He pinched the man's skin and watched the white mark slowly fade away, and then examined the man's eyes. "Goddamn!" He sat back down. "Shirley, listen. Can you get out of the corner without moving him? He's not a drunk, and he knows my name."

Shirley dropped out of sight under the table and reappeared on Peter's side without further comment. Peter mentally chalked a large checkmark next to her name. "What *is* wrong with him?" she asked. "Where do you know him from?"

"I've never seen him before, as best as I can remember. He's high on bounce, and I don't think he's ever coming down."

"Bounce?" I've heard of it, but I don't know anything about dope."

"No high school experimentation?"

"Listen," Shirley said. "To you this is the twenty-second century, but in Bay Ridge it's still 2030. My mother thinks that cannabis drives you crazy, masturbation causes pimples, and a girl who isn't married by the age of sixteen is a whore. You tell her different."

"I'll tell you about bounce," Peter said. "Don't worry about him; he isn't really there until he starts talking."

* * *

Phenylhydroxydimethylcerebrenol, as it was listed in the *Leeds Handbook of Biochemical Engineering*, Sixth Edition, abbreviated PHD by some unknown humorist, had the street name "bounce." It was a multiple mystery. First, in structure. Bounce had been partially analyzed. It had multiple carbon rings somewhere in the middle and atoms of lithium and copper somewhere in the chain, which seemed to stretch erratically from here to there, depending on the sample being analyzed. It refused to analyze any further without giving conflicting and confusing results—and nobody knew or could come up with a decent theory as to why.

Next, in origin. Nobody knew where it came from except whoever was distributing it. It was impossible to tell whether it was a natural or synthetic product, which made very little difference except that biochemists would have liked to shake the hand of anyone able to synthesize it.

The effect was known, but generally not believed. When taken in nanogram doses, the white crystalline powder removed the conscious mind from its moving peg between past and future, and placed it somewhere (somewhen?) to the left of time. A very enticing drug did not remove problems but put them in a nicer, broader perspective. It was not physiologically addictive, but seemed to be highly psychologically habituating. The effects were cumulative, and, when sufficiently accumulated, further doses of the drug became superfluous.

The gentleman sitting opposite Peter and Shirley was at the superfluous stage. Further doses of the drug would do nothing for him, and nothing known to man would bring him back to the spot known as the present for anything but a brief visit. He simultaneously existed at all points on his lifeline, and could see ahead and behind his own physical existence for a variable distance.

When it was established that this was indeed what happened— about three years after the drug's mysterious introduction some ten years ago—when the first bouncers refused to come down and serious research was done to determine just where they were—various people had various schemes to profit from this condition. Some attempted to benefit the human race, most tried to better themselves; none were markedly successful. The bouncers would not communicate except when *they* had something to say. They bounced into reality and left just as suddenly, staying long enough to perform vital bodily functions (when they thought of it) and hold conversations of varying lengths. Sometimes one disjointed sentence. Sometimes they conversed for weeks at a time. The people they spoke to might be there, might have been there yesterday, or might be coming there tomorrow. The bouncers tried to be exact, but one day is such a short span out of eternity.

Some of those who managed to converse with bouncers felt as though they had just shared a mystical experience and glimpsed, from a distance, a great beauty. Others were merely annoyed by the random,

seemingly meaningless phrases. Seldom did either group feel as though
they had acquired any useful information or accomplished anything
like an exchange of ideas. But still, when a bouncer wants to talk to you
by name, it would probably be wise to listen. Somewhere in the intricate skein of words arranged by one who could see both ends of a
conversation and was likely to work symmetrically toward the middle,
one who probably didn't have a clear idea of when the conversation was
taking place, one who saw all of your deeds and could be aware of none
of your hopes; somewhere in this pattern could lie your future.

                              *   *   *

The waitress returned to the table bearing Shirley's toasted Danish
and sniffed audibly as she set it down. Daisy-Bee Coffeehouse Number
27,956, she was clearly thinking, is a high-class place, and doesn't cater
to bums.

"Our friend has arrived," Peter said. "He would like a hamburger—
no, a cheeseburger—and a glass of natural milk." The waitress sniffed
again, and left.

"That's very hard to believe," Shirley said. "I mean, one doesn't
think of time as something you can travel in, except forward at a set
rate."

"Don't think of him as physically traveling through time," Peter
said. "His body goes along at the same rate, in the same way, as yours
or mine. It tends to get to more interesting places, since he knows
when things are going to happen. But their time sense is badly warped.
Sometimes you'll see a group of bouncers gathered on a street corner
waiting expectantly—well, perhaps interestedly is a better word—and
you know that *something* is going to happen soon. Then again, you
might see one hurrying toward a spot where an event happened a few
days ago. Bad timing, or something."

"What sort of things do they go to? Explosions, fires, Vandal happenings?"

"Not usually. They seem to go for more subtle events, things that are
more important on a long time scale, if less immediately exciting.
Twenty-three of them gathered at the Berlin Zoo two years ago; I think
that's the most ever seen together at one time."

"What happened?"

"An African elephant died. It wasn't until sometime later that it was generally realized that it was the last African elephant." He sipped at his coffee and stared at the gaunt face across the table. The bouncer stared back at him, and Peter wondered what he was seeing. "Then last year four of them showed up at the Los Angeles County Museum. That was two days before the quake."

"Do they only show up at tragedies?" Shirley asked.

"No. They come to ends and beginnings. It's just that it's much easier to tell an end than a beginning. Last year three of them visited the maternity ward of a hospital in New Delhi. Obviously they came to see a particular newborn child, but no one could tell which child. Then again, there were six of them in the room when the American Senator Dooley, Chairman of the Space Committee, had the oath of office administered to him for his fourth or fifth term—something like that. Never attended any of his other ceremonies. Nobody knew how they got there, but then no one wanted to throw them out. The reporters tried interviewing the six of them for a while, but couldn't figure out what they were doing there."

"Wouldn't they talk?"

"Sure they'd talk. I'll get you the crystal if you like; it makes less sense than Dutch Schultz's dying words."

"Who?"

"Dutch Schultz. He was a famous gangster in the 1930s or '40s who was shot by a rival gang. His last words were taped by a police stenographer and later published in a book of parodies as a parody of Gertrude Stein."

"I've heard of her, at least," Shirley said. "She's the American lesbian who went to Paris to find intellectual freedom, and then wrote a cookbook and nonsense poetry under the name of George Sand."

"Something like that," Peter admitted cautiously.

The bouncer stirred. "I thank you, Pe-ter. Pe-ter. Pe-ter Ly-on. Lyon. Peter Lyon." His voice was thin and whispery, with a rustling quality reminiscent of a light breeze over dried grass.

"He wants to tell me something," Peter said. "Or, possibly, he thinks he already has." He leaned forward and covered the bony hand with his own. "What is it? What do you want to tell me? Can I do something for you?"

"Pet-er. There's no body here. No body. My, isn't it beautiful. All alone." He was silent for a minute, and then his eyes slowly focused on

Peter. "You must watch. Watch. Warned is armed. The girl is dead. Take the blue case. Is that it?"

"That already happened," Peter told him. "Look!" He lifted the blue protect case up to the table and showed it to the bouncer. "I have the case."

"That's it," the bouncer affirmed. "Take it. Do not leave it behind. Important. The girl will be dead. Is dead. That is not it?"

"Here's your burger!" the waitress announced, sliding the plate in front of the dirty emaciated seer. "Milk." She wrote out the check, slapped it facedown, and departed.

"I hope I'm not the girl he's talking about," Shirley said, staring with an awed fascination at the bouncer.

"You're not," Peter assured her. He leaned forward and put the bouncer's hand on the sandwich. "Eat!" he said firmly. "Eat now!" He leaned back, and the bouncer picked up the cheeseburger and started mechanically eating it, his eyes unfocused and disinterested. He dripped on the table and on himself.

Shirley slid back under the table to the other side and adjusted a large paper napkin around the gaunt man like a great bib. "I don't think I'd like to be like he is," she said. "Does he know what he's doing, or what's happening around him?"

"In some ways not, in some ways better than you or I. He's very prone to accept and follow simple suggestions like 'Eat' or 'Walk' or the like. Anything more complex he'll simply forget before he carries it out."

"You mean anyone can order him around?"

"I suppose so, but who'd bother? The only thing a bouncer is useful for is information, and that you can't understand even when they want to give it."

"Why do you know so much about this PHD stuff?"

That's what I like, Peter thought. *A nice direct girl. Ah well, she's probably what I deserve.* "I took the stuff for a while," he told her. "Not enough for any noticeable cumulative effect, but enough to get very interested in the process. I stopped well before any permanent symptoms developed—frightened away by what I'd read about it. I have no more idea of what's going to happen tomorrow than you, and a damn poor memory for what happened yesterday. Ask me about my sixth birthday and I'm a whiz."

All through this the gaunt man ate; his fingers grasping, his arm lifting and lowering, his jaw chewing, and his mind traveling throughout the breadth of time, an impotent observer of one small segment of Mankind's triumphal march toward the heat death of the Universe. Bouncers shambling along a street were known to suddenly stop and stare at a person, a building, a random artifact, or a patch of empty space, and start to laugh and laugh and laugh until someone led them away. They seldom cry. Neither physical pain nor personal tragedy can touch them. Nobody knows what it is that makes them cry. It is not good to watch a bouncer cry.

"What's it like, taking PHD?"

"I know this is going to sound puerile, but it is almost impossible to describe. It's difficult to remember just what it was like. Even the next day it's difficult to remember. There is a disorientation, as though everything were pulled away from you and turned to a new angle. There is a change in stress and importance. And you become vaguely aware of a new way to measure things: Besides weight, or height, or bulk, there is permanence."

"You mean like being aware of time?"

"No. Not that, really. One is always aware of time. This just twists the awareness into a new—shape. I told you it was hard to describe." Peter thought back to his college days. "There's a kind of stretching and a fuzziness around the edges of events, as though they're all happening at once and you're watching the parts move. The more you take, the wider this fuzziness becomes, and the harder to tell where one specific thing leaves off and another begins. It's like floating up through a layer of fog. The higher you get the more you can see, but the less clearly you can see any one thing. I understand there's a breakthrough point, which our friend here must have passed, after which everything becomes clear again; it's just that there's so much of it."

The gaunt man finished eating, and Peter placed the glass of milk in his hand. "Now drink!" And he did.

Peter leaned forward and stared into the man's eyes. "Hello," he said. "Hello." A greeting, a call to attract attention, a plea for recognition, a return of recognition: "Hello, hello, hello . . ."

The bouncer focused on the table, and his gaze slowly moved up to Peter's face. He moved his hand out to tug at Peter's sleeve, knocking over the milk glass unnoticed: "Hello. Pe-ter." Shirley picked up the glass and removed the napkin from his chin; he didn't notice. "Hello. Thank you, Pe-ter."

("He's thanking you for the food," Shirley whispered. "I doubt it," Peter answered. "Just listen.")

"You are here. Pivot. Blue case pivot. You pivot. Is this clear? Cowlike noises clear?"

"Listen," Peter said, speaking as distinctly as he could. "What am I the pivot to? What are you thanking me for?"

The gaunt man turned and stared at him, and for a moment Peter felt that he had made contact. "The stars!" the bouncer said. "Can you hear them? You should. You. The stars!" He made a gesture with his arm that almost upset the sugar. "I give you the Earth. We are all alone now. When. Isn't it pretty?"

The bouncer stood up, his eyes now focused on infinity. "I go to watch things drip apart," he said. "It clears, mandible-clacking clarity, when I am there. And sometimes I am there. Welcome, Pe-ter." He shuffled through the door humming a tune that had yet to be written.

"Well!" Shirley said, patting her hair into place. "You must lead an interesting life."

"It's an old Chinese curse," Peter told her, remembering what Escobaga had said. "May you live in interesting times."

*　　*　　*

The next morning they took a cable car to Northend in Marin and rented an electric for the ride out to the S for TF outing in a national park area north of the city. The parking lot was already filling up when they arrived. Suspended between two redwood trees, a large banner hung thirty meters over the entrance to the park:

WELCOME ALL TO THE MONTHLY OUTING OF
THE SOCIETY FOR TOTAL FREEDOM

The reverse side of the banner, Peter noticed as they passed under it, was covered with an imaginative variety of obscene cartoons.

The park began as a chain of linked glades, leading deeper and deeper into a dense redwood forest. A path, expensively constructed to look natural, went along a narrow glen from one of the inner glades to a large grassy clearing entirely surrounded by *Sequoia sempervirens*. It was majestic and beautiful; an open-air cathedral with 150-meter-tall arches, and a sky-blue vault. The two hundred or so society members, in different stages of cavort around the clearing, were reduced in perspective to the appearance of church mice frolicking in the nave of St. Paul's.

The ground crunched underfoot with a layer of drying leaves, needles, and cones; and the air held the presence of sequoia. All sounds were muted by the natural baffle chamber of the surrounding woods, and the lack of a visible sun, shut out by the surrounding great trees, gave a majestically gloomy feeling over all. It was somehow sad, Peter thought, that no Druid priest had ever seen a sequoia.

"Come on, let's register," Shirley said, dragging Peter over to a portable table, standing on thin aluminum legs between two great trees. The skinny woman who had been behind the desk in the S for TF office was now behind the table. She had let down her hair and, in a peasant blouse and wraparound skirt, looked as if she were ready for great things.

"I'm so glad you decided to come," she said. "And you, Miss Vermont, it's so good to see you here. I hope you both have a rewarding time. Let's see, Mr.—ah, oh yes—Lyon. You're not a member. There's a twenty-dollar fee for nonmembers. It's to help pay for the rental of the park and the insurance; we're forced to take out a great deal of insurance. Heaven only knows what they think is liable to happen, but whatever it is we're insured for it." She took Peter's twenty and waved him off. "Now go have fun, you two. And remember—be good! Being good takes constant practice!" She chuckled happily as they left the table.

Peter and Shirley wandered around the field holding hands, stopping to listen to a discussion group gathered in a circle on the grass arguing over very basic sexual politics, on the order of who had the right to do what, and with which, and to whom. They stood at the rear of a group watching an animated demonstration of "How the Romans Did It Under Nero." They listened briefly to a young long-haired woman with a wary expression who was lecturing on "Complete Sexual Freedom as the Basis for a Free Society," and to a pinched-faced man with bright eyes who was speaking earnestly on the theme "Migration: Somewhere There's a Place for Us."

"You want to leave Earth?" Peter asked as they wandered away.

"If there is somewhere to go," Shirley said. "Why not? But there really is noplace to go. One can't migrate to the space colonies; they're as restrictive as Earth itself. In many ways, more restrictive. I can't really believe that the government is hiding the secret of faster-than-light travel, like so many of these people seem to think. Why should they? But, when it is developed, I think I might like to migrate to a fresh planet where the population isn't so inhibited. After all, there'll be enough to go around. Everyone will be able to have just the sort of place they like."

A bell rang, a deep, sonorous sound with ponderous overtones. Peter looked around but couldn't find the bell. It sounded again. "Time!" someone shouted into a microphone, and the echo "Time!" came back from the trees. Aha! Both bell and voice were amplified. Now that Peter was able to cast out the vision of a giant church bell suspended beneath a steeple-tree, he spotted both ringer and speaker. A small scurrying gentleman with a handheld public address system was instructing the Totally Free:

"Time, everyone, time. The first Event. Everyone pair up. Complete nudity is the rule. The rest will follow as the night the day. Remember: We are totally free. Come on, everyone, don't be the last to divest! Free yourselves of the encumbrances of everyday life. Enjoy! What are we here for?"

"What are we here for?" Peter asked Shirley.

"We have to pair up," she said.

"I thought we were paired up."

"You don't have to pick me," she informed him. "We just come in two-by-two to make sure the odds are even, if you know what I mean."

"I want you," Peter decided.

"That's nice. Me too. I mean, the other way."

"What do we do now?"

"See what all the others are doing?" she asked. Peter could hardly help noticing the acre of people busily removing garments. "We take our clothes off. Turn around."

"Turn around?"

"I told you I have hang-ups. Turn around."

Peter turned around and started taking his clothes off, stacking them in a neat pile on the grass. Total freedom, he thought, had peculiar penalties. In modern society, where casual nudity was an accepted fact of life, people shouldn't make such a big deal out of removing their clothes. The people who band together to fight for total sexual freedom are the people who feel they don't have it. The repressed people who have to be directed to be free.

"I'm ready," Shirley said.

He turned back. "So you are."

"You are too," she said. "That's nice. I thought we'd like each other." She came into his arms, and they fell together onto the leaves. Somewhere someone sang.

> *To be free, to be free,*
> *To be totally free;*
> *Oh isn't it grand to be free?*
> *Like a bird, like a bee,*
> *Like a diclinous tree;*
> *There's you and there's me, and we're free!*
>
> *To be in, to be out,*
> *To be up and about;*
> *Oh isn't life grand when you're free?*
> *To be male, to be fe-,*
> *To be you, to be me;*
> *To feel and to taste and to see.*
>
> *To be free, you and me,*
> *He and she, two or three;*
> *Oh isn't it fun when we're free?*
> *Like the waves of the sea*
> *As they crash over we*
> *With a smash, and a dash, and we're free!*

Peter had a strong memory of martial music being played sometime during the next twenty minutes, but he was never sure if it really happened. It could have. Perhaps it should have. Shirley seemed to remove her hang-ups with her clothes, and she really *did* seem to be fond of Peter. They laughed and cried in alternating minutes, and came together and separated, and rolled over each on the other, and possessed each other, and made wild, glorious love. And made happy, contented love.

Then they sat, each forming a rest for the other, and talked. The others about them were still paired or tripled or more, but they took no notice of others.

"Should we get dressed?" Peter asked after a while.

"Why?" asked Shirley. "Not yet. I like looking at you."

"That is a valid point," he said, running his hand along her inner thigh. "And the grass is comfortable."

"Yes. And you have that blue case to use as a pillow. Do you take that thing everywhere you go? Everywhere?"

Peter nodded. "You should see me playing tennis. Or swimming."

"Do you like the Society?" Shirley asked. "I hope you do."

Peter thought about it for a minute. He felt guilty at having come to the Society for Total Freedom under false pretenses, just to put them under observation. But this was balanced by the fact that he had no idea what he was looking for—except that someone might try to steal the blue case. But did he like the Society? No, he thought it was silly. But he liked Shirley. "Let me take you away from all this," he said, rolling over to look at her.

"Really?"

"Yes," Peter said, deciding that anything less than honesty was—dishonest. "I like—I am very fond of you. Already. But the Society doesn't turn me on much. Free sex among the stars isn't that much of a motivating force for me."

"Let's put our clothes on," she said. "Turn around."

INTERLUDE

The four hundred men and women of Baker Company formed a ragged line four-deep in the company street and stood stiffly at a vague approximation of attention: eyes straight ahead, shoulders back, fingers along the uniform seams of their ill-fitting khaki trousers. Before them, their first sergeant, in a deep-blue uniform jacket with large brass buttons and excessive gold stripes, strutted like a malevolent bantam rooster.

"You call yourselves soldiers, *mes petites,*" he snarled at them. "You are nothing more than sissyboys and sissygirls. Not a one of you can run twenty kilometers with a full pack before breakfast. *Zut alors!* And you will get no more time to practice. Basic training is over for you troops. Tomorrow you move up to the front lines. The major will speak with you now. Ten-*shun!*"

The major stepped in front of them, his uniform thrice as resplendent as the sergeant's, his rows of medals gleaming in the early morning light. "Congratulations," he said, his voice amplified by his lapel mike to a cracking boom. "When you came to War Games Theme Park two weeks ago, you were civilians in search of adventure, using your two-month yearly vacation to experience in full the glories and hardships of battle. Now you have become soldiers. Welcome to World War I. You will spend the next six weeks in battlefield conditions as realistic as we can make them. Those of you who live through it will truly have lived! Today we're shipping you to the Ardennes. Tomorrow you go over the top."

A little man stepped out of the ranks. "I don't think I want to go any more," he said in a tired voice.

"What's that?"

"Sir, I don't think I want to go—sir."

"You should have read your contract more carefully. For the next six weeks, trooper, your ass is ours. Sergeant—put that dissident on permanent KP. And make sure he goes over the top in the first wave."

The troops of Baker Company, along with the troops of Able, Charlie, Dog, and Foxtrot companies, were crowded into rickety wooden third-class carriages, and pulled around and around the perimeter of the War Games Theme Park by a sooty, ancient locomotive at twenty kilometers an hour. Various landmarks were changed ahead of them each time around to give the impression of traveling a great distance. Finally, after dark, the train stopped and they were detrained at a rearline trench, where they were allowed to sleep. From somewhere in the immediate distance came the *crump* of artillery and the chatter of machine guns. An occasional star shell lit up the surroundings. They did not sleep well.

The next morning, at dawn, they were chivied along miles of the zigzag communications trench to the front line. Rolling waves of thick white fog gave a mystical quality to the earthenwork defenses. The bloody, bedraggled-looking troops that they relieved staggered into the communications trench and started back without a word.

At six o'clock they were lined up against the outer wall and told to fix bayonets. At six-fifteen the major walked down the line to give an encouraging speech. At six-thirty a whistle blew, and was immediately echoed all up and down the line. The two-week soldiers scrambled up the rope ladders and went over the top.

The fog had not yet lifted, and the troops could not see farther than the tangle of barbed wire in front of them. It was unearthily quiet as they went forward.

And then, from the pseudo-Boche trenches ahead of them, the deadly coughing of the water-cooled, nine-millimeter machine guns began. Nickel-jacketed bullets mowed down the khaki-clad soldiers like a scythe blade through grain. Soon the guns stopped, and the only sound was the crying of the wounded.

During the course of the morning, those who were able crawled back to their trench and rolled in. It was noon before a truce party came out to no-man's-land to take away the dead and wounded.

"Tomorrow it'll be our turn," one of the survivors muttered, cleaning his mud-caked uniform off as best he could with his mud-caked hands. "Tomorrow they attack us! We'll get those Boche bastards!"

"You know"—his companion, a little balding man, leaned over to him—"I'm having fun, really I am. But next year I think I'll just go to the beach."

TWELVE

Peter stopped feeling like an idiot three seconds after he crossed the drawbridge, walked under the great portcullis, and found himself inside the long hall that led to the outer bailey.

He had felt foolish ever since Escobaga had helped him get into the costume. It consisted of tights, pointed shoes, a loose, balloon-sleeved sort of jacket with scalloped edges, a long cloak, a weird-looking hat, and a ninety-centimeter broadsword swinging at his left side.

Peter had stared at himself in the mirror, and then turned to Escobaga. "I won't go," he had said. "You can do this one yourself!"

"Pshaw!" Escobaga had replied. "Of course you'll go, my boy. That's what youth is all about. You don't want to waste your youth by *not* doing things. You'll have nothing to talk about in your old age. Plenty of time not to do things when you're physically incapable."

"You don't look physically incapable to me," Peter had said. "You go."

Escobaga had looked sad and shaken his head. "Clothes do not make the man. The man makes the clothes. You look quite handsome, actually. Trust me."

Peter had allowed himself to be cajoled, and here he was; walking across the outer bailey of Castle Hightower, the residence of Tismane of the Far Reaches, King of the Western Empire and Hereditary Emperor of the Universal Monarchist Society. And all at once he didn't feel silly. He was dressed as a man should be dressed who has just crossed a drawbridge, walked under a portcullis, and strode across an outer bailey. Except for the blue protect case, which went with him everywhere at Escobaga's insistence and looked definitely out of place. He was dressed as those around him were dressed—those not wearing half-armor and standing around holding pikestaffs. The outer bailey, he discovered, was a large semicleared space between the castle walls and the castle buildings, which were known as the keep. Somewhere on the other side of these massive walls, Peter assumed, there would be another clear space called the inner bailey. Otherwise the area he was crossing would just be "the bailey."

In the far corner of the outer bailey, near a pen full of goats, were a group of men clad in full armor and wielding swords and shields, who were engaged two-by-two in what looked to be a stylized ritual of a battle. A sort of grand knight ballet. Peter stood watching it for a couple of minutes before continuing on to the inner portcullis.

The serjeant of the guard, a tall, dolorous-looking man wearing chain mail and a porkpie helm, and sporting a two-foot shortsword in an ornate leather scabbard, stopped Peter at the gate. "Ho there, stranger," he said, leaning over the half-door to the guardhouse and smiling a friendly smile. "Whence cometh you? Where goeth you?"

"I cometh from San Francisco," Peter told him. "I goeth to see King Tismane. I haveth an appointment."

The serjeant consulted a clipboard. "You hight Peter Lyon? That right? You be vender?"

"Do we have to talk like this?" Peter demanded.

"It gets to you after a while," the serjeant of the guard admitted. "You kind of forget you're doing it. Here, wait a minute." He rummaged on a shelf behind him, and produced a plastic-bound booklet. "Here's a vocabulary with some sample sentences so you can get the hang of it."

"Thanks," Peter said. "Who talks like this?"

"We do," the serjeant told him. "Just us."

"I am not one to comment on another man's hobby," Peter said, "but this rather looks like an obsession."

The serjeant of the guard nodded. "It's very interesting, people's reactions," he said. "First they think we're crazy. Then they think it looks like fun, so they come to a couple of tourneys. Then, when they see how seriously some of us take it, they think we're crazy again. Then some of them see that we're not any crazier than anyone else, and at least we're enjoying ourselves, so they join. Full-time. Except for their straight jobs, of course."

"What are those men doing out there?" Peter asked, pointing to the ongoing ballet in the outer bailey.

"Men and women," the guard said. "You couldn't tell, of course, in their armor. They are practicing full-armor fighting techniques for the next tourney."

"You let women fight?"

"We don't insist upon it, but if a given lady wishes to fight, who are we to deny her the privilege?"

"What is your straight job?" Peter asked.

"I'm a cop," the serjeant said, looking embarrassed, "a hippo."

Peter smiled appreciatively. "So," he said. "Just a short hop from the Hemispheric Police to serjeant of the guard in a twelfth-century castle. Sort of a busman's holiday, isn't it?"

"Remember, it's a twelfth-century castle with electricity and hot water," the serjeant said. "All of the advantages of the Middle Ages with none of the disadvantages. And it's much easier to make status, and achieve something you feel good about, within the Society than in the real Middle Ages. Or, you may note, than in the real world today. Come, let me check that briefcase for you, and then I'll take you to His Royal Highness."

The protect case? Peter gloated. This was the first time that anyone had expressed an interest in the case, and Escobaga seemed to think that the bad guys—whoever they were—might have just such an interest. "Why?" he demanded.

"Why what?"

"Why do you want to check the protect case?"

"Oh, is it one of those high-tech jobbies?" The serjeant looked interested. "Because it's an anachronism, that's why. Same reason as why we won't let visitors in unless they dress properly. A blue protect case doesn't go with a brown doublet."

"It has my stuff in it," Peter said.

"Tell you what," the serjeant said. "I'll loan you this sheepskin shoulder bag. Put the blue thing in there, and take it with you. Then you'll only be inwardly anachronistic, like the rest of us."

A little disappointed that the serjeant hadn't tried to keep the blue case, and thus qualified for a higher level of suspicion, Peter stuffed it into the bulky sheepskin, draped it over his shoulder, and followed the serjeant into the castle.

King Tismane was a large man in all dimensions. If bulk were indicative of status, Tismane would an emperor be. His personal empire—the embodiment of his self—was vast. But it was a hard, firm vastness. Nothing of the flabby monarch about Tismane. His was an exercised, controlled bulk that wore its kingly garments well and radiated great self-confidence.

"We are pleased to meet you, Mr. Lyon," King Tismane said, holding his great flipper of a hand out to Peter, who wasn't sure whether to shake it or kiss it. It took Peter a second to remember that kings said "we" where the rest of us would say "I." He shook the hand, which did not seem to offend the king.

"You, We understand, are trying to sell Us something. Is that correct?"

"Not exactly," Peter explained. "I represent the Fanciful Figures Factory in Marin. We manufacture historical artifacts and science-fiction paraphernalia for motion pictures, realities, telly, and the like. We are trying to ascertain whether it would be worth our while to create a line of products for your—ah—organization." Which was basically all true. There was a company called the Fanciful Figures Factory, and he did represent it—at the moment. It was one of the smaller, more obscure divisions of the great Griffin.

"What sort of artifacts?" the king demanded. "What type of paraphernalia are we talking about?"

"Well, we make anything that is needed. Our machine shop is quite impressive; computer-guided microcutters, implosion forming chambers, free-polymer metal-forming phages"—Peter produced the words as though he had some idea of what they meant. "But, of course, price is the question. Anything we can put into semiproduction is considerably cheaper than a one-shot."

"I can see that, of course," King Tismane said. "I take it we are not talking about reproduction pieces here, stuff just for show. We're talking about good, honest swords and maces that can bash the daylights out of anyone they hit; and substantial but lightweight armor that can protect a man from anything from the blow of a battle-ax to the punch of a hi-vee slug. Is that the sort of thing you had in mind?"

"You're looking for body armor that really is body armor," Peter commented. "Why do you need anything that heavy, when you must know that it is much more expensive?"

"A piece of insubstantial but showy plate won't do a man much good during a tourney," the king said. "As it is, we average three knights killed on the Field of Honor every month. Usually the unskilled, 'tis true, during the Grand Melee after the scheduled bouts."

"Every month?"

"Yes." King Tismane smiled. "My lad, it is clear that you haven't done your homework properly, have you? You have only the slightest idea of what goes on within this organization."

"I had hoped to learn a lot more," Peter admitted.

"Well. You must come to one of our tourneys. As my guest. And bring someone. Don't look alarmed; you don't have to fight if you don't want to. As a matter of fact, we frown upon it during the first visit. Here, this booklet will tell you how to dress and behave. Although your current garb is excellent . . . *excellent.* Here, I am going to call Lord Desmond the Drear; he is our current seneschal for procurement. Talk with him before you go."

Lord Desmond the Drear was a short, round, black, gay gentleman who bounced when he walked, and giggled when he talked, and was able to produce large amounts of excitement about everything. *Everything.* He walked Peter around the inner keep to the side exit to the outer bailey, and then over to a door in the wall to the left, which led to the storeroom and sales office of the Western Empire Imperial Outfitters, Inc., PURVEYORS OF FINE OFFENSIVE DEVICES, according to a plaque on the wall over the door, TO HIS ROYAL HIGHNESS TISMANE OF THE FAR REACHES, KING OF THE WESTERN EMPIRE AND HEREDITARY EMPEROR OF THE UNIVERSAL MONARCHIST SOCIETY. There were a set of plaques on the far wall testifying to the previous Royal Highnesses that the firm had purveyed to. Peter went over to inspect them.

"It seems that you have had an awful lot of monarchs over the past few years," he said.

"A new one every Royal Ascension Tournament," Lord Desmond told him. "Roughly every year and a half. The date of the Royal Ascension varies according to an extremely complex formula. It's sort of an election by battle."

"You use the term 'hereditary' in an unusual fashion," Peter commented.

"Call it a foible," the Drear explained. "Now, let me show you the difference between tourney weapons and dress weapons. Here, for example, is a tourney sword." He pulled a meter-long broadsword from a bin and passed it to Peter. "Observe that it is both flexible and blunt.

Although it looks as though it could do great damage, it is made from plasticized aluminum, and is no more dangerous than so much hickory."

"I would not particularly enjoy being batted around with a hickory stick," Peter commented.

"True," Lord Desmond said, nodding his round balding head. "But, when well-padded and armored on the tourney field, you are not liable to greater damage than an occasional broken rib. Unless you are inexperienced, stupid, or careless. We give lessons and practice sessions for anyone who wishes to learn to fight, but we can't do much about the stupid or careless. They weed themselves out. Whereas, with a real steel blade, such as we carry for dress wear"—he pulled his own sword from its scabbard and passed it gingerly to Peter—"an incautious hack by the most well-intentioned opponent could cost you an arm or leg. An ill-directed stab could kill."

"A strange dichotomy," Peter said. "Your battle weapons can merely bruise, but your dress weapons can kill."

"A strange world we live in," Lord Desmond said, "where going about in public is more dangerous than holding a private battle between consenting adults. The dress weapons serve as defense on the public streets. You'd be surprised how few muggers are willing to jump a man armed with a one-meter blade."

"Not really," Peter said.

Desmond waved the clerk away and settled behind the desk himself. He handed Peter sheets of technical data on weapons and armor, none of which Peter understood, and pulled out a series of pamphlets, booklets, and leaflets, all of which Peter stowed in the sheepskin bag hiding his blue protect case. "Go over it with your production people," Desmond said. "We have over five hundred thousand members—and that's just on this continent. That should be a large enough base for your company to do a little miniproduction."

"I would think so," Peter agreed.

"Come to our tourney this Sunday. Actually it's an overnight—Saturday and Sunday—but the first day's for members only. Sunday we have another group joining us. Invited guests, you know. So we'll be set up to show off to visitors."

"Where?" Peter asked.

"At Agberg Park in the Oakland hills. There'll be plenty of room.

It's the off-season; we're only expecting a couple of thousand people to show up."

"I'll be looking forward to it," Peter promised truthfully.

Suddenly a whistle went off, and Desmond the Drear jumped to his feet. "The Vandal alarm!" he shouted. "You wait here!" And, drawing his sword, he rushed back out to the outer bailey.

Peter peered through the doorway and saw a big black balloon with a round gondola that looked like an oversized pie plate suspended from it. The balloon was settling with an awful inevitability right in the center of the outer bailey.

Peter went over to where Desmond was standing, one of a ring of men that had formed around where the balloon—or, at least, the gondola—would touch down. The group that had been batting at each other when Peter first came through the outer bailey had dropped their practice swords and retrieved their more-deadly dress swords. But they kept the heavy body-covering shields well in front of them as they faced the object.

"What is that thing?" Peter asked.

"No way of telling," Lord Desmond told him. "Could be a giant bomb. Could be a troop of cavalry. Could be the world's largest pizza. No telling what these jokers will send us."

"The Vandals? Are you sure it's them?"

"Sure? No. But they try some stunt or other just about once a month. Our existence seems to offend them."

The ropes coming down from the balloon all terminated in a large ring, which was connected to the gondola below. When the giant pie plate gondola, which was about fifteen meters in diameter, was about two meters above the clear space, the large ring suddenly parted. The balloon was immediately lofted skyward, and the gondola fell with a metallic *thunk* to the ground below.

For a long moment nothing happened. The circle of medievalists waited silently, swords drawn and shields up, for what the pie plate would reveal. Peter noticed that King Tismane had appeared and, with three burly knights, was standing in front of what seemed to be a door in the newly grounded gondola.

There was a series of snapping sounds from within the object, and the door sprang open and then, with a mighty clank, came loose and fell to the ground.

When the dust had cleared, a figure appeared in the doorway. Everyone tensed and raised their swords a bit higher. Peter casually put the bulk of Lord Desmond between him and the open door.

The figure was a short balding man in a puffy-sleeved yellow tunic, a wide blue sash, a patchwork vest, and purple pantaloons. The latest fashions in any major city in the North Western Semisphere. He looked, Peter reflected, like an advertising executive.

The short man stuck a purple floppy hat with a large white feather firmly on his head, turned back into the pie plate, and yelled, "We're here!" to someone inside, and then took a step forward. "Greetings!" he said, raising his hands high in the universal gesture of friendship. "We cometh in peace. Do you understand me?"

"Of course we understand you," King Tismane barked, lowering his sword just a bit. "What the hell are you doing here?"

"We cometh to you from the far future," the man said. "We weren't sure whether our English had diverged too greatly from yours to allow for easy communication. They assured us that it hadn't, Shakespeare and all—but you wouldn't know about Shakespeare yet—but such a thing is, after all, a judgment call, and one man's accent—"

"Who assured you that it hadn't?" the king interrupted. "And just where, or when, do you claim to be from?"

"Well," the man said. "I must say that you are taking it more calmly than we expected." He turned back to the inside of the pie plate. "Okay, everybody. Let's emerge!"

The man came forward, and more men and women appeared in the doorway behind him. "Don't be shocked," the man said, heading toward King Tismane, "but we cometh from the twenty-second century. There are many ways in which we can help you, here, with our superior knowledge." He took a disposable cigarette lighter from his pocket and flicked it in Tismane's face. "I can make fire!" he said.

Lord Desmond reached over and plucked the cigarette lighter from the man's fist. "Why so can I, or so can any man," he said, "but can you put it out?"

"What's that?" the man asked, jumping back.

Lord Desmond shrugged. *"Henry the Fourth*, Part One," he explained.

Peter noticed that the knights who had assembled to protect the castle were dispursing, grumbling under their collective breaths. About twenty people had come out of the pie plate, and they were clustered about in a tight group, looking with fascination and wonder at the walls and battlements of what they thought was the past.

"Damn!" Tismane said. "What are we to do with you?"

"With our superior knowledge," the man told him, "we can help you build a better society."

"That will certainly be nice," the king said. "But there's something I think you'd better know."

PLATO............ARCHIMEDES............RAMSES IV............LEO XIV
CHRISTOPHER MARLOWE..............AMBROSE BIERCE..............
LING TSU
GILGAMESH........HELENA BLAVATSKY.......ROBERT AGBERG

WHAT TRAITS DO THESE PEOPLE SHARE?

WHAT CAN *YOU* LEARN FROM THEM?

And why are we asking you about these particular people?

They were all successful in their chosen profession (in some cases, that's putting it mildly), they all were "geniuses"—that is, they shared knowledge that the rest of us do not have—and they all disappeared from view at the end of highly productive lives.

WHERE DID THEY GO?

Are you ready for forbidden knowledge? Will you profit from sharing secrets others cannot—or will not—understand?

If you think so, contact: SCRIBE

SEEKERS OF THE TRUE MU
424–144 Grosbittle Avenue
San Jose, CA., N.A.
N.W. Semisphere 3/3-92945-8936-582

ADVERTISEMENT   *ADVERTISEMENT*

THIRTEEN

"I spent the whole day there," Peter complained to Escobaga, "and learned more than I want to know about modern-day tournaments, and chain mail, and heraldry, and I have no idea whether I learned anything of any use to our employer. Why? Because you have not bothered to take me into your confidence enough for me to have any real idea of just what I'm supposed to be looking for."

"Just speak your report into that little gadget I have provided," Escobaga told him, "and let others worry about its utility. 'The Bird of Time has but a little way / To flutter, and the Bird is on the Wing.' "

"What?"

"Or, perhaps, the wing is on the bird. I've never been too clear about that. At any rate, the people upstairs—I use that expression figuratively, you understand—have trimmed down the list. Your next assignment is to come from this abbreviated version. Take your choice." He handed Peter a slip of paper. "One from Column A, so to speak."

"Whatever I'm supposed to uncover, I doubt whether these Monarchist people know it," Peter said. "They can't keep a secret. Anything they know, they write a booklet about. I must have been given thirty booklets, pamphlets, leaflets, and assorted papers during my day there. They have some sort of fascination for the printed word."

"The best way to conceal the devious," Escobaga said, mopping up the last of the egg on his plate with the last of his toast, "is among the ordinary."

"What does that mean?" Peter asked.

"How should I know?" Escobaga said. "It sounded good, so I said it. I can't be expected to understand everything I say."

Peter thought about that for a moment. "You know," he commented, "what you just said is a perfect example of what you just said."

"Now, stop that, boy," Escobaga said sharply. "You're beginning to sound like me."

"What about that tournament in Oakland on Sunday? Do you want me to go?"

"Of course. But that's Sunday. Five days from now. A lot of water to send through the tubes between now and then."

Peter signaled to the waiter in the boatel coffee shop. "I have a fine little apartment in Broxton," he told Escobaga. "Am I ever going to see it again?"

"When you took a job as courier with Griffin Universal," Escobaga said, "you knew it entailed a bit of travel."

The waiter, a slender young man who was proudly raising his first mustache, came over and refilled their coffee cups. "Anything else?" he asked.

"Were those real eggs?" Escobaga asked, staring intently at the young man.

"Of course," the waiter said, looking puzzled. "At these prices, what else would they be?"

"They could be," Escobaga said. "Any number of things. Bring the check."

"A bit of travel?" Peter scowled. "I haven't been home in months. And I don't exactly seem to be functioning as a courier any longer. The trouble is, I don't know just what it is I *am* functioning as. I spend my days visiting certain groups, from a list compiled elsewhere, for reasons they won't tell me, looking for I don't know what. I need to know what I'm doing, and, if possible, why. Please enlighten me on that, if you don't mind. If you can't do that, at least tell me what *you're* doing."

"What I'm doing?" Escobaga finished his coffee. "I am carried on the company's rolls as an expeditor, so I suppose I must be expediting. Whatever that is. What you're doing? You're helping us catch whoever killed that young Thai girl. Isn't that what you wanted?"

"You're not interested in the Thai girl," Peter said.

"Of course I'm not," Escobaga said. "If that was a more-encompassing 'you,' then I confess that Mr. Parker and his fellow Powers That Be in Griffin Universal are probably not overly interested either. But it would seem that their interests and yours overlap, in that in accomplishing what they want, you will probably stumble over the killers of your Thai girl. Or so they assure me."

"Things seem to be stretching away from the main point," Peter said. "I don't see how what I am doing now has any relation to that poor girl's death. I would like to believe you, but I don't."

"I'm shocked," Escobaga said. "Shocked, hurt, and indignant. So, you desire to be put in the know, so to speak. Is that it?"

"That's right," Peter agreed. "I want to know what I'm doing, and why."

Escobaga leaned back in his chair and thought, his eyes closed, his lips moving slowly in and out. Finally he opened his eyes again. "Can do," he said. "A bit more, anyway. Try to let you understand. I don't have the full story myself, you realize."

"I didn't," Peter said. "I always thought you knew it all."

"A vicious rumor," Escobaga told him. "Perhaps, as we're going to be here a bit longer, I should have a muffin." He called the waiter back over.

"Well?" Peter asked.

Escobaga stared at Peter, considering his face. "Somewhere," he said finally, "within the vastness that is Griffin Universal, there is a fink."

"A traitor?"

"Were Griffin Universal a government, then the term would be traitor. We'll settle for fink. A blueberry muffin, I think," he told the waiter. "Warm it a bit, and bring some butter on the side. Real butter, mind."

The waiter looked offended and scurried off. "This fink," Escobaga continued, "is, we believe, highly placed within the organization. Somewhere in the operational level. Has access to meaningful company secrets."

"What sort of secrets?" Peter asked.

"The sort that neither you nor I have any interest in knowing," Escobaga told him. "The sort that were to be concealed in your protect case. No, I take that back. What our informant had, obviously, was not the secret data itself, but merely the knowledge that it was to be transported within the case."

"Then he must be at a fairly low stratum of this high level, if you see what I mean," Peter commented.

Escobaga shook his head. "You haven't thought it out," he said. "It's those at the top who have no knowledge of mere operational details, or mundane technical specifications, and no need to know. So there is no telling what level this person is, except that, to have access to the basic knowledge of the existence of this secret at all he must be fairly high up." He paused in his explanation to accept the muffin, and started buttering it.

"So our fink passed the word to his friends that this information that they wanted would be transported from Bangkok on such-and-such a date in such-and-such a manner. And they tried to get it. In the process killing two people, which is not of great importance in this day and age, the value of a human life being about the same as that of a parking space."

"It's meaningful to me," Peter muttered.

"And the interesting thing about all this is: They didn't get it."

"Didn't get what?"

Escobaga took a scornful bite of muffin. "Whatever it was in the Bangkok office that they were after. They didn't find it there."

"How do you know? Just because they left it behind? Maybe they copied it, or took a picture of it, or whatever."

"Apparently," Escobaga said, "they didn't. It seems that whatever this knowledge is, it would make waves. If they knew, then by their actions we would know them. Do you see?"

"Darkly," Peter said.

"So the Powers That Be, hopefully excluding the company fink, have spread the word that the secret—whatever it is—was in the protect case all the time. *And* that you are presently carrying it around."

"Now, why would I do that?" Peter asked.

"Because you don't know," Escobaga told him.

"But if *they* know, wouldn't they take it away from me? I mean, won't it look phony that I still have the case, and whatever is supposedly in it?"

"Maybe," Escobaga admitted. "They're trying to make it look like an oversight, that one hand doesn't know what the other is doing. An all-too-common occurrence in an organization the size of Griffin, and hence believable. They hope. They're hoping that the fink will put the two bits of information together and feel very clever, and never think he might be being hand-fed, as it were."

"And so I'm supposed to carry the case around until someone kills me for it?"

"Tries to obtain it in some fashion. We hope, however, that there will be no bloodshed." Escobaga said.

"Yes," Peter agreed. "I, myself, hope that. Am I to stand out of the way and let somebody steal the case?"

"Oh heavens no," Escobaga said, throwing up his hands in mock horror and getting muffin crumbs all over his shirt. "We've been over this before. You are to make every effort to protect it, as though it were of some real importance to you. Not as though you thought it contained the crown jewels, of course, since you're not supposed to know, but more than if it merely contained your lunch."

"The time we went over this before it was not mentioned that someone might be trying to kill me for the case. That's awfully final for a man of my youth."

"Don't let that happen," Escobaga said, wagging a finger at Peter. "I shall be dreadfully annoyed. You have no idea how much paperwork is involved if an employee gets killed."

"Then all these organizations I'm spending my days visiting are merely window dressing?"

"I don't think so," Escobaga said. "Those godlike creatures in corporate headquarters up on the two hundred forty-fifth floor of Griffin Spire are spending too much effort picking your targets for it to be a mere diversion. They have some object in mind, which they have not deigned to inform me of. Although, being of sound mind and possessing a reasoning and curious nature, I have stared at these lists and evolved a clue."

"You have?"

"Didn't I just say so?" Escobaga's muffin was finished, and he picked up the last few crumbs with his forefinger, and then stared at the empty plate wistfully and looked annoyed.

"Share it with me. And don't look so unhappy. There's always lunch."

"Food?" Escobaga said. "I have no interest in food. Have you looked over the list?"

"Looked it over? I've stared at it till my eyes hurt. The only thing I can see that these organizations have in common is that they're nut groups, mostly. But that isn't even universal. Some of them are merely sort of fringe societies, without being actually nuts. Like those people today."

"Ah, 'tis true, 'tis true. But, remember what I pointed out to you? Amongst all these essential nuttinesses, is there not one common thread that stands out?"

"I don't know anything about these groups, except the ones I've been to. One of them is interested in the Middle Ages, and another in sex. Except for the fact that they probably had sex in the Middle Ages, I see no connection that cries out for attention."

"Well," Escobaga said, "I have researched these groups myself, and have compiled a dossier on each. And there is a common link, as I told you on Verne. The ensuing excitement probably drove it from your mind."

"I would be more impressed," Peter said, "did I not know that your research consisted of one phone call to the Griffin Universal Data Bank. And I'm not the one who threw up when the restaurant tilted."

Escobaga looked offended. "Two phone calls," he said. "And it is unkind of you to refer to a physical disability. And the cleverness came not in acquiring the data, but in studying and interpreting it. If you would like to go through the mass of printout yourself—"

"Spare me," Peter said. "Impress me with your knowledge. Share with me the results of your research. Please."

Escobaga shook his head. "You're right," he said. "I should stop acting like a prima donna. Here, let me show you." He pulled the master list out of his pocket and unfolded it on the table. "Even some of the names are indicative," he said, stabbing his stubby forefinger at the words.

"Like what? And what do they indicate?"

"Like Ad Astra Inc., and the Brotherhood of the Void, for example. "Or here: the Neues Verein für Raumschiffahrt aus California."

"It doesn't say to me whatever it says to you," Peter commented. "For one thing, I don't speak German. That is German?"

"It is. It's the New Society for Space Travel of California."

"I didn't realize that you'd had a recent influx of German immigrants hereabouts," Peter said.

"Not at all," Escobaga explained. "The name was picked for historical verisimilitude. One of the first groups to take the idea of space travel seriously was the original Verein für Raumschiffahrt, which was formed in Germany before the Second World War. During the war, it evolved into the group that dropped V-2 rockets on London, but no-body's perfect."

"So all these groups have an interest in space," Peter said. "So you told me that before, and I still say so what?"

"Not just 'space,' " Escobaga said. "They are not interested in Tranquillity City on the Moon, or any of the bagel-like marvels that trail us in orbit like so many puppies; their little hearts do not beat faster at thoughts of the penal colonies on Mars, or the research station on Ganymede, or U.N.W.S. Io Observatory, or Farbase."

"Ah!" Peter said, wondering what the hell Escobaga was leading up to.

"Ah, indeed. Perhaps you begin to see the light? These groups are not content with our paltry Solar System; they want the stars."

"Ah!" Peter said. "They believe the stories."

"They do. Or they would like to. Some people believe in Spiritualism, some in perpetual motion, some in the Revealed Word of God, some in the Dignity of Labor; these people believe in Faster-Than-Light. Alien planets circling distant-suns are calling them. The evil government, or some other evil group, is trying to keep them apart."

"I've heard those stories," Peter said. "How do you suppose things like that get started?"

Escobaga shrugged. "It seems to be an essential part of the human psyche to believe in myths," he said. "The catalog is endless. Some believe that Moses parted the Red Sea"—he made a parting gesture with his arms, and narrowly missed knocking a water glass off the table. "Some that Christ rose from the dead. There are those who think that God spoke to a woman named Mary Baker Eddy, for reasons of His own.

"In the sixteenth century, many people believed that other people were witches with supernatural powers, and had them burned to death. Although why these people would hold still to be burned to death if they had supernatural powers was never explained.

"In the seventeenth century, tens of thousands of people died fighting each other over their interpretations of the Word of God; and all of these people called themselves Christians. In the eighteenth century serious astronomers still had to pretend to an interest and belief in astrology to get court backing for their observatories. In the nineteenth century, Spiritualism sprang full-blown into an expectant world, and otherwise intelligent people spent large amounts of time and money in the attempt to talk to dead relatives.

"In the twentieth century, there were the suppressed inventions, most of them having to do with automobiles, which were the fetish objects of the period: a pill that would turn plain water into gasoline in your gas tank, a battery that would last a hundred times as long without discharging, miracle spark plugs, a miracle carburetor, miracle tires— more miracles than were performed by any saint. If you had put them all together, you would have had a car that could run five times around the world on a pint of water, with no tire wear.

"In the twenty-first century, there were the Chroniclers, who believed that the spirits of the dead were inhabiting the other planets of the Solar System. And the Children of Gung, who believed that true wisdom could only be attained by sitting cross-legged on a pallet at least two meters off the floor and repeating the word 'gung' over and over again. At its peak, there were supposedly over fifty million of them. That's a lot of gung.

"And now, in the twenty-second century, what do we have?"

"Is that a rhetorical question?" Peter asked.

"We have all of the above, and more," Escobaga said, continuing his rush of rhetoric unabated. "Today, when there are human colonies, or at least research stations, on or in orbit about all ten planets, the Flat Earth Society still has thousands of members. Today you can leave an astrology parlor in New York and enter a Spiritualist Church in London less than two hours later through the Transatlantic Tunnel. It must be very reassuring to know that.

"It seems that there is a sort of cosmic system of checks and balances. With every advance in human technology, there comes a corresponding advance in human nuttiness. If we ever reach the time where some of us understand everything, most of us will know nothing. And will insist upon it."

"I've never heard you sound bitter before," Peter commented. "It's usually more of a maudlin sarcasm. Besides, how do you know they're wrong? Maybe there really is a faster-than-light drive. Maybe some government or major corporation really is suppressing it."

Escobaga thought that over for a second. "Maybe," he acknowledged finally. "If I had a secret like that, I wouldn't spread it around."

"Why not?" Peter asked.

Escobaga grinned. "There are some things," he said, "man was not meant to know!"

FOURTEEN

Senator Pedro Dooley stood alone by the large picture window in his inner office and stared down at the Washington Mall and the various buildings of the Smithsonian surrounding it. It was a view he seldom tired of, but for some reason this was one of the times. "Seamus," he called.

"Yes, Senator?" the soothingly inhuman voice in the wall replied.

"Seamus, I'm tired of looking at this view. Pull up something else for me, will you?"

"Of course, Senator, if you require it." Seamus paused. Had it been human, it might be thought to be considering. "The Lincoln Memorial is quite impressive," it said. "The sensor is temporarily out at the Roosevelt Memorial, but I have hours of it on disk, if you'd like a replay."

"No, Seamus, not recorded, and not Roosevelt. Nor Lincoln, if it comes to that. Nothing inspiring. Rather something restful, and conducive to deep thinking. I have some deep thinking to do, and I'm going to need all the help I can get."

The window blanked for a moment, and then a woodland scene appeared, complete with chirping birds and babbling brook in the distance. "I imagine you will find this restful, Senator," Seamus said. "It's somewhere in northern Maine."

Dooley went over to his desk chair, sat down in it, and then swiveled around to stare at the window. "Tell me something, Seamus," he said.

"If I can, Senator," the office computer replied.

"You are part of the same system that all the other senators have, is that right? The S.C.C.C.?"

"That is correct, Senator," Seamus replied. "I am a unit of the Senate Chambers Computer Complex."

"Now, I don't follow this computer stuff much," Dooley said. "I mean, if something works, there's no call to have to know how to rip it apart and know how it works. I can't fix my own car, or copter, or dishwasher, or office, if any of them break. I mean, it's enough for me to know how to handle people. I've always thought that machines should be able to handle themselves."

"Yes, Senator," the voice in the wall said. "I agree."

"Thank you, Seamus. But what I'm asking is: How tied up with the S.C.C.C. are you? Is it one giant computer that services all the Senate in some kind of time-sharing deal?"

"No, Senator. Each unit is separate, and we share only the main data bank. I am what I am, and, such as I am, I'm all yours for as long as you hold office."

"Well, what about this data bank thing? Just how private are our little conversations? I know you remember everything. But how easy would it be for someone else to get ahold of your memories?"

"Impossible, Senator," Seamus said.

"Now, Seamus," Dooley said, "ain't nothing's impossible."

"All my information is encrypted before it is stored," Seamus said. "There is a finite possibility that the crypt could be broken, by a computer the size of an Omicron, if it worked steadily at it for the next fourteen thousand years."

"Is that a big computer, the Omicron?" Dooley asked.

"The biggest," Seamus replied.

Dooley thought that over. "I'm going to take you at your word, Seamus," he said. "I need to talk to someone . . . something. Seamus, I've got a problem."

"Wouldn't you find it more useful, Senator, to speak with a fellow human being?" asked Seamus, its low pleasant voice seeming to come from somewhere a few inches away from Dooley's right ear.

"Frankly, I would, Seamus," Dooley said. "But I don't know, at the moment, who to trust. You are the only intelligent thing in this Universe, right now, that I think I can trust. And I'm not too sure about you."

"If you like," Seamus said, "I can triply encrypt any data you give me that pertains to this problem."

"Giving me an extra twenty-eight thousand years, eh?" Dooley said. "No, I reckon if I'm going to trust you at all, fourteen thousand is enough."

"Then, what seems to be the problem, Senator? Perhaps you'd like to lie down on the office couch while you speak about it. You might find that more restful."

"Don't give me none of that psychology crap, Seamus," Dooley said. "Ain't no problems with my psyche, or whatever."

"Sorry," Seamus said.

"That's okay," Dooley said. "The problem is, Seamus, that I'm being lied to by a bunch of experts, and I can't figure out what's behind it."

"I see," Seamus said. "Would you like to go on with that? How does it make you feel?"

Dooley glared around the room. "Now, cut that out!" he said. "I'm not crazy. Not everyone who thinks he's being lied to is a paranoid. Especially if he's a United States senator."

"Sorry." Seamus said. "There's some kind of program deep in my system that goes into operation when you say you have a problem. I will suppress it."

"See that you do," Dooley said. "What I need is a sounding board, not a psychiatrist."

"Who is lying to you?" Seamus asked.

"The Board of Directors of Griffin Universal. Not all of them, just all the ones I've met."

"I see," Seamus said. "And what are they lying about?"

"That," Senator Dooley said, "is the problem. I can't be sure."

"You went there last week to watch the results of the deep-space probe," Seamus said. "The very existence of the Deep-Space Probe Program is classified Utmost Secret."

"How did you know?" Dooley asked the computer that animated his office.

"I keep track of your appointments."

"Oh. Of course. That's right."

"What happened at the meeting?" Seamus prompted. "You have filed no notes on it."

"I don't know," Dooley said. "I know what they want me to think happened. I know I saw some data screens—and very pretty they were, too—and shook hands with some very impressive corporate executives. I know that the information from the *Gone With the Wind* signal torpedo was just what everybody expected it to be. They did a good job of looking disappointed, and they tried to look surprised, but they sure as hell didn't. If there's one thing I know, it's human nature—and that's not human nature."

"What's a '*Gone With the Wind* signal torpedo'?" Seamus asked.

"I'll take that triple protection you were talking about," Dooley said. "I'm not supposed to talk about this."

"Passing information to your office computer is not considered a conversation," Seamus said. "Since I am conscribed from making use of or even discussing the information with anyone else."

"Hell," Dooley said. "I'm not even supposed to *dream* about this stuff."

"As you will," the soft voice said. "For your information and guidance, allow me to point out that the S.C.C.C. system is cleared to receive and process information through Utmost Secret, Crypto-Crypto, Mesa-Atomic Codeword."

"This is not a secret of the United States Government," Senator Dooley said. "This is a secret of Griffin Universal, and they take their secrets seriously."

"As you will," the soft voice said. Computers do not argue.

Dooley stared out at the Maine woods for a couple of minutes. "The *Gone With the Wind,*" he said quietly, "is an unmanned experimental faster-than-light ship that has supposedly been sent out to explore the ternary star system in Perseus that we know as Algol. It is the second such probe sent out. The first is, even now, in orbit around one of the stars. The smallest one. Or so the Board of Directors of Griffin Universal would have me think."

"So," Seamus said. "That's what a deep-space probe is."

"Indeed it is," Dooley said. "And the torpedo is a three-meter long homing device that supposedly comes back here and tells us what the *Gone With the Wind* has found. If we waited for radio transmission from the ship, it would take over a hundred years to arrive." Dooley lapsed back into silence, until the computer clicked at him encouragingly.

Senator Dooley stood up and began pacing back and forth behind his desk. "On the *Gone With the Wind*," he continued, "along with scads of your electronic brethren, there was a small menagerie. Everything from a jar of paramecia to a pig. The *Gone With the Wind* is the fifteenth or sixteenth vessel to explore faster-than-light travel. At least, the sixteenth one that Griffin Universal is telling us about. It seems that inanimate objects and electronic fields can withstand the stresses involved, but no living matter can. In each of the previous vessels that carried living things, the living organisms died, down to the last bacillus. Nobody knows why; they just come back dead. The Griffin people were trying a new variant on the process with this one. But, according to the data on the signal torpedo, the creatures, to a cell, were just as dead."

"Fascinating," the office computer named Seamus said.

"That is what the returning torpedo reported to us. But I have my doubts."

"Yes? What is it you doubt?"

"I don't know. That's the problem. But my sensitive nose detected the faint smell of corruption. There was something they were selling me, separately and collectively. Pencannon, Lettmore, Darthwaite, Parker, and Landau." He counted the names off on his fingers. "The man in charge of the deep-space project, and four of the richest, most powerful, most respected men in the country, directors of Griffin Universal. The raw data was coming in as we all stood there, and they all knew it wasn't true."

"How could you tell that, Senator?"

"They gave me what I like to call 'impure reactions.' When you are truly surprised, your reaction is pure, honest. When you are merely acting surprised, your reaction is impure; it sort of has overlays. I can't be any clearer than that, because it's a highly subjective and very difficult thing to describe."

"I see, Senator."

"Yes? I wish I did. What, exactly, are they lying about? And why are they lying? And why to me? Is the *Gone With the Wind* project phony? Are they sending those torpedos from some secret base really no farther out than Neptune?"

Dooley dropped back into his chair. "They want something from me. They must be running this charade for a reason. And, since I have

nothing of value to anyone outside of my position as a United States
senator, they want something from the government. Something they
shouldn't have. What could it be?"

"I don't know, Senator," his computer told him.

"It was only a rhetorical question," Dooley said. "You don't have to
reply to rhetorical questions. Now, the only way I relate to them, the
only reason they try to make me feel like a United States senator *is*
meaningful in their world, is my chairmanship of the Senate Select
Deep Space Committee."

"That may well be so, Senator," Seamus said. "But you might consider—"

"Quiet!" Senator Dooley ordered. "Be respectful and listen. Sounding boards talk less and listen more. It's the way of the world."

"Sorry," the soft voice murmured.

"Now, the Deep Space Committee is studying the Space Projects
Appropriations Bill for next year, a subject the Griffin people scrupu-
lously avoided mentioning. Or perhaps they really don't care. Their
yearly budget for space activities is more than ten times the United
States Government's. What else? There's the Space Lanes, Markers,
and Signals treaty with the United Nations. Now, let's see—what's in
that that might interest Griffin?"

"Was that also a rhetorical question?" the office computer enquired.

"Well, actually, it was, but you might as well reply. Read it off to
me."

"Very good, Senator. 'THE UNITED NATIONS JOINT TREATY
ON THE ESTABLISHMENT OF ROUTES AND LANES
THROUGH THE HEAVILY TRAVELED AREAS OF THE SO-
LAR SYSTEM, AND REVISING THE UNIVERSAL CODE OF
MARKERS, SIGNS, ELECTRONIC AND VISIBLE SIGNALS, BY
WHICH SUCH TRAFFIC IS REGULATED UNDER THE PRO-
VISIONS OF THE DEEP SPACE TREATY OF 2067.

PREAMBLE:
Inasmuch as it is to the common good and welfare of all signature
nations to the Deep Space Treaty of 2067 to regulate such traffic
as operates under its provisions for the safety, security, and comfort of those who travel the space lanes, we the undersigned do
hereby—' "

"I don't want to hear it word-for-word," Dooley interrupted. "It's a hundred and forty pages long. Just give me a rundown. A précis."

"Sorry, Senator. The treaty runs down like this:

"First: Outer Space is defined as being all that space without the atmosphere of Earth and within the Oort Cloud. This takes three pages.

"Second: The United Nations Space Service is given authority to enforce such regulations as are brought into being by this treaty, any future amendments to this treaty, or any future treaty or section or amendment that may affect travel in Outer Space. This takes nine pages.

"Third: The Constitution and Charter of the Space Service is amended. This takes three pages, and a separate unattached document addendum of two hundred twenty pages.

"Fourth: Deep Space is held to be the Common Heritage of All Humanity, to be administered jointly for the good of all. This provision specifically exempts a certain list of pre-existing colonial possessions and the territory on the surface of the gas giants and beyond the Oort Cloud, as free enterprise must be encouraged to make such areas profitable before they can be taken over for the public good. This took six pages.

"Fifth: . . ."

"Wait a minute!" Senator Dooley lay down flat on his back on the carpet and stared at the white ceiling. "There's something there. That Oort Cloud was mentioned a time or two. Let me think."

"Of course, Senator."

"I have an idea," Dooley said, rolling over onto his substantial stomach. "I am formulating a notion. I believe I know where I was being misled, and why. This may not be so, but if it is, the Board of Directors of Griffin Universal are the worst bunch of dastards it has ever been my privilege to know, and I'm going to be the next President of the United States.

"That's very exciting, Senator," Seamus said.

"I have some deep thinking to do," Senator Dooley said. "Turn up the gain on that waterfall."

INTERLUDE

The usual image of the passage of time is one of gradual evolution—one event sliding imperceptibly into another, until enough small changes have added up to produce the one large, perceptible change. So the planets formed, condensing gradually from a ring of cosmic dust. So the protozoa, over millions of years, evolved into multicelled plants and animals. So tribes evolved into city-states, and city-states into nations.

So it was believed.

It is now known, in that corner of the scientific world where the newest science is giggled over for years before it makes its way into textbooks and the popular press, that this is not so. Not in cosmology, not in climatology, not in chemistry, not in geology, not in human affairs. The Cosmos is not so constructed.

The way it actually works is this: Things go along pretty much the way they have been going for some time, event after event taking place, holding center stage, and then making way for the next—each of interest to those who live through it, but having little noticeable effect on the status quo ante. Then, all at once, from somewhere out of left field, one last thing happens, and *blam*—everything rips apart, and you can't pick up the pieces.

Interstellar gas remains interstellar gas until ripples from a passing shock wave, spreading from a distant supernova, cause it to condense into new stars and planets in a few millions of years—a mere blink of the cosmic eye.

The temperature of a sheet of newspaper can be slowly raised from absolute zero to 233° Centigrade (450° Fahrenheit), with no perceptible change beyond a little drying and browning—but one more degree will cause it to burst into flame and be consumed. Proving, if you like, that the arrow of time is not reversible.

A pressure crack in the side of a glacier will grow at the rate of, perhaps, three or four meters a year; but then will come that last centimeter that suddenly rends the glacier apart and, in a matter of seconds, sends a ten-kilometer chunk of ice into the shipping lanes.

Think of the death of Archduke Ferdinand, just one more in a long series of pointless assassinations.

Think of the almost microscopic union of a single sperm and ovum.

Think of the mighty and prolific dinosaurs, rulers of all they surveyed for a hundred million years.

Think of a rat cage, a perfectly normal rat colony full of healthy, happy white rats. You overload the colony, and they get irritable. Then you put in the one rat too many. Suddenly the rats practice child molestation, homosexuality, cannibalism, and a whole host of other human traits.

The planet Earth is become like an overcrowded rat cage. Not in sheer numbers, although thirty-two billion of anything is an impressive mass, but in psychological pressure. The cage bars are imaginary, but they are as strong as steel.

The Earth is a sphere, and we enhabit the outside of it, which is rapidly filling up—and there is no place to go where anybody would really want to go.

Oh, if you are lucky enough, and skilled enough, you might get a place in one of the space stations, or planetary sites, and have the privilege of spending the rest of your life in a confined space, living on hydroponic food and recycled water and air, and never again seeing the sky.

The colonization of the Solar System has been a washout. The big New Frontiers movement of the '20s that was designed to open up the planets slowly fizzled out. Not that Mars couldn't be made livable, but that there was no way to pay for it. You can't tax the thirty-two billion people on Earth indefinitely to support a couple of million on Mars; they won't stand for it. And it would take hundreds of years and untold billions of dollars to produce anything like a breathable atmosphere on Mars.

And the other planets were even worse.

For a while it looked as though space cities might make it. A variety of deep-space doughnuts, spheroids, and truncated cylinders of all sizes up to twenty-six kilometers in circumference were placed into various approximations of Earth orbit around the sun. Living in these tiny, inside-out worlds produced some interesting psychoses, but given time it might have worked out. A potentially infinite number of space cities swarming around the sun like bees around a queen looked to become the future of Mankind.

But then came the *Cosmogorsk* accident.

On Wednesday, May 16, 2035, at six-sixteen and eighteen seconds, Greenwich, a nickel-iron asteroid about the size of a large truck struck the two-centimeter-thick cupraluminum skin of the cylindrical space city *Cosmogorsk* at a relative speed of nineteen kilometers a second. A tenth of a second later it was out the other side and away, minus about 2 percent of its velocity and 4 percent of its mass.

The asteroid did surprisingly little physical damage to the interior of the huge space colony; which, with a length of seven kilometers, and a radius of slightly over three kilometers, was the second-largest human-made object in solar orbit at that time. It missed the solar collector field on each side of the great cylinder. It came nowhere near the small atomic power plant.

But in the two minutes immediately after the penetration 26,419 people died. The only survivors were two men and a woman who were in a recompression chamber after having spent three days in a low-atmosphere work vehicle, and one neurotic man who kept a spare air cylinder and skin suit by his bed.

The deaths, as far as could be worked out, were caused by a bizarre and certainly unrepeatable series of coincidences. The main patcher unit, a safety device that automatically blew up large sticky-plastic balloons and cast them adrift when a drop in air pressure indicated a puncture, had been capped following a routine inspection. The four secondary patcher units, closer to the skin of the city, could not handle holes of quite this size; their patch bubbles just blew out into space. The shock wave from the collision knocked out the alarm-and-preserve system, which should have automatically sealed the safety air hatches. Molten cupraluminum drops penetrated one of the main air reservoirs, and the whistle of the escaping air set up a vibration in the framework of the city that shorted out most of the electronic equipment. And, with no electronics, all the remaining safety backups went.

They learned a lot from the accident. Cosmic cities are much safer today.

The only trouble is, nobody will voluntarily move to one. It was pointed out in all the disaster reports that, had the asteroid struck any major city on Earth, the devastation would have been much worse, but to no avail. As the *Hindenberg* disaster marked the end of lighter-than-air travel for a hundred years, so the *Cosmogorsk* tragedy killed the future of deep-space colonization.

It was shortly after that that the planet broke out in a rash of pranks, stunts, and large-scale practical jokes. At first merely annoying and bedeviling, the stunts soon became increasingly deadly. They were incoherent and random acts of malicious mischief—some clever, some merely vicious—with many of the most imaginative done on a much larger scale than had ever been seen before.

"We are not going to allow this country to be taken over by disorganized vandals," the President of the United States declared after the Ogallala Outrage.

The Society of Organized Vandals appeared a month later. And have been with us ever since. They, as a noted TV commentator has observed, add a sense of piquant expectation to the dreariness of everyday life. Nobody knows for sure where they come from, who the members are, how to go about joining them if you want to, or where they get their money. Some of their japes cost millions. Some are murderous, others merely disruptive. All are possessed of a certain *élan* that speaks of a joyous sense of purpose.

The official emblem of the Society of Organized Vandals is a half-closed eye, with the motto: "When You Least Expect It."

The official emblem of the Society of Organized Vandals is a clenched fist, with the motto: "You'll Get Yours."

The official emblem of the Society of Organized Vandals is a stylized mushroom cloud, with the motto: "Easy Come, Easy Go."

The official emblem of the Society of Organized Vandals is the cartoon character Porky Pig, waving, in 3-D, with the motto: "Th-th-th-th-that's All, F-f-f-folks!"

The Society of Organized Vandals have no official emblem or motto —it's all a hoax.

There really is no Society of Organized Vandals, there aren't even any Organized Vandals—just a long series of copycat acts of creative vandalism.

The Society of Organized Vandals really does exist, but it is a small part of a supersecret organization that is trying to bring down the world government—what there is of it. It really isn't much of a government at all, more of a holding action.

Take your choice.

* * *

But *somebody* is doing *something*.

* * *

It was quarter to eleven on Sunday morning, and the Faithful were gathering for the Doctrinal Prayer and Healing Service at the Church of the Heavenly Scripture of the Revealed Word of Our Lord, a Not-For-Profit Florida Corporation. Some ten thousand lucky enough to have tickets had come in person to the great Crystal Cathedral itself. Spreading out over four city blocks, in the middle of its own two-hundred-acre plot of land in Prayerville, Oklahoma, the twenty-story structure glittered in the clear morning sunlight, presenting photo opportunities from almost every angle.

The rest of the Faithful, numbering about a hundred and twenty million, attended the service in front of their television sets. Beamed live to two privately owned satellites, distributed instantaneously throughout the world by the Revealed Word of Our Lord television network, sent by tightbeam to fourteen off-world colonies, including both Ganymede and Callisto, the weekly Healing Service of the Reverend JimmyBob Marvel rivaled in ratings a professional football game. Not a post season game, of course, not even a game between two top-ranked teams. Say a game between two teams toward the bottom of the ratings on an off-night.

Still, a hundred and twenty million people is a respectable draw. And the people watching the football games don't pay for the privilege. Most of Reverend Marvel's watchers did. Many only sent in five bucks a week, but some of them tithed themselves. Only a couple of million, but every little bit helps. It is expensive to preach the Revealed Word. Those on the list as tithers could expect the Lord, with the Reverend Marvel's assistance, to heal them of just about anything. Even those who only gave five or ten bucks a week could expect to receive a yearly invitation to "take your vacation with the Lord," and a discount coupon entitling them to half-price reductions on tickets to the Sunday services. They would fly into Prayerville a few days early, stay at one of the glittery chrome-and-plastic motels on the strip from the airport to the Cathedral grounds (all owned by a separate Church corporation), and have a chance to donate to the new University that the Reverend JimmyBob was building, under the Lord's explicit instructions.

At ten minutes before airtime the Reverend Waldo Sikes, JimmyBob's second-in-ecclesiastical-command, came out to warm up the live congregation. By the time the theme music started, and the exterior shots of the Crystal Cathedral were being shown behind the credit roll, ten thousand voices in the Great Hall had been adequately rehearsed in responsive reading, in roaring in unison, and in showing approval.

The interior cameras came on as the Reverend JimmyBob came through a small door into the vast chancel. "And now, brethren and sistren," Waldo Sikes voice boomed over the internal address system, "once again we bring to you, in compassion and healing and humility for His Word, the Reverend JimmyBob Marvel!"

JimmyBob walked calmly and sweetly before the altar, and smiled his famous smile, and held his right hand out—fingers spread, palm forward—and the chorus of a thousand trained voices broke into "I Spent the Night in a Motel with Jesus," and the crowd went wild.

The television viewpoint switched from a side view to a low front view as JimmyBob came to his glass pulpit and silently faced his audience. The hymn ended, and slowly the crowd grew silent. The picture on the television screen was awe-inspiring: JimmyBob centered behind his glass pulpit, framed by the chorus to his left (stage left); the line of sick and lame waiting to be healed to his right; and, above him, the giant solid-gold crucifix, with Jesus smiling proudly down through his pain, secure in the knowledge that the Reverend JimmyBob Marvel was on his side.

JimmyBob's sermon for this Sunday was on the theme "Evolution: Just a Theory—Or a Tool of the Devil?" And he really ripped into those scientists. His words and image, carried on electronic wings to the six corners of the Solar System, told his viewers of the Satan waiting below, waiting to pounce on those who do not take the Lord's message to their hearts. Below what, he didn't say.

Suddenly, as he reached the part about the witches among us, there was a loud snapping noise, which echoed through the Cathedral, bounced into the microphones, and started on its way out to the moons of Jupiter.

The sound had seemed to come from somewhere above. Everyone looked up, looked around, looked for something that could have caused the sound. The Reverend Marvel looked annoyed. He didn't like anything to come between him and his pitch.

No one could see anything wrong, but some in the audience shifted nervously in their seats. An unidentified snapping sound in an all-glass cathedral is enough to make even a Believer a trifle nervous.

There it was again—a bit louder this time. *Snap!* Like a dry twig breaking. A *thick* dry twig. The Reverend JimmyBob did a heroic job of keeping up with his sermon—after all, the commercial break had to come on time—but he had lost his audience.

Someone in one of the front pews screamed, and pointed up at JimmyBob. Someone else picked it up, screaming and pointing. There was a scattering of hands throughout the front rows, pointing up at JimmyBob, and the screaming grew.

No, wait, it wasn't *at* JimmyBob they were pointing, it was *above* him. Somewhere over his head.

JimmyBob would have been other than human if he could have resisted that. Pausing pregnantly in his sermon, he turned around and looked up.

The nails through the palms of the solid-gold Jesus had ripped out, and the solid-gold Jesus was leaning forward, away from the solid-gold cross. At this new angle, He no longer seemed to be smiling benevolently at JimmyBob; but, rather, He was glaring at him with an expression of anger.

Or was it the angle?

The statue of Jesus reached down and pulled the nail from its foot, and then dropped lightly onto the chancel floor. It had amazing grace for a gold statue. Those close enough could see that it was definitely glaring at JimmyBob, with an unpleasant expression on its face. It pointed a great accusing hand straight at JimmyBob. *"Pharisee,"* it intoned, its voice booming through the great hall.

JimmyBob's television producer, from his place high above the scene in a control booth, had the presence of mind to throw the master switch, yelling, "Get a disk of an old service going out—quick!" to his production assistant.

"Excuse me," the chief engineer, a union man, interrupted. "It's still going out."

"What?"

"It's still going out. The signal."

"What do you mean, it's still going out? Don't give me that crap. I just pulled the master switch."

"I don't care what you just pulled, Meisterkopf," the chief engineer told him. "This monitor shows the local pickup—and that mess down there is still being picked up."

"Sabotage!" the producer yelped, while below him on the chancel floor chaos reigned.

The Reverend JimmyBob Marvel, for the first time in some forty years, was struck dumb. He stared motionlessly at the six-meter-tall Christlike apparition that stalked across the marble floor of the chancel toward him. For a solid-gold statue, it was surprisingly light on its feet. "I was gypped," JimmyBob muttered into his microphone. "That thing can't be solid-gold."

Reaching down, the statue grabbed JimmyBob by the throat and lifted him high into the air. "How dare you," it thundered, "erect my statue in this temple of Mammon? I shall not stay!" And, dropping JimmyBob to the ground like a sack of wet cornmeal, the six-meter golden Christ strode down the central aisle of the Cathedral and out the great crystal front doors.

The outdoor cameras picked up the statue's exodus from the Cathedral and followed it down the great drive toward the front gates. In the production booth, the producer had by now given up trying to figure out what was happening—or, more precisely, how and why it was happening—and just sat slumped back in a chair and stared into the monitor.

With the cameras full on it, the golden figure lofted majestically into the air, turned toward the west, and sped off, gaining speed and altitude as it went, until it disappeared into a cloud.

With a little *chirp*ing sound, the Great Crystal Cathedral began to fall apart. Slowly, as though it were being disassembled by a giant unseen hand, the Cathedral shed pieces, which tumbled to the ground. Ten thousand people began to pour out the great front doors, the lesser side doors, and a few even through the back doors, while the building came to pieces around them. Most of them made it.

FIFTEEN

When Saralu Ngaxu decided that it would be a good idea to leave her place and style of employment for a while, she gave the matter much thought. It would not do to just walk out. Nor would it be satisfactory to ask for a leave of absence, or to request what would seem to be a sudden and unplanned vacation. Those same considerations that prompted her to wish to be elsewhere for a while also made her realize that extreme discretion and a bit of wit were required in the execution of her plan.

It is not easy to make secret plans when you know you're being watched most of the time, and you're not sure just when that is. But Saralu was of strong-minded and devious stock.

The sudden illness of her father came as a distinct shock. Mr. Vileonder, the supervisor of the Buckton Nondenominational Orphanage of Southern Africa, called her to his office and handed her the pink flimsy that had been forwarded from the Federated Censorship Office. YOUR FATHER IS VERY SICK. COME AT ONCE. MOTHER, it read.

"I'm sorry to be the one to break the news to you," Mr. Vileonder told her. "This is not a usual part of my duties. Ordinarily, of course, some relative could have just called you or blipped a message. But you come from Kenya, you see, which is in the CAU, and officially we *are* still at war with the CAU. So the border is closed to all electronic communications."

"That's silly," Saralu said, waving the pink sheet of paper in front of her like a red flag hoping for a bull. "Cleared for delivery by the

Federated Censorship Office? And this took two days? There hasn't been a hostile act between the People's Federated Protectorate of South Africa and the Central African Union for—what?—twenty years? And now I'm kept from getting direct word of my daddy because of a war that they're not even really fighting!"

"I understand your sentiment, Miss Ngaxu," Mr. Vileonder said. "It is most unfortunate. Most. We will do what we can for you here. Of course you will take an emergency leave of absence. Take as long as you need. I am even now arranging transportation for you. Indirectly, of course. You'll fly from here to Brazil, which is a neutral country. From there you can easily board a plane for Kenya."

"That's kind of you," Saralu said, forbearing mentioning that she could cross the borders of both countries, and the four in between, in less time and with less trouble than the continent-hopping solution Vileonder was proposing.

Two days later she stood at Daddy Exx's bedside in the intensive care unit of Mombasa Ritual Hospital, looking down at his recumbent form. His eyes were closed, and there was a tube up his right nostril, a tube in his mouth, two in each arm, and assorted and various electronic connections disappearing under the starched white sheets.

Emma Ngaxu, Saralu's mother, patted her gently on the arm, and then shooed the doctor and two nurses out of the room. "Let's leave them alone," she said. "They were very close."

As the door closed behind the last of the others, Saralu leaned forward. "Hello, Daddy," she said softly.

William Blakely Exx opened his eyes. With his right hand he reached up and pulled the tubes from his nose and mouth. "What the eff is going on here, daughter?" he demanded.

"I needed your help, Daddy," she said, leaning over and kissing him on the cheek. "That's why I got word to you to think of some excuse to get me out of there for a while. I knew you'd know what to do."

"What I ought to do is turn you over my knee," Bill Exx grumbled, sitting up and pulling all the tubes and electrodes off his body, " 'less you got a real good reason for this." Saralu noticed that the intricate electronic monitors didn't miss a beat as the electrodes came off. Her father was very good at the details.

"I do, Daddy," Saralu told him. "I got a real good reason."

Bill Exx grinned. "I know you do, honey," he said. "I told your mammy you've got brains and judgment enough for any two men, aside from being the prettiest girl from here to Pluto. And there ain't anywhere else."

Saralu smiled and sniffled. "I know you did, Daddy. You're a strange mixture of a man. You'd never understand if I tried to explain to you why saying I'm smarter than any two *men* is sexist—"

"What do you mean—"

"But at the same time," Saralu said, putting her hand gently over her father's mouth, "remember what else you said? Mommy said it went something like this . . ."—she lowered her voice two octaves— " 'If my baby needs my help, why, she's going to get it. I don't give a damn how many sonabitches gets in the way!' "

"Might have been something like that," Bill Exx said, pulling the blanket aside and swinging his legs over the edge of the bed. "You're not going to bitch about my calling you my baby, now, are you?"

"Course not, Daddy."

"Okay, then, what's going on? And how long I gotta stay in the hospital to give you an excuse for being here? And what for do you need an excuse anyway?"

"I need some help, Daddy. There's some very strange stuff has come plunking down where I work, and it's connected to some other stuff, and I want to find out what's behind it."

"That's the vaguest description of events that I have heard of in some time. What sort of stuff, daughter? Never mind, tell me over dinner. I've got to get dressed."

"I thought you were going to stay here," Saralu said. "In case anyone's checking up on me. Which I think is quite possible."

"Don't worry, daughter," Bill Exx said, getting up and going to the closet. "I ain't going to let you down. I been here for three days already, and I got it figured out to a fine edge. All day long I stay here. At night I leave here in these togs, and slip back to the bungalow for dinner and spend the night, and nobody notices." He took a khaki policeman's uniform from the hanger. "And my double slips in and takes my place until I get back in the morning."

"You have a double?"

"Why sure, honey." Her father grinned a wide grin, showing all his teeth. "Doesn't everybody?"

The Exx–Ngaxu bungalow was a two-story, sixteen-room house in the upper-class suburb of Dastubi Watti. It was shaped like a U with the open end closed by a wall, to provide a completely private inner courtyard. After dinner, in a room open to the inner courtyard to catch the cool evening breeze, Saralu settled down to explain to her parents why she had passed word out to them to stage this elaborate charade.

"You ever have a feeling, I mean a real, deep-gut feeling, that something is very wrong?" she asked. "When you can't explain why, or exactly what it is?"

"Feelings like that saved my life more than once," Bill Exx said. "Ain't nothing to sneer at."

"I think it's your subconscious acting on information that your conscious mind doesn't know how to properly evaluate," Emma Ngaxu said. "The accuracy rate of hunches is amazingly high, I understand."

Saralu went over to the balcony and stared down at the courtyard. The central fountain was turned on, and the hidden light tubes made the streams of water iridesce in an ever-changing pattern of primary colors. That fountain had been there as long as she could remember. When she was a teenager she had thought it awfully gaudy and middle-class, and she used to turn it off before her friends came over. Now she realized how much she had missed that fountain.

"I don't know how much of this is hunches, or subconscious reading of facts," she said. "I just know that when people are doing something that doesn't seem to make sense to you, and they keep doing it regardless, then there's got to be something about it that you don't understand."

Bill Exx nodded. "Go on, daughter," he said. "Lay it all out, and let us look at it."

"Well, okay. First of all, all the offices are bugged."

"In the orphanage?" Emma asked, looking surprised.

"That's right. And I'm being watched."

"Who would want to do that? Who cares what goes on in an orphanage?"

"Now, wait a minute," Bill Exx said. "Didn't you tell me that those used to be some kind of government buildings? Maybe the bugs are a hangover from the bad old days."

"They might have been installed when the building went up," Saralu said, digging into her shoulder pouch, "but they're active now, Daddy." She held up a gold brush-tip pen. "The back end of this is a bug detector. It glows when there is an active bug in your area. Not an old, defunct bug, but an active, even-now-in-use bug. I keep it in my bag, and it glows a lot."

Bill Exx shook his head. "Can't argue with science," he said. "What else?"

Saralu put her bag down and rubbed her hands together. "Let me describe for you how the orphanage works," she said, "sort of in rough detail:

"We get all kinds of children from all over Southern Africa at Buckton. Since it was originally founded by the United Nations after the breakup, it isn't strictly a government institution, even though the government is running it now. We have black children, and white children, and colored children, and mixed children. The only thing that matters to the orphanage is that a child is under seventeen with no home. And there are a lot of them in Southern Africa today."

"Very commendable," her father said. "Course, there are a lot of them everywhere. A lot of people of all kinds wherever you turn. Black people, white people, yellow people, mixed people, young people, old people; setting up housekeeping where there used to be elephants, and eland, and gazelles, and lions, and such."

"Shut up, Bill," her mother added. "Let the girl talk."

Saralu paused to consider. She had been thinking this out for months, but she had never talked to anyone about it. There was nobody at the orphanage to trust. The words would sound strange. "We do not categorize the children by race," she said. "That's part of the old United Nations agreement; besides, everyone in the Protectorate spends much of their time trying to pretend that they don't care and it doesn't matter. Therefore, officially there are no black children, or white children, or the rest."

"They all gray, are they?" Bill Exx asked, leaning forward with interest.

Saralu smiled at her father. "That's kind of it," she said. "We hide our children from the future behind a façade of dull neutrality. The system is far from perfect. I am working to change it. But that is not what has me concerned. We have over twenty thousand children at Buckton at any one time. And nowhere on the records of these children does it say anything about their race."

"Very commendable," Bill Exx repeated, stretching to his feet. He

went over to the far wall and poked at it experimentally until it opened
into a wet bar. Then he poured himself a double shot of bourbon and
papaya nectar and gave each of his women a glass of chilled white wine.

"Stay with me, Daddy. This is kind of subtle, and I'm not sure it will
come across as strong as it should in the telling. But if you lived with it
day by day, and saw it growing after the suspicion hit you, then—"

"Don't put your old daddy down, daughter," Bill Exx said. "I can
wrench the truth from a subtlety as fast as any man. Just lay it out for
me."

"Okay, Daddy. I'm sorry. Well, let me tell you what we do with
these kids. At the orphanage they live in bungalows, about forty kids
and a housemother to each bungalow, and go to school."

"With twenty thousand kids, that's an awful lot of bungalows," her
mother said.

"Over five hundred," Saralu said. She took a healthy swig from her
wine glass, and then continued. "Twenty to a block, and twenty-seven
blocks at the moment. We treat them as well as we can, which is not
badly, but after all it *is* an orphanage. Our primary goal is to find
adoptive or foster homes for these kids."

"Of course," Emma said. Bill Exx just quietly sipped his bourbon.

"The first thing I noticed," Saralu went on, "was that there was a
pattern of secret marks on the children's files. And that these marks
indicated the race of the child."

"Humph!" Daddy Exx said. "All children are gray, but some are
grayer than others."

"How do you leave secret marks in a computer file?" her mother
asked.

"It's very subtle," Saralu said. "There's a box on the form that's
labeled 'Introduced by.' And the name in that box is something like
'M. Randall,' or 'T. Sturgeon.' But 'Introduced by' doesn't do anything. It is useless and redundant information. There are other boxes
for the parent's names and other relatives' names, and for the
caseworkers involved. So who is supposed to have introduced who to
whom?

"Well, I figured it out. The name is a fake. Only the first initial
means anything: It specifies the race of the child."

"Why?"

"That's what I want to find out. I know more than they want me to

—whoever they are—but not nearly enough. I've found out some more interesting facts about whatever is happening; enough to develop a theory, but it's only half an explanation. I need to find the other half."

"What else have you found out?" her mother asked.

"A couple of things. First, the security. Forget about the fact that I'm being watched. I could be paranoid, or it could be something unconnected with the institution."

"Like what?" her father asked.

"Well—for instance, the People's Federated Protectorate could have decided that I'm a CAU spy."

"That's silly," her mother said.

"Of course," she agreed. "Maybe one of the security guards just likes to look at my body."

"Er—umph," Daddy Exx said, trying not to look shocked. Somehow it sounds different when coming from your own daughter.

"Even if I don't make anything out of the fact that *I'm* being watched," Saralu said, "there's still entirely too much security around. Much more than we have any rational need for, if we're only protecting poor unwanted children. The excess security seems directed at the staff, which makes no sense at all. We don't need to be protected, and we don't need to be watched. We are handling a commodity that, unfortunately, is of no practical value to anybody else. Nobody wants thousands of orphans."

"Have you asked the people in charge about it?" her mother asked.

"That's the Protectorate staff. Civil Service types. They say it's for our protection," Saralu said. "After all, there's a war on."

"Sounds like a lot of mendacious bullshit to me, daughter," Daddy Exx said, taking a healthy sip of his bourbon and nectar. "Always watch out when someone else says he's doing something to help you, when you didn't ask him to. Especially governments. Sometimes they're so conceited about it they don't even bother telling you, they just put up signs: 'For your protection, patrons must wear shoes.' 'For your convenience, everyone entering this building will be searched.' 'For your safety, all citizens must report to the prefect of police within twenty-four hours any change of address.' Dictators are people who know what's good for you, and are determined that you're going to have some of it."

"Then there's the school," Saralu said.

"What school?"

"It's actually a good thing," Saralu said, "or would be, if it was doing what it was supposed to. If I hadn't been sensitized by this other stuff, I probably wouldn't have thought anything of it. But I was, so I did. It's called the Higher Outreach Primary School, run by a group who call themselves the Higher Outreach Society. Dedicated to helping people all over the world fully use their true abilities and achieve their true goals."

"Do-gooders," Daddy Exx said. "I smell, at the very least, a mouse. There's entirely too much altruism loose in that institution of yours, daughter."

"The Higher Outreach Primary School, which is in a city called San Jose in the state of California, United States of America, is a high-class boarding school. They have, according to their catalog, which is in our library, over six thousand students. Most of these students go on to the Higher Outreach Secondary School, which is in Ojai, California, about two hundred and fifty kilometers down the coast."

"What is it that this fancy boarding school is doing for your orphans?" Daddy Exx asked. "Let's get down to cases."

"It is, supposedly, taking in about fifty a semester."

"Out of the goodness of their hearts?"

"Something like that."

"Now, both of you," Emma Ngaxu interrupted. "Let's not let our cynicism carry us away. There are nice people in this overcrowded world of ours. Some. I've even met one or two in the course of my life."

"All the children selected to go to this school," Saralu said, "are black. Every one."

"It is not outside the realm of possibility," Emma said. "After all, fifty out of six thousand. There can't be more than—what?—5 or 10 percent whites at the school."

"And 5 percent Oriental, and about 20 percent mixed races. And besides, it's been going on for about four years now, which makes about four hundred kids gone. Every single one of them pure, unadulterated black stock. If that's a coincidence, then I'm the Bishop of Ulster."

"You make a strong case, daughter," her mother said. "Somebody's collecting Ambroses."

"Huh?" Both father and daughter swung around to look at her.

"A twentieth-century writer named Fort used to unearth and assemble odd facts," she explained. "Once he noticed that, in a given period of time, an unusual number of men named Ambrose had disappeared from home. His explanation: Somebody was collecting Ambroses."

"You never cease to amaze me, Ms. Ngaxu," Bill Exx told his wife. "That's why it is always a pleasure to come home to you—on those rare occasions that I find you home when I arrive."

"Thank you, Mr. Exx," she replied. "And I must say that life with you has never been dull. A greater compliment I do not know."

"Sometimes I wonder about you two," Saralu told her parents. "But, to get back to my story: The other thing about these Ambroses is, not only are they all black, but they're all high-grade morons."

"How's that?" Daddy Exx asked.

"We have a wide range of kids," Saralu said. "Some geniuses, some idiots, and everything in between. The smartest kid in the place right now registers one ninety-five on the Bradford-Conant Absolute Intelligence Scale; the dumbest somewhere around sixty-five. Below that and they have to be institutionalized. The smartest kid happens to be black. In the dumbest range, we've got a couple of each."

"So?"

"All the kids picked for the Higher Outreach Primary School, or, at least, all the ones whose brain scans I've checked, register between seventy and ninety—which is high-grade moron to dull normal."

"Somebody's collecting dumb Ambroses," her mother said, getting up to refill her wine glass. "Black dumb Ambroses."

"I don't like it," her father said. "The ripe odor of evil chicanery rises from your story like swamp gasses rise from a swamp. Something is wrong. What are these kids like when they come back? What do they have to say about their experiences?"

"There aren't any of them have come back yet," Saralu said.

"Son-of-a-bitch," Daddy Exx said, articulating each syllable clearly and distinctly. "We are going to have to find out what in the name of various unmentionable deities is going on there. Is this Higher Outreach mingus some kind of remedial school?"

"Not according to their catalog," Saralu told him. "The kids that pay to go there are no stupider than the average rich kid."

"I'll find out about it," Daddy Exx promised. "I'll have my people get to work on it tomorrow. Should have something by the end of the week. You going to stay around for a while?"

"Why, Daddy," Saralu said, "how can I leave you while you're so sick? I wouldn't feel right."

SIXTEEN

After a hard three days of talking to single-minded people about things that fascinated them but did not interest him, and achieving no noticeable result, Peter went out with Shirley Vermont on Saturday night. How they entertained themselves, and what personal discoveries they made, is of no concern to us, but let us note that Peter was feeling at peace with himself and the world when he went out Sunday morning to rent a car. "I'll be ready by the time you get back," Shirley promised. "I thought my wardrobe was up to anything, but medieval is a problem."

Robinson's Vehicle Rental, "Anything from a Scooter to an Orbiter —by the Hour, Day, Month, Year, or Decade," was on Clay Street, a couple of blocks from Shirley's apartment. The manager, Mr. Clute, a happy man with a droopy mustache, rented him a boxy little electric rollabout designed for local travel. "It's good for tourists," he said. "Complete map and memory of local streets and traffic conditions. Updated daily. Just tell it where you want to go. If you end up in Los Angeles, you'll have to get an area update."

"I'm not going to Los Angeles," Peter told him. "Just the Oakland hills."

"It's this button," Mr. Clute said. "The small update fee will be put on your credit account."

"Honest," Peter said. "I'm not going to Los Angeles. I'd fly to Los Angeles, or take the monorail. I don't like to drive that much."

"Listen," Mr. Clute said. "You don't have to be ashamed of going to

Los Angeles. It's all right with me if you go to Los Angeles. There's no extra charge. Although I'd recommend that you take a hypled, rather than an electric. More serviceable over long distances. Only a little more money."

"The electric will be fine," Peter said. "Thank you for the advice. I'll have it back to you tomorrow morning at the latest."

The manager shrugged. "Just give a call if you want to keep it longer," he said, and escorted him out to the car.

Peter stuck the plastic access card into the slot on the dash and fastened his seat belt. The words VOICE ACQUISITION PROGRAM lit up in the windshield in front of him. He stared at it. For a minute nothing happened. Then a tinny voice from his left said, "Well? Say something."

Peter jumped as far as the seat belt would allow. "What?" he said.

"It doesn't matter," the voice told him. "Anything you'd like. I just have to be sure I can understand your words before anything happens where I have to. Recite a poem."

Still slightly startled, Peter ransacked his memory for a poem. "Gaily bedight, / A gallant knight, / In search of Eldorado," he recited.

"Try again," the car advised. "Either you have exceeded my vocabulary, or we are fated never to communicate on a sound basis."

"We'll give it a shot," Peter said:

> When I was a babe in the arms of time,
> My cradle was an eternity of Earth in Spring,
> My nursery songs were paeans in rhyme,
> Ceaseless murmurs of remembering.
>
> The bright rose petals of joy were strewn,
> And rainbows of butterflies sparkled the air.
> Time stretched out an endless noon
> Of Jam, and Trumpets, and Ladies Fair.
>
> There were dragons to fight, and bears and things,
> And trackless forests were every tree.
> There were goblins, and imps, and magic rings,
> And nothing was twice, and love was free.

"How's that?"

"I'm not sure about the 'pans in rhyme,' " the car said, "but I think

I've got you pegged. We won't go into the 'thistle sifters sifting sandy thistles by the thousands.' Where do you want to go?"

"I'll take it on manual for the first part," Peter said. "It's just a few blocks."

"Okay," the car said doubtfully. It turned itself on, and the legend on the windshield faded out.

Shirley was waiting in front of the large apartment building that housed her tiny apartment. She was dressed in a long, full green skirt and a peasant blouse. "It's the closest to medieval I could manage," she told Peter. "It's from my folk dancing days."

"It's lovely," Peter said. "You're lovely." He drove back to the boatel so he could change into his medieval costume, then they started out for Agberg Park and the Universal Monarchist Society tournament.

"Do you wish to go the fastest way, or the scenic route?" the car asked. Peter noted that the car pronounced the "c" in "scenic."

"What is the difference in time?" Shirley asked.

"About eighteen seconds," the car replied.

"Let's go for scenic," she decided.

"All right," the electric said, and started off.

"Say," Peter said. "How come you didn't make her recite a poem, or something?"

"I've been listening since she entered me," the car said. "Nice voice."

* * *

Agberg Park was a soupçon of raw nature, way up in the hills of Oakland. The original Agberg estate—two large stone-faced houses and about forty acres of land, surrounded by a high stone wall—had been built in the mid-twentieth century as a retreat by Milton Spengerfall, about whom nothing whatever is remembered except that, for some reason, he was known as "The Toad King." It then fell into the hands of Robert Agberg, the multimillionaire author of historical romances. Agberg, a reclusive figure who wrote under the *noms de dactylographie* of Dottie Osborne and Lacie Camisole, would only leave the grounds of his estate to add another cactus or succulent to his extensive collection. His four hundred and thirty-seven known books were translated into forty-one languages and French, and the least of them sold over twenty million copies in English. More than a hundred of them were dramatized by movies, television, or one of the other mechanical arts during his lifetime.

In his will Agberg left the entire estate—house, grounds, and wall—to the newly founded Agberg Foundation, with the proviso that it be turned into a private park and expanded as circumstance and money permitted. The park was to be leased at nominal cost to "Unusual and Interesting Groups" who had need of the space, with special consideration given to groups that, for whatever reason, would have difficulty leasing public land. "I have spent my life entertaining my fellow man," Agberg wrote in his will, "and I think it's high time that he entertained me for a while."

It took over fifty years to adjudicate the will since Agberg, the day after his sixtieth birthday, disappeared from his house and was never seen again. Every time an interested relative would go to court to have him declared legally dead so that his extensive property could be divided, his publisher would receive a new manuscript from him, or his wife would get a postcard from some unlikely place. What really happened to him is not known to this day, although there is a recurring legend that he actually became the first American Pope, Leo XIV. The only basis for this story is the fact that the obscure Dominican Father Calvin Knox, who was acclaimed Pope after the third ballot showed a hopeless tie between the Brazilian nun Sister Juan and the Coptic Bishop the Right Reverend Father Xenophon, had no known history before his ordination, when in his sixties, two years before. There is also the tantalizing, but objectively meaningless fact that His Holiness Pope Leo XIV, after ten years' service as God's emmissary, also disappeared. His last known words, "If I had known it was going to be like this, I would have stayed in Kansas," are believed to be a literary reference rather than a statement of antecedents.

The park had by now grown to over eight hundred acres, and to the original two buildings, garage, and greenhouses had been added a stable, a merry-go-round, and, during the "Roman" seventies, a *thermarum, tepidarium,* and *thermopolium.* The swimming pool had been enlarged to hold either a pod of hippopotami or a crocodile of small children. The garage had been enlarged, mostly underground, to hold three or four hundred vehicles.

Peter and Shirley learned these fascinating facts, and much more, within ten minutes of arriving at the gate of Agberg Park. A moving arrow guided their rented electric to a slot in the underground parking garage, and a series of instructional signs appeared, and were verbally reiterated, while they removed themselves from the boxy vehicle.

PLEASE LOCK YOUR CAR appeared on the wall before them. *"It would be best if you would keep your vehicle locked while you are removed from it"* was mechanically murmured in the air as they walked to the elevator.

"It's nice to know someone cares," Peter told Shirley.

"They're just trying to avoid liability," she said.

DISMOCK FUEL DISKS IF STAYING OVERNITE glowed on the wall as they turned the corner. *"If you are planning an overnight stay, please remember to dismock the fuel disks if yours is a hypled vehicle. Thank you for your attention,"* the air murmured as they passed.

"I hate to admit that our car is just an electric," Peter whispered to Shirley. "I might offend the wall."

"You might offend the car," Shirley whispered back.

Upstairs in the entrance hall, a large glassed-in area decorated with glowing illustrations of the original covers of Dottie Osborne and Lacie Camisole books, Peter's invitation was inspected and removed from him by a small, taciturn, elderly man with a close-cropped spade beard, who was garbed in jeans, sandals, and a flowered print shirt that said AGBERG across the back. He led them to seats in a compartment in the first car of the three-car miniature railroad train that was the approved way to arrive at the tournament site.

As the train filled up with other arrivals, they were treated to the short lecture on the history of Agberg Park, complete with pictures flashed onto the wall of their compartment. It was as though the present directors of the Agberg Foundation were worried that Robert Agberg might suddenly show up and they wanted to prove that they cared.

"They really led exciting lives back in those days," Shirley said, watching the hundred-and-fifty-year-old photographs and film clips of famous coronations, assassinations, invasions, inventions, sporting events, and entertainments that had happened during the known life span of Robert Agberg.

"He was a recluse," Peter reminded her. "He probably never got any closer to any of these happenings than we are right now."

"But he could have gone, if he'd wanted to," Shirley said, watching a twenty-second clip of the Beatles talking to Ed Sullivan. "These things were happening around him. He could have attended any of them if he wished. He chose to stay home, but he was a world-famous writer. Think of who may have come to visit him: Churchill, Truman, Einstein, Woody Allen, Charlie Chaplin, Mark Twain, Max Maven, William Shatner, Albert Payson Terhune—"

"I think you have several periods mixed up there," Peter said, "but I get your idea. Although, in fairness, I don't think he could have chosen to attend most of the news items—the blowing up of the *Hindenberg,* for example. He would have had to have advance warning that it was going to explode to show up. Or he would have had to have been on bounce, which wasn't invented, or discovered, or whatever at that time. And if he had been a bounce user, he couldn't have written all those books and made all that money, and left it to open a park, so you never would have heard of him in the first place."

"Such is fame," Shirley said.

The train traveled through thick clusters of dusty-green eucalyptus to debouch on the edge of a considerable grassy clearing with a brook running scenically along the far side. Around the perimeter of the clearing were a double rank of tents of a wild variety of sizes and shapes, all done in gay colors, with banners and pendants flying from all possible—and some improbable—projections. Some of the tents, for all Peter knew, might have been of a medieval pattern. Some clearly were much more modern. Some had never been seen before outside of the bizarre minds of their creators.

The eucalyptus smell was strong in Peter's nostrils as he got out of the compartment. He was not fond of the odor—for some reason, it made him think of undefined alien places where peculiar people did unspeakable things.

"Australia," Shirley said when he told her that. "The eucalyptus is native to Australia, not California. It was brought here a couple of hundred years ago as a crop, but it turned out to be a weed. It grows faster than anything and shuts out all the native trees."

WELCOME VISITORS, a large banner hung between two pikestaves proclaimed, TO THE LISTS OF CHIVALRY. Underneath that, a handprinted sign had been taped to one of the staves. WANDER ABOUT AND ENJOY YOURSELVES, it said, BUT PLEASE STAY OFF THE FIELD OF COMBAT UNLESS YOU INTEND TO FIGHT. Under that, someone had

added, IF YOU ARE GOING TO FIGHT, READ THE RULES OF COMBAT AND
FOLLOW THEM. —KING TISMANE.

The midget train steamed away, leaving the thirty or forty people
who had detrained clustered together before a long wooden table that
stood between them and the field. It did not exactly cut them off from
entering the field, since one could go around it from either side, but it
was clearly placed to be dealt with before proceeding. The table held
an impressive assortment of books, pamphlets, leaflets, instruction
sheets, instruction disks, photographs, and less identifiable objects. Behind the table four earnest middle-aged medievals were giving away,
selling, and thrusting upon those who looked like they needed them the
various impedimenta of the tabletop. A scattering of teenage boys and
girls in medieval dress were going among the newcomers and offering
assistance. Those new arrivals who were dressed in modern clothes were
offered an assortment of more-or-less medieval coverings from a small
tent behind the table. Monks' robes for the men, and a kind of coverall
long dress for the women.

A pretty blond girl of fourteen or fifteen in an elaborate puffy blouse
and layers of long skirt, with a small name tag over her left breast that
affirmed her to be MAID ASTRID, came up to Peter and Shirley. "Hi,"
she said. "Welcome to the tourney." She surveyed their costumes. Peter was wearing the tights and jacket he had worn to Castle Hightower,
with his ever-present blue case semiconcealed in a canvas shoulder bag,
while Shirley's long-skirted folk garment seemed to fit in adequately
with the surrounding feminine garb. "You look good," Maid Astrid
said. "Have you been here before?"

"No," Peter admitted.

"Well, just wander around and do whatever seems right. There's no
formality here. Except in the lists, of course. But I assume you don't
intend to fight. You're not exactly dressed for it. Although you can rent
armor, if you really want to. And we do have basic bashing lessons for
neophytes over in that corner, across there."

"Is there any objection to just watching?" Shirley asked.

"Of course not. Come, let me present you to King Tismane."

"How did you know?" Peter asked.

"Know what?" Maid Astrid replied.

"That we are special guests of King Tismane?"

"Oh, are you? I didn't know. *Everybody* gets presented. It's protocol."

"I see," Peter said.

The presentation was brief, as King Tismane was very involved in eating small meat pastries, drinking mead from a golden chalice, and fondling a pair of giggling maids-in-waiting, one of whom had mastered the technique of blushing every time the king said anything. Although, with what the king was saying, it did not take much art for a comparatively innocent young girl to blush. He did remember Peter. "Lord Peter," he said, waving the large hand with the mug of mead. "Glad you could come. Enjoy yourself. If you need anything, just ask. Maid Astrid, I appoint you to look after Lord Peter and his lady, and see that they want for nothing while they are here. They are my guests." And that was that.

Maid Astrid took them for a slow walk around the field and gave them a running commentary on all they saw. "Each of these tents belongs to one of the households of the Society," she said. "Except that some of them have more than one tent, and some households have members here at this tourney, but didn't erect a tent."

They paused to admire an ornate red-and-yellow-striped tent done in a strong Moorish style, and then strolled on. "What, exactly, constitutes a household?" Peter asked.

"I can tell you roughly," Maid Astrid said, "but not exactly. The way the Society grew over the past century, very few things got to be exact."

"Just how old is the Universal Monarchist Society?" Shirley asked. "And where did it come from?"

"And, incidentally," Peter added, "if it's not too personal, just what are you a maid of?"

"All work, I sometimes think," Astrid said.

They stopped in front of a wide tent done in tessellated black and white diamonds. There were a pair of long wooden tables with accompanying benches on each side of the tent. "Okay," Astrid said. "Let me take it from the top. Here. Let's sit down and have something to drink. I recommend the wine. Stay away from the mead. I'm going to have a Stella soda, but they'll open it in back and put it in a mug. Plasticans are considered an unacceptable anachronism."

"We can just sit here and drink these people's food?" Peter asked.

"This is the public tent," Astrid explained. "It isn't marked 'cause that's an anachronism too. And it's not overly crowded 'cause the households mostly bring their own food. And then some. There's quite a bit of rivalry as to who cooks the most medieval—and yet edible— provender."

A slender young man in a red-and-white doublet and brown tights, who projected the air of waiting to be asked to do handsprings or flips, or some other complex athletic maneuver, came over and took their order—and hop-skip-and-jumped back into the tent.

"A household," Astrid told them, "is, sort of, the smallest collective unit that is a member of the society. The blazons on the banners in front of the tents are the households' official arms. If there's more than one, then it's the one flying from the staff to the left of the door. Above a household would be a dukedom—which can be one or more households; a principality; and a kingdom. Over that is just the corporation itself."

"But the information I got from King Tismane and Desmond the Drear—there was this whole armful of pamphlets—says that I can just join the Society. None of it mentions households, I don't think."

"That's certainly right," Astrid agreed. "And officially, the households are meaningless. But practically and socially, they are all. If you join the Society, you would be called Goodman Peter and Goodwoman Shirley—they're both slurred together, and pronounced like 'Gomman' and 'Gwamman.' That's kind of like being a serf, except that we don't have serfs here. To get a better title, it's easiest to be in a household."

"But King Tismane called me 'Lord Peter,' " Peter remembered.

"That was a courtesy, because you are a guest," Astrid said. "If you joined, you'd be a gomman until you achieved rank."

"Well, what makes you a maid?" Shirley asked.

The hyperactive waiter brought their various beverages and tumbled away. Peter and Shirley were trying the white wine at Astrid's suggestion.

"Members of households who are under sixteen are maids if they're female, or pages if they're male. Sometime between sixteen and twenty, one can become a knight—if one earns it."

"What about the girls?" Shirley asked.

"The girls, too. There are feminine ways of earning knighthood, if one doesn't feel like entering the lists."

"The lists?"

"Fighting," Astrid explained. "To become a knight that way, you have to enter in single combat three times, or a melee ten times, and come out with distinction."

"What sort of distinction?" Peter asked.

"That means that you didn't make a complete ass of yourself, and you didn't run, and you didn't get killed. Getting killed is very bad form."

"I can imagine," Peter said.

"Well, anyway," Astrid said, "in order to fight in single combat, or in anything but an open melee, you just about have to be in a household. In order to make rank any other way, or to rise above knight, you just about have to be in a household. And *everybody's* a knight."

"How do you join a household?" Shirley asked.

"Well, I was born into mine," Astrid told her. "I'm the daughter of Archduke VanRijn. That's our tent over there; the blue one with the gold trim. Our family has held the throne sixteen times. Daddy has been king himself three times; that's what makes him an archduke. And Mommy is a Royal Duchess; that's because she's descended from one of the Twelve Families."

"The Twelve Families?"

"The founders of the Society. Way back in nineteen hundred and sixty-nine. And the Twelve Families is actually the twelve original households. There were something like seventeen or eighteen families involved, but a couple of them sort of doubled up. They still do. Even in real life—I mean, outside the Society. A Society household may end up all living together."

"Like Hightower," Peter said.

"That's right," Astrid agreed. "It becomes like a vast game that you play all the time. It takes up your life. Society politics are much more important to the people here than who gets elected President of the United States, or the United Nations, or anything. Besides, how else can you get to live in a real—or sort of real—castle?"

They continued their walk, carrying their mugs of wine, and Maid Astrid pointed out the various households and the tents they occupied. "There's Von Hoefflischkeit, one of the Founding Families. Their device is two beer steins touching on a field of suds. The next tent, the clear plastic one, is the Earl of the North Western Marches."

"How seriously are these titles taken?" Shirley asked.

"Within the Society, completely seriously," Astrid said. "Outside, of course, they're not."

"Hah!" a voice from somewhere past them called. "Lord Peter!" Peter turned. It was Lord Desmond the Drear, sprawled happily in a canvas chair by the side of a tent. "Glad you came," he yelled. "Come on over and let me refresh your mugs and offer you a bite of something medieval and hearty."

They paused in their guided tour to sit with Lord Desmond and eat thick meat pies. Astrid, seeing that they were in good—if plump— hands, excused herself and ran off to her household tent. Lord Desmond was delighted to meet Shirley, and got involved in a long discussion with her on medieval cooking; what parts of it should be revived, and what parts are better left interred. "Cooking and fighting are my two passions," he told them. "Although both mainly as spectator sports these days. Which reminds me—" He pushed himself up from his chair and entered his tent, returning with a plump red-cheeked woman and a folder of papers.

"My wife," he introduced, "the Lady Miranda Desmond. A truly Southern belle. My dear, let me present Lord Peter and Lady Shirley. They are guests of His Majesty."

"That is my husband's little joke," Lady Miranda said, shaking hands with them. "I am from Brazil. But that was years ago."

"Lord Peter," Desmond said, drawing him aside, "I have here some specs that I've worked up concerning equipment that your company might be interested in making for us. Lances and armor, and such. Also some heavier stuff that you just might want to price out, although we won't need it for a while."

Lady Miranda took Shirley away for further discussions of cooking, so that the men could have their boring old man talk. Peter sighed. This sort of man talk he found just as boring, but he had to feign interest. He was *supposed* to be interested. It was what he was there for. If only someone would make a swipe at his blue protect case. If only he didn't feel so silly lugging it around all over the place. If only he felt that something he was doing was having some success at finding out who killed the Thai girl, and why she was killed. If only he'd kept his job selling educational robots to private schools instead of giving in to a yen to travel around the world as a courier. Griffin Universal owned Rob Roy, "The Teacher's Friend Robot Company," and they believed in promoting from within. But was this really a promotion?

Someone was staring at him. Peter could feel it like a physical sensation. He turned around.

A small white-haired woman dressed in a brown sack of no determinate age (either the woman or the sack) was standing off to one side of the Desmond tent. Her gaze was intent and unblinking, but to say it was aimed at Peter would be saying more than could be told. Her eyes were fixed on where Peter was sitting, but when he shifted to the left or right her gaze did not track.

"Who is that?" asked Lord Desmond the Drear.

"I was about to ask you something along the same lines," Peter said.

"Aha!" Desmond said. "An interloper. We know how to handle such. We will have her produce antecedents, or she shall be ejected from the tourney."

"No—wait—" Peter said. "I don't know what she's doing here, but I think she's a bouncer. Removing her would serve no useful purpose."

"Hmm," Desmond said. He stepped over to examine the woman, who did not seem to notice his presence. "You may be right," he said. "I have only the slightest experience with these people. She seems to be looking at you. Or should I say, staring? Could that be?"

"I suppose," Peter said. "It wouldn't be the first time."

Desmond murmured something into the lapel of his tunic, and a minute later Peter saw Astrid striding across the greensward in the company of a tall blond man with piercing eyes and an attitude of complete control. His air of authority may have been aided by the fact that he was in full armor, a Germanic-looking full body suit done in matte black.

"Sorry to pull you away from whatever you were doing, VanRijn," Lord Desmond said, "but you did say that you wanted to be notified whenever any of these bouncers showed up."

"That's so, that's so," Lord VanRijn said. He glared suspiciously at Peter.

"This is Peter Lyon, Daddy," Astrid said. "He's a guest of King Tismane."

Lord VanRijn stuck out his powerful right hand. "Welcome to the Society, Lord Peter," he said. "I hope you're enjoying yourself."

"Pretty much," Peter said. He introduced VanRijn to Shirley, who had emerged from the tent to see what all the excitement was.

"Lord VanRijn is our Secret Service," Lord Desmond explained to them. "All suspicious happenings are to be reported to him. It was felt by His Previous Majesty that any self-respecting medieval kingdom should have a Secret Service, and since Lord VanRijn occupies a similar position in the Mundane World, he seemed the ideal choice."

"The Mundane World?" Shirley asked.

"Ah yes. A little redundancy we use to mean everything outside of the Society. Here I am Lord Desmond the Drear, and occupy the important post of seneschal of procurement, for instance. In the Mundane World, I am but a postal clerk."

"That's his personal conceit," Astrid said. "Uncle Des is really postmaster-in-chief in charge of electronic communications for the North Western Semisphere."

"Just a glorified postal clerk," Desmond insisted, but smiling with pleasure that Astrid had the good sense to puncture his little charade.

While the conversation was going on, Lord VanRijn had gone over to examine the woman in white. He walked around her, studying her from several different angles, and waved his hand in front of her face. She appeared not to notice, and kept staring at the chair Peter had been sitting in. Lord VanRijn moved the chair. She stared at the space it had occupied.

"These people," VanRijn said, shaking his head. "It's a miracle to me that they stay alive. They know so much, and yet they can't even take care of themselves. Some of them soil themselves, you know; they can't be bothered finding a toilet. They usually manage to eat and drink enough to stay alive, but they don't care *what* they eat. At all. And they get strange diseases that other people don't get. Schwenk's syndrome has never been seen on someone who wasn't a PHD user. It's a fascinating puzzle."

"What is?" Shirley asked.

"What the stuff is, where it comes from, why it has the effects it has, that sort of thing."

"Are you a policeman in the, ah, Mundane World?" Shirley asked.

"Indirectly," Lord VanRijn said. "I am the C.O.O. of the Continental Protective Services Group. We supply private guards. Some small countries contract their police force to us."

"C.O.O.?" Shirley asked.

"Chief Operations Officer."

"Why the interest in bouncers?" Peter asked.

"They've been showing up at Society tournaments recently," Lord VanRijn said. "For no reason that any of us can figure out. There's one of them in my tent now, being fed goulash and talking to the wall. The east wall, for some reason. If we try turning him around, he goes back to it."

"One of them knew Peter's name," Shirley said, taking Peter's hand. "We were in a restaurant and he came over and started talking to Peter."

"Is that right?" Lord VanRijn looked interested. "Listen, I'd like to talk to you about that, if you have the time. Not right now, because I have to go bash a few heads in a minute."

"Sure," Peter said. "Who am I to argue with a man who's preparing to bash a few heads?"

VanRijn laughed. "It's not as bad as it sounds. We're going to have a peer's melee—for baronets and up—and they'll expect me to show up. I'm leader of the Blues. That's what I'm all dressed up for."

"Of course," Peter said.

"Here—" Lord VanRijn patted himself on the armor for a moment, and then looked embarrassed. "Astrid, honey, would you please run back to my tent and get one of my cards—my mundane business cards —out of my carryall? Bring it over and give it to Mr. Lyon."

"Sure thing, Daddy," Astrid said, and she was off like a young gazelle.

"Come see me in the office, if you have a chance," VanRijn said. "We have an open assignment on bounce and bouncers, and I should be doing something to earn the money. Every extra bit of information is mist for the grill, as they say."

"Who's collecting information on bouncers?" Peter asked.

"We don't give the names of our clients," VanRijn said. "Think of it as a useful safeguard that you'll want yourself when you become a client."

"You sound awfully sure that I'm going to need a guard service," Peter said.

"Call it professional optimism. I had to go to a Foglest seminar on Friday, and I'm afraid some of it wore off."

"Well," Lord Desmond said. "Ditmar Fogle?"

"That's him. The Chairman of the Board is a fanatic Foglest, and insists upon inflicting it on the rest of us."

"With the truth-teller, and the whole business?"

"With Ditmar Fogle himself. 'The Will Is the Life, and the Life is the Universal All.' 'The Will to Success Can Beat Any Failure.' 'Try—Believe—Strive—Succeed.' It's enough to make any sane man puke."

"I was a Foglest," Lord Desmond said.

"Oh. Listen, I didn't mean to insult you, old man. I'm sure there's good—"

"No no," Desmond said. "You are absolutely right. I was hypnotized, or something. When I came out of it, I found I'd been involved with the group for six months and about fifty thousand dollars. My wife was ready to leave me, and my children were looking at me as though I were some kind of freak. All in all, it was a very instructive experience."

VanRijn shrugged. "Today's nut cult, tomorrow's major religion," he said. "What can I tell you? If we could bottle the personal magnetism that these people, these philosophies, possess, and use it only for good causes, we'd have the world straightened out in six months. But then, we'd be the ones picking the good causes, wouldn't we? *'Quis custodiet ipsos Custodes?'* as Juvenal so cleverly put it. I must go back to my tent and prepare for the bout." He shook hands with Peter and Shirley, slapped Desmond on the back, and strode away.

A minute later Astrid returned and handed Peter her father's business card. "Daddy says please come, he really would like to speak to you. He's fascinated by the bouncers, and every little bit of information helps."

Peter examined the plasticine. THE CONTINENTAL PROTECTIVE SERVICE, it said, PAUL WINSTON VANRIJN, OPERATIONS. The office address was in the downtown San Francisco area; one of the bright, tall new buildings that had just started going up in the area devastated by the "Big Mother" Earthquake of 1997. Escobaga had been very eloquent on the subject only the other evening. For a hundred years they had allowed nothing taller than sixty stories; but they forget. With the next quake overdue, building permits were easier than ever to get. Oh sure, the buildings were supposedly quakeproof; but, as Escobaga had put it, "If you can't get better than even money, bet on the quake."

"Tell your father that I will look forward to seeing him," Peter said. "I, also, am very interested in the bouncers. Maybe we can both learn something."

"My father listens much better than he talks," Astrid said. "It's an occupational whatchamacallit."

A man dressed in motley with a long red cape strode out to the middle of the field and blew briefly on a trumpet. "Hear ye!" he shouted, striding about the field as he spoke. His voice was being picked up by a mike somewhere on his person and floated over the area on a network of small, strategically placed speakers. "Hear ye, one and all! The noble and gentle Lord Pandibar would have it known that he finds the style and opinions of the earnest and forthright Lord Quintile the Seldom Ready to be totally unacceptable. Lord Quintile has likewise advised me that he feels that the ideas and habits of Lord Pandibar do not bear discussion. Each is determined that the other shall see the error of his ways.

"Since discussion and calm reason has proved fruitless, each of these two noble lords is resolved to establish the rightness of his cause on the Field of Honor. I ask now, before the bloodshed commences, whether it is not possible to reconcile your difficulties? I shall give you a minute to consider."

"Well!" Shirley said. "Who is he? Are they going to fight?"

"This is all formula," Lord Desmond told her. "It's leading into the melee. He is the herald, and it's his job to announce the fights and see that protocol is followed."

A minute later the herald came back onto the field. "Hear ye!" he bellowed into his microphone. "Both sides refusing to see the sweet light of reason, we will now fall back on that ancient and honest saying: 'Might makes right.' Lord Pandibar has appealed to the Blues to champion him, and they will use a blue sash as their device, while Lord Quintile the Seldom Ready has the aid and assistance of the Reds, who will, of course, don red sashes for their part.

"Standard melee rules will apply. No hitting when an opponent is down, or has surrendered. If an opponent loses his helm, there will be no blows to the head, but a combatant who is dishelmed must leave the field of combat as soon as possible. All weapons carried onto the field must have been approved by the seneschal of battles beforehand. There will be no exceptions to this rule, and failure to obey it will be regarded most seriously. All fighting will cease immediately upon stepping out-side of the boundaries of the field, which are marked by red pennants and chalked lines on the ground. This rule will not be broken, upon pain of the king's displeasure.

"The coin having been flipped, Lord Quintile the Seldom Ready has chosen the north end, and Lord Pandibar and his host will assault from the south. When both sides are ready, I will lower the red banner."

An assistant herald stood by the side of the field, holding up a tall staff with a gold-rimmed red flag atop. "That's the battle flag," Astrid explained. "It is always lowered to start a melee."

The two sides assembled at each end of the field, about sixty fighters to a side. While the herald spoke, two assistant heralds had been going around the field sticking up bamboo poles about three meters long topped by triangular red pennants, and marking the space between with a powdered chalk linemaker. The final area marked off was about twice as long and half again as wide as a football field.

"Are you ready?" the herald inquired loudly.

"Ready!" someone yelled from the South End Gang.

A knight in bright red armor emerged from the northern group. "Not ready yet," he called, waving. A soft chuckle spread over the field, quickly turning into a wave of energetic laughter.

"Lord Quintile is not yet ready!" the herald announced over the noise.

About two minutes later the red knight came forward again. "We're ready now," he announced.

"Very good," the herald said. "Both sides are ready. Watch for the signal!" He nodded to his assistant with the red battle flag and strolled off the field. As he reached the border, the flag was dropped.

The two hosts rushed toward each other with furious energy, in irregular battle lines, swords over their heads, shields raised. They met with a sound like "Night on Bald Mountain," played with hammers and wrenches on ash cans.

"Ah, the din of battle," Lord Desmond yelled. "It's music to my ears!"

SEVENTEEN

Thirty-two light-years from the Earth, in the direction of the constellation Pisces, slightly to the north of the dorsal fin, the slightly red sun Ragnorak swam in the universal void with its complement of planets, comets, moons, asteroids, space dust, and detritus. Its four main planets, as humans classify such things, were Atlantis, Hyperborea, Barsoom, and Mu. Atlantis and Hyperborea were gas giants with multiple moons, the former 14 percent larger than Jupiter, almost at the threshold of igniting itself and becoming a star; the latter a hair smaller than Saturn, but with a finer set of rings. Barsoom was small, moonless, dull red, dry, and cratered, and chased its tail in the corona of Ragnorak. In another ten million years it would spiral in and be consumed.

Mu was 2 percent larger than Earth, and had 1.5 percent less surface gravity. It had three moons: Plato, which was three-quarters the size of Luna, Ramses, three-eights the size, and Marat, a tiny one in a close, retrograde orbit. Mu's average distance from Ragnorak was 1.6 A.U., which was just right to keep water a liquid over most of its surface. And there was water over most of its surface; roughly 87 percent. Of the 13 percent of the rock mantle that thrust above the water, 3 percent was under a sheet of ice at the South Pole, and the remaining 10 percent was distributed among two land masses in the Northern Hemisphere, and a belt of thousands of tiny volcanic islands that straddled the Equator.

The two large land masses were the continents of East and West Mu, and the major settlement on East Mu, the larger continent, was the metropolis of New Mu, which now contained in excess of four thousand people. The second-largest settlement was Port Thebes, the spaceport, on a small island of the same name at the Equator, which had a permanent population of over a thousand. The rest of the

Muvian population was spread out about East Mu, trying to figure out what crops grow best in reddish light, with some small groups practicing oceanic husbandry on the equatorial islands.

*   *   *

Dilbert Walweb, the captain of the gashopper *Ra*, Lord Commander of the Galactic Seas, and Procurator of the Inner Circle of the Seekers of the True Mu, leaned back in the con chair, closed his eyes, and prayed a silent prayer as the ship prepared to come out of interstitial drive somewhere around Ragnorak. Bright blue darts shined inside his eyelids, and strange distant geometric shapes appeared. Interstitial space getting in its last kicks. He swallowed twice, took a deep breath, and killed the drive.

A violent wave of nausea passed through his body. Most people didn't have that reaction, but he did—every time. He opened his eyes to look around the bridge. Reassured that its appearance had returned to normal, he flicked the GENERAL CALL switch on his intercom. "This is the captain," he announced in as close as he could approximate his normal, calm, low captain's voice. "As you can tell, we have just deflogged the interstitial drive, and are in normal space somewhere close to Ragnorak and Mu. As soon as we finish computing orbital relationships and distances, I will announce our estimated docking time at Fort Fort, the transfer satellite. It will probably be somewhere between a week and a month. That is all for now."

Captain Walweb flicked off the intercom and leaned forward in his con chair. "Well?" he asked. "Where are we?"

Tepping, the electronics officer, was hunched over the scanner boards with McAlister, the navigation officer, and the two electronics mates. At the captain's words, he turned around, doing little to conceal his annoyance at the interruption. "We are conducting a survey of the scanner screens, as you ordered, sir," he said. "As soon as we have something, you'll be the first to know."

Captain Walweb bit off an angry retort. It would do no good. *If this were the Navy*—he thought. But his Navy days were long behind him, and he was more often on the receiving end than the giving end of angry retorts in those ancient and halcyon days. Which was all for the best now, wasn't it? Here he was commanding the only gashopper in the Seekers' fleet, while if he'd stayed in the Combined Forces Space

Navy, he might—just might—have made it up to First Officer on an Inner Planets tug.

"If you would be so good, Mister Tepping, would you put the scanners up on the big screen?" Walweb asked sweetly. "Start with the forward scanner. I'll rotate them from my console. I don't want to distract you from your work."

These were passive scanners, electronic cameras receiving and interpreting light and other radiation emitted by the surrounding Universe. The screens on the active scanners, such as radar, would probably not come alive for some time yet. The odds of any object being close enough for their radar beam to have reached it and returned in the brief time that they had been out of interstitial space were slight—and it would have been very disconcerting were any planet-sized or stellar-sized object to prove to be that close.

The big screen came to life with a view of what the forward scanners saw in front of the *Ra:* distant varicolored points of light.

"Stars," Captain Walweb muttered. "And not a one of them looking significantly larger than any other." He toggled the port scanners on, with the same result. The dozen or so officers and crew members on the bridge were all standing around trying to pretend that they had something to do, that they were not holding their collective breaths and staring at the big board, hoping to see something that looked like a very large, *very close,* red star.

The starboard scanners centered on the Dynsdale Cluster, a group of hundreds of stars, mostly bright blue or pure white, which danced together in the cosmic void. Was it Walweb's imagination, or were they just a bit larger—and thus considerably closer—than they should have been? Perhaps the screens were set to a slight magnification. Walweb chose to hope so.

The topside and bottom scanners merely showed an unrelieved star field, with nothing unusually close or unusually red. Only one more chance to earn his money the easy way.

Captain Walweb toggled the rear scanner onto the big screen—and let out an involuntary gasp. One of the crew—it was the pharmacist's mate, who should have been in the sick bay, and not on the bridge—screamed.

A large circle was cut out of the sky directly behind them. Matte

black, and fringed with a dimly sparkling corona of red and orange, it
almost filled the big screen.

"What the Hell—" Walweb said explosively.

"Atlantis," Miz McAlister, the navigation officer, told him, frowning
a disapproval at his cursing. "We are on the far side of Atlantis. It is
screening us from a view of Ragnorak. We have, so to speak, created
our own solar eclipse. Actually, this is quite fortuitous."

"How do you figure that?" Walweb demanded.

"Elementary celestial mechanics. The gravity well of Atlantis will
absorb much of out forward momentum, and we can use it to slingshot
ourselves inward toward Mu. There are several options."

"Come here, if you don't mind, Miz McAlister," Walweb said, "and
let us discuss these options of yours without shouting."

McAlister stepped over to the con chair. "Let me bring the orbits up
on your board, Captain," she said.

"Belay that!" Walweb snapped in a hoarse whisper. "You know what
this means?"

"To what are you referring?"

"To the appearance of that monster on the aft screen! What it
means, Navigation Officer McAlister, is that, while in interstitial space,
we have passed through the normal space locations of a red star and a
giant gas planet. It means that, had we come out of the drive a fraction
of a second earlier, we would have been squashed like an egg roll and
burned to an atomic crisp. I don't like it!"

"It may mean that, or it may not," McAlister said coolly. "We don't
know whether there is a one-to-one correspondence between the two
spaces. There probably is not. We don't know whether there is a mass
deflector built into the drive. And there probably is."

"There's entirely too much that we don't know," Captain Walweb
said in a petulant, but very low, voice. There were things that the crew
and passengers were not meant to overhear. "We don't know how the
interstitial drive works in the first place. We don't know how to go
anywhere in a gashopper that we haven't already been. We don't know
how to make repairs if the thing breaks—may the Elder Gods forbid!
We don't know how to make course corrections with any reliability.
Every time we make the trip from Earth to Mu, we try to correct for
the change in relative positions, and we're guessing."

"My 'guessing' has been pretty good so far," Miz McAlister commented frigidly. "If you think you can do any better yourself, you're certainly welcome to try."

"Don't get sensitive, McAlister. You're a ship's officer, not a woman. I didn't mean to disparage your skills at any rate. It is quite possible that anyone else, working with the slight data at our disposal, would have put us smack in the middle of one of those two vast objects to our stern." The captain waved his thick hands in the air and waggled their stubby fingers. "I think you're doing an incredible job. For the love of oysters, McAlister, you know we couldn't do this without you. But it's all—what do you say?—empirical. We don't know the theory behind it. And when you don't know the theory—when you don't know *why* you're doing something—you're liable to make a mistake."

"Well, it's not my fault that when the Seekers stole a gashopper they didn't get the repair manuals or the Interstitial Navigation Charts," Miz McAlister said firmly. "It sounds like sloppy planning to me. Now, if you'll excuse me, Captain, I have to plot an orbit."

Due to the cleverness of Navigation Officer McAlister and the presence of a gas giant only half a million kilometers away to use as a gravity slingshot, the trip to Fort Fort orbit took only five days, which was the shortest that had been achieved since the first year and a half of operation, when the *Ra*, then known as the *Harpist in the Wind*, was still part of the Griffin Universal fleet, and the direction and distance calibrations were done by someone who knew how gashoppers worked.

Adolf Castow Merriam, Princeps and Imperator of Mu, known as "A.C." to those privileged to associate with him, was waiting at Port Thebes when the transatmosphere shuttle came down from Fort Fort. Standing on the speaker's dias in the purple toga with the gold trim that was his robe of office, he gave his usual "Welcome to Mu, Fellow Seekers" speech to the two hundred colonists who had been aboard the *Ra*. Then, before any of them could corner him and start asking the interminable, dreary questions to which he had no answer, he left the platform and went to look for Captain Walweb.

Walweb had just passed his personal hand baggage to one of the young Negro porters, and was settling down to enjoy a large crème de menthe and soda in the operations lounge, when Merriam found him. "Well?" Merriam demanded.

"Well, what?" Walweb replied, in a surly refusal to understand.

"Well, old man, what's the news? First, any trouble with the gashopper? Second, any further information on how to run the thing? Did our man in Griffin come through? Come on, old man, you know what I want to know. I gave up being a dentist when I left Earth. Don't make me start pulling teeth to find out what I want to know."

"Is that a threat?" Walweb demanded. "Are you resorting to threats? I don't have to put up with this, you know. You're not the one who has to go through hell every trip, wondering whether we're going to make it or end up somewhere in the Cosmic Void."

"A threat? What in the name of various Elder Gods are you talking about? Pulling teeth? That's an expression, old man. A metaphor, don't you know? No more than a careless simile. Don't get on your hobbyhorse now. You're not the only one affected by our common problems. You don't know what it feels like to be stranded here without knowing from one day to the next if you're going to be—ah—stranded here."

"I thought you were happy here," Walweb said. "You ought to be. You're the big cheese." He stared with disfavor at his now empty glass and put it down. "Let's go next door where we can talk. This isn't exactly private."

"Oh, don't misunderstand me. I *am* happy here," Merriam said, following Walweb into the corridor. "I never want to go back to Earth. But that doesn't mean that I no longer want to be able to hear from Earth. To get new goods and new people from Earth. You are my lifeline, Procurator Walweb." They went into the office of the chief of operations, who was out supervising the unloading of the shuttle, and fixed themselves a couple of tall glasses of bourbon and rainwater from his private stock.

"You think you've got it rough?" Walweb asked, settling in behind the C of O's desk and putting his feet up. "I never know where the hell we're going to come out of interstitial space when we turn off that drive. This time we almost ended up inside that damn red sun of yours. If we don't figure out how to navigate in interstitial space pretty soon, I'm going to go flippy-dippy. And what if the drive breaks? Nobody knows where we'd end up then. At least, nobody on Mu."

"I take it that this means that our attempt to get the drive specifications has been a failure?" Merriam asked.

"As far as I know," Walweb said. "Nobody ever tells me anything. I suppose if we had the specs, someone would have come along to look over the gashopper before we headed out. But you can never tell. The Inner Circle never tells me what it's doing, or why, and I'm on it. Oh, that reminds me—" He reached into his jacket pocket and pulled out a sealed envelope. "This is from them. For you. Probably goes into all that."

Merriam sighed and shook his head. "Sometimes you amaze me," he said. "Our need for a ship's captain must have been severe when you got the job."

"So it was," Walweb agreed. "If you think I don't have the right attitude, you're not alone. The goddamn Navy didn't think so either. But I'm here and they're there. And so what?"

"So what indeed." Merriam took the envelope and opened it. It contained a data crystal, which he shook out onto his palm and dropped into the reader built into the corner of the desk.

The device hummed thoughtfully for a minute, and then beeped twice and filled the screen with verbal garbage. Then it overwrote a second layer of garbage on the first, and a third on the second. Then the three layers wiped clear, leaving only a blinking question mark centered on the screen.

"Why they bother with all this stuff," Captain Walweb said, "when they could have just told me whatever they wanted and let me pass it on to you, is more than I know."

Merriam typed in a code word and waited expectantly. "Protocol, old man," he explained. "Need to know. Chain of command. Rightful order of precedence. All that sort of thing."

MESSAGE #1 OF 24—ACTUALITY
lit up on the screen, which then went blank for a moment, and cleared to reveal a man's face. "Hello, A.C.," the man said.

"Dynast Blakesley!" Merriam said.

"I thought I should speak to you myself," Dynast Blakesley, President of the Seekers of the True Mu, and Chairman of the Inner Council, continued, staring somewhat over Merriam's right shoulder. "Try to explain to you what's been happening, and just where we are at right now, as near as anybody can tell. This is most secret, and very private, of course."

The speaker paused, and Merriam turned to Walweb. "Secret," he repeated.

Walweb nodded. "I'll lock the door," he said. "No telling who might be trying to listen in."

Merriam nodded back. "You can never tell," he agreed. Trying to be subtle to Walweb was an utter waste of time, and Merriam didn't feel up to ordering him out of the room. He'd just have to hope that the message contained nothing that Walweb shouldn't know.

"As you know, our agent inside of Griffin Universal has been trying to locate the information we need," the speaker said. "He received word that a copy of the current Interstitial Space Navigation Charts was being sent on microguppy from a subsidiary office in Bangkok to the research facility in San Francisco. We attempted to intercept this information."

"I know," Merriam told the screen, sounding aggrieved. "What happened?"

"He can't hear you," Walweb volunteered. "It's only a recording."

"Unfortunately," the face on the screen continued, "the incompetents we hired in Bangkok discorporated two people in the attempt. On top of which, they failed to obtain the data. I take full responsibility for the error in judgment. The miscreants are being chastized."

"Wonderful!" Captain Walweb commented. "So we continue to stumble blindly through interstitial space."

"There is, however, some hope," the face went on. "Our contact within Griffin Universal has established that the desired data was actually concealed in a blue protect case that was in the office. Griffin's Section G, which controls this information, believes that the case has been retired. However, our man has discovered that the courier involved is still carrying the case about. He has, you see, no idea that there is anything of importance concealed in it. It seems it's hidden in a false top to an interior compartment.

"So our job is clear: to locate the courier and disassociate him from his blue case. This is now being worked on, with some fair hope of success."

The Chairman of the Inner Council paused and stared intently out of the screen at Princeps and Imperator Merriam. "A.C.," he said, "I want you to know that I am looking forward to the day when I can be there with you to share the dangers—and the rewards—of creating a New Mu. We all know and appreciate the great job you're doing. I need a full report from you on conditions there on Mu; any changes, anything unusual or unexpected; and more particularly on any possible additional export potential for any of the indigenous flora or fauna. Remembering, of course, that it *must* be possible to conceal its point of origin. Our present exports, secret though they are, go a long way toward paying for Program New Mu.

"We also need constant feedback on the success of our Second Homes program. I hope that you are having it adequately monitored. The only true judge of the success of the training here is in the results there."

"What's that?" Walweb asked. "I don't know about this Second Homes stuff."

"It's the black kids," Merriam told him.

"Them young Neeegro servants?" Walweb asked. (He pronounced it "Neeegro.")

"That's right," Merriam agreed. "I'll explain later. Let me hear the rest of this."

Walweb poured himself another drink.

"We will have another group of young, ah, students ready to send along to their second homes next trip," Blakesley continued. "It is a shame that the great public service we are doing will go unrecorded— at least here on Earth. I am looking forward to the day when I can pass the mantle on to another, and give up this great task, and come to join you there on Mu."

"I'll bet *you're* not looking forward to it," Walweb said, nudging Merriam. "He might want your job!"

"Don't be silly," Merriam snapped.

"The rest of this data crystal is, er, data," the Chairman of the Inner Council said. "I'll be talking to you again soon. Bye!" He waved his hand, and the screen went blank.

"No big news there," Captain Walweb said. "I don't know about these people. They can steal a kilometer-and-a-half-long gashopper from under the nose of the Griffin, but they can't locate an instruction manual, or a properly programmed navigation chip."

"Which part are you complaining about?" Merriam asked. "The fact that they are thieves, or the fact that they are such inefficient thieves?"

"Don't be funny," Walweb explained. "You don't have to drive a four-million-cubic-meter bag of rare gas through the Cosmos on prayer and hunches."

EIGHTEEN

"Here is the report from my agents about that Higher Outreach Primary School. There is something very strange going on there," Daddy Exx said, waving a tablet reader over the breakfast table at Saralu.

"What sort of strange?" Saralu asked. She took the reader from him and held it in front of her, tilting it forward and back. "The light's bad on this side of the table. I can't read this thing."

"It's self-illuminating, and you've got to hold the corner to turn it on," her father told her. "Here—like this." He took her right hand and moved it to the lower-right-hand corner of the rectangular tablet.

"Oh." She shook her head. Daddy Exx could never resist a new gadget. Which meant that, if she stayed away for more than six months or so, she couldn't work the house when she got back.

She read the report carefully and studied the pictures. The report was better than she had expected, even from a top American detective agency, with only a week's work. The pictures didn't actually show anything useful; they just served to add an air of verisimilitude. She put the reader down and drank her coffee, then picked it up and read the report again. "It is strange," she said. "I can't think what it might mean. Unless they're cannibals."

"Don't put anything past a group of white people, daughter," Daddy Exx said. "If cannibals seems like the most logical answer to you, then cannibals is what they probably are."

"I wish it were that simple," Saralu said. "Not that I wish a bunch of poor orphans have been eaten for dinner; but that, whatever the truth is, it turns out to be that obvious. It won't."

"How many of your pure black stock kids do you figure the orphanage has sent this school?" Daddy Exx asked.

"Should be about four hundred," she said. "Black children with low IQs, being taken care of by these Higher Outreach people."

"But there are less than a hundred there, according to my detectives," Bill Exx said.

"That's what it says," Saralu agreed. "This a good agency?"

"The best," Daddy Exx told her. "I own it."

"Then what has happened to three hundred kids?"

"Have a piece of mango pie," her father suggested. "Nothing like mango pie for breakfast to clear the mind."

"You know anything about this group that your men say are behind the schools?" Saralu asked, helping herself to a slice of pie. "These Seekers of the True Mu?"

"Not a thing, daughter," Bill Exx said.

"I think I'd better go find out," Saralu said. Her sharp white teeth took a healthy bite out of the triangle of pie.

"Whatever you say," Daddy Exx agreed.

* * *

Lying prone on his ample stomach on a rooftop three buildings away and across the street, William Jesse Harker extended the lens of his sneakscope cautiously over the ledge and peered into the tiny screen. This was not an ideal point of view. It was not—if it came to that—an ideal point of anything. The roof was hard, and sloping, and exposed, and grainy, and covered with a thick layer of fine white dust that covered his viewscreen and made him sneeze. Harker took a large semiwhite handkerchief from a back pocket and applied it to his nose, his eyes, and the tiny screen. He had the uncomfortable feeling that he was here paying for his sins.

When the girl, Saralu, had taken leave to come to visit her sick father, Harker's employers had suggested that he follow and keep watching. But this was not the sort of watching that he had come to need. The brief, distant glimpses he got of the tall black girl merely strengthened his itch, and didn't help scratch it at all.

He had sinned. He had told his superiors that there was something suspicious in Saralu's behavior when there was not, merely to satisfy his own needs, his own lusts. And now, for punishment, he got to follow her from a block away when she went to the hospital to visit her father; he got to peer electronically at her in her parents' home while she sat with her mother and some male who looked enough like her father to be an uncle—not that Harker could tell these people apart.

The punishment was fitting. Somewhere in the back of his head, Harker could hear his Calvinist grandfather pronouncing something about "sowing" and "reaping," not to mention the shrill voice of his mother telling him it was "dirty" to peep through windows.

And now Harker would have to follow this beautiful black woman around from a distance, without even the expectation of a sight of her seminaked body to fuel his fantasies. And he still couldn't let go; he was still not master of his own compulsions. He couldn't bring himself to tell his superiors that Saralu Ngaxu was beyond reproach. For then he couldn't watch her at all—and that would drive him crazy.

He sighed and rolled over, and put his eye back to the tiny screen.

INTERLUDE

Thirty small faces, ranging in hue from light brown to black, sat placidly in the small antiseptic classroom and listened with varying degrees of attention to the large white face in front of them.

"You have been picked," the white face told them, one hand fluffing the dark circle of carefully coiffed hair surrounding it, "to take part in a great experiment. You boys and girls are very lucky to have this opportunity. Those poor orphans that you left behind at the Buckton Nondenominational Orphanage in the People's Federated Protectorate of South Africa will envy you the chance that you are getting. First, here you are in the United States of America, known far and wide as God's Country. Second, you are going to receive three months' training and instruction that will fit you for meaningful jobs in a brand-new world that we are creating. Not many people have such a chance. Then you will receive further training and job guidance in your new location; a wonderful place, where we all live and work in harmony, each in his or her assigned place, according to the instructions of the Council of Mu and the wisdom of the Elder Gods."

The pudding of brown and black faces stared up unemotionally at the white lady as she kept speaking. They seemed to understand what she was saying, but they didn't seem to care.

A large man took over from the lady. "I am Mr. Tropp, your proctor in charge of discipline," he told them. "You'll have no trouble with me if you follow your instructions. Do what those placed over you tell you to do—cheerfully, rapidly, and well, putting your whole heart into it— and you will be at peace with your instructors, your masters, and your gods. Fail to do what you are told, or do it badly, and you are at war with me—and it is a war you cannot hope to win.

"Now it's time to take your medication. From now on it will be given intramuscularly; that is, by injection. But that means you'll only have to take it once a month. Line up to my right, and roll up your sleeves."

NINETEEN

"A little Theosophy," Escobaga said, "a little astrology, a little Christian Science, and maybe just a dab of Rosicrucianism. Put them all together, with a touch of broad-based innocence, and a couple of hundred bucks a month to spend on the Greater Truth, and you have a Seeker. They seem to be doing very well."

Michael Wong Escobaga had parked his ancient alcohol-burning automobile across from the main entrance to the Seekers' headquarters complex in Palo Alto. It seemed right, Peter reflected, that a vehicle belonging to Escobaga would be alcohol-powered.

SEEKERS OF THE TRUE MU < > TEMPLE AND MUSEUM, said the sign

done in wrought-iron tracery over the vast main gate. In smaller print on the right-hand gatepost was added: VISITORS WELCOME TUESDAYS AND THURSDAYS, 10–6. On the left-hand gatepost, a square white plastic sign gave the black Gothic-lettered warning: ADMINISTRATION BUILDINGS CLOSED TO THE PUBLIC. CALL FOR APPOINTMENT.

"It being barely past eleven of a Tuesday," Escobaga said, "What say we go into that there temple and/or museum and look around?"

"That's why I'm here," Peter said, lifting his blue protect case from the backseat and opening his door. "What I'm not sure of is why you're with me."

"Just following orders, my friend. The Powers That Speak to Us on High—I refer in this vague fashion to the gentleman we both hold in reverence—Mr. Parker—and those gentlemen he holds in reverence—and so on up the Griffinish line—have decided that we should pay special attention to the Seekers. Why they would suddenly decide this, they say not. Of what they consider special attention to consist, they say not. Very good, they are, at putting one on one's mettle by dint of insufficient information and vague instructions."

"A trait that seems to be catching," Peter commented.

"And so," Escobaga continued, blandly ignoring Peter, "I join you in this endeavor. The best sort of special attention—the very best—is doing it yourself. And so I give up the life of an intelligence grub, a seeker of truth among the dusty records of our civilization, and get back to fieldwork. The joy of once again feeling the wind in my hair, the sun beating on my face, is not to be underestimated, if at all."

Peter had the feeling that he so often had when talking with Escobaga that the conversation had somehow taken a left turn while he was still going straight. "I'll take your word for it," he said. "What now?"

"We enter and show an intelligent interest in our surroundings, same as any gullible layman might, and keep our eyes open and our various senses peeled. Much as you have been doing at all our previous locations, but doubled, as there are now a brace of us."

Escobaga locked his car with meticulous care, and they crossed over to the museum entrance. A pair of large brass-cased doors opened to the cool, strategically lighted entrance hall. They signed the visitor's log just inside the door, and entered. The room was large and finished in white marble, and the concealed lighting was placed to leave large areas in shadow, making the room seem even larger. There were four or five other visitors in the hall, looking doubtfully about, as though uncertain of where to begin. Behind the desk at the door and a counter by the far wall were a few Seekers, selling things, giving things out, and answering questions. They were dressed in loose white robes and sandals, and looked very relaxed and comfortable.

Peter and Michael Wong walked leisurely to the center of the room and looked around. "Remember, we are tourists," Escobaga whispered. "Look disinterested. Try to slouch."

Four doorways led out of the hall: two in front of them, and one each in the left and right walls. They were labeled, clockwise from the left, first: ANTEDILUVIAN ARTIFACTS; second: THE CIVILIZATION OF MU BEFORE THE DESTRUCTION—A RECONSTRUCTION; third: MUSEUM SHOP; and fourth: RELICS OF ANCIENT ASTRONAUTS.

"Do we do this together," Peter asked, "or do we split up and each take a separate path through the museum?"

"I think we shall wander through this garden of earthly delights arm in arm," Escobaga said. "Figuratively, of course. That way we can point out to each other such anomies and anomalies as we find and discuss whether they are worthy of further note. Shall we begin with the Antediluvian Artifacts?"

Through the arched doorway to their left they entered a room of musty dark wood cabinets with glass tops and dark wood displays with glass fronts, badly lighted from within. "Not very exciting," Peter said. "They haven't designed museums like this in a hundred years."

"Hmmm," Escobaga agreed. "That's so. Very clever indeed, I think."

Peter looked at him. "Clever?"

"Just so. Thus do they create the illusion of age and respectability. Let us look this over, and see what else they are trying to sell us."

Peter went over and peered into the glass top of the nearest cabinet. A large stone frog peered back at him. The neatly typed card beneath it explained that it was a Stone Frog—representative of the god Mesomoma who, with his twin brother Tomomoma, guarded the gates of Atlantis. Discovered in plowed field by E. W. Harp, Deal, New Jersey, July 19, 2014. From the Blakesley Collection. How, Peter wondered, did they know it was Meso and not Tomo? Perhaps Tomo disliked having his effigy carved. Would that make him chisel-shy?

The rest of the case held more frogs, done in stone, lead, iron, brass, and terra cotta; in size from one centimeter to over twenty from snout to stern. A card on the side of the case explained how their worldwide dispersal proved the existence of an early Atlantean civilization.

The next case contained a collection of ancient Atlantean objects that had been found by divers on the floor of the Mediterranean. There was a flat round stone about twelve centimeters across with a small hole neatly drilled through it somewhere near the center, a small gold amulet in the shape of a money clip, the clay handle to a "ceremonial flask," an unidentifiable bit of twisted aluminium, and some early Greek coins.

Peter read the long explanatory text and stared at the objects in fascination.

"Don't overdo it, my boy," Escobaga whispered out of the corner of his mouth. "You look like a teenager who's seeing his first burlesque show. Not an appropriate response when staring at a bunch of assorted rocks and crockery."

"It is truly wonderful," Peter said. "These people see evidence of lost civilizations in everything."

Escobaga shrugged. "Some people see God in every bush; these people see Mu. 'To each his own,' as my sainted mother used to say."

The next room, THE CIVILIZATION OF MU BEFORE THE DESTRUCTION —A RECONSTRUCTION, contained a variety of panoramas, diaramas, models, maps, and charts of the continent of Mu and its principal cities as it looked before it disappeared beneath the waves of either the Pacific, Antarctic, or Indian oceans, depending. The architecture looked like a Bauhaus rendering of ancient Greece; the costumes on the pictured and modeled Muvians looked like Buck Rogers visits Ramses III. There were intricate little models of ancient Muvian craftsmen plying their ancient Muvian crafts: potting, weaving, brewing, soldering printed circuit boards, and boarding flying saucers to travel to distant planets.

Peter looked at one of the model displays, showing a noble Mu family at dinner, and then the next, showing the innards of a Muvian grain warehouse. "That's interesting," he said. "I think we have a little unconscious racism here."

"Don't be too sure it's unconscious," Escobaga said, peering down to examine Peter's find. "The taint of bigotry runs deep in some of the nicest people."

"Notice the slaves in these two scenes," Peter said, pointing to the little figures serving dinner and lugging grain. "They all seem to be smaller and darker than the nobles."

"They are not slaves," Escobaga commented. "I just read a long explication of Muvian society on that wall over there. The Muvians didn't believe in slavery. Mu was a theocratic democracy, whatever that is."

"Then who are all those little brown people waiting on the big white people?" Peter asked.

Escobaga shrugged. "The ways of the Elder Gods are mysterious," he said.

"That's my other question," Peter said, leaning up against the glass case. "Who are these Elder Gods?"

"Clearly a bunch of gods older than the undifferentiated mass," Escobaga explained. "The answer to that gets into the problems of space-time, relativity theory, and why only one sock comes back from the wash when you know you sent two in."

"Oh," Peter said.

A short blond girl with a practiced smile came up to them. She was wearing the loose white robes of the Seekers, and a gold pin on her shoulder that said:

MARIA
I AM HERE TO HELP YOU

"Hello," she said. "I would like to help you."

Escobaga smiled avuncularly at her. "What did you have in mind?" he asked.

"You are"—she consulted a data board—"Michael Escoboggle and Peter Lyon?"

Escobaga bowed. "Michael Escoboggle at your service."

"And you're Mr. Lyon?"

Peter nodded.

"We try to talk to as many of our guests as we can," the girl said. She looked to be somewhere between eighteen and twenty-one, and very earnest. "So many people look at the museum artifacts and just see— things. They don't understand who we are, or what our message is."

"So you are a sort of tour guide?" Peter asked.

"Sort of," the girl agreed. "My name is Maria. I'd like to show you around, and describe our view of the Universe for you. I think you'll find it interesting."

"I'm sure we will," Peter said.

"Good," Maria said. "Then let's go. Just how much do you know about our Society, or what we do?"

"My friend, Mr. Escoboggle, is the expert," Peter said. "I'm just tagging along."

Maria turned to Escoboga. "You're not a member," she told him, after a cursory glance at his jacket.

"No no," Escobaga assured her. "I don't know the secret handshake or wear the members-only lapel pin. I'm just an outsider who is interested in things Muvian."

"Well," Maria said. "Then there's no point in making you listen to the introductory talk. Come this way. I'll show you something of what the Society is doing now, and what we hope to accomplish."

"That would be delightful," Escobaga said. "Lead the way, fair lady."

They twisted in and out among the display cases, as Maria led them across several of the public halls to a door marked PRIVATE. "Through here," she said. "I think you'll find this interesting."

She opened the door, and Peter stepped in. "Say!" he said. "This is just a clos—"

Maria squirted him in the face with a small plastic bulb, and everything expanded, and grew more colorful, and he lost all interest in speech or movement. Slowly, very slowly, he slid to the floor.

TWENTY

Senator Pedro Dooley stood at the foot of the oval table and looked at each of the twelve men seated around it. One at a time, carefully, he examined each face. They were serene faces, knowledgeable faces, confident faces. They were the faces of the Board of Directors of Griffin Universal, probably the dozen most powerful men in the world today. "I should warn you," he stated carefully, "that a crystal containing everything I know, and all I surmise, is in safe hands, and copies will be delivered to all of the major news organizations in case I fail to, ah, return from this meeting in due time. You could never control all of them quickly enough to prevent its release."

"Senator Dooley," said Mr. Pencannon, sounding sad. "Senator Dooley, what must you think of us? What must you suspect us of? We are not a gang of thugs, Senator. We are the leaders of a respected multinational corporation. Have we not always dealt honestly and uprightly with you, even to revealing to you and your government information that the general public should not know? Whatever you think you have found out, Senator, share it with us, and we can work out the details amicably, I'm sure."

Three burly men had silently entered the room behind Dooley while Pencannon was speaking, and they stood awaiting a nod from Pencannon.

"Allow me to also point out," Dooley continued, "that I have been dosed with antighor, and if you try to torture me or use truth drugs to discover the location of the crystal, I will certainly go unconscious for a period long enough to release the crystal, or possibly die. Which you will find hard to explain."

Pencannon smiled suavely at Dooley, and shook his head slightly, at which the three toughs retreated from the room. "How can we be sure that you're telling the truth, Senator?" he asked.

"If you have nothing to hide, and no evil intentions toward me, why should you care?" Dooley replied, leaning heavily on the chair in front of him.

"A point," Pencannon conceded, continuing his revision of his estimate of the senator's intelligence. "A distinct point." He would have to keep in mind, in future dealings, that for politicians, showing intelligence was not necessarily a virtue. "What, exactly, is it that you think you have discovered, and what do you intend to do about it? Or, more to the point, what do you expect us to do about it?"

The other eleven board members sat mutely around the table, observing. Their expressions were impossible to read. Dooley could not tell which were figurehead and which were movers, so he directed his remarks only to Pencannon. "I don't believe in bluffing," he said with a straight face, "so I will lay my cards on the table. Griffin Universal is running faster-than-light ships on the interstitial drive. You would have us think that the drive kills all living things. This is not so. Those are manned ships. Griffin has colonized at least one, and probably several, star systems. What criteria Griffin is using for selecting the colonists, I do not know. For some reason, Griffin is keeping this a secret from the rest of this overcrowded planet, and acting as God. The ships themselves never approach Earth any closer than Pluto orbit, and the famous one-gee shuttles service them."

The Griffin board members stared at each other, while Dooley held his breath. If he was drastically wrong on any of his guesses, they would know he was only guessing, and laugh him out of the room while denying everything. But he *had* to be right. A jigsaw puzzle has only one solution, and, once you orient the pieces the right way, it falls into place.

"Is this what's in your letter?" Pencannon asked, expressionlessly.

"That—and the proofs," Dooley said, mentally crossing his fingers.

"What proofs?"

"Come on," Dooley said casually. "They are complex, but can be followed. Since you know I'm right, they are irrelevant for the purposes of this discussion. Even if I'm off slightly on a couple of the facts, they're close enough so they can be investigated and the exact truth determined."

"If it were true—if we really had a faster-than-light drive that could carry living things—why would we be hiding it? What motive would we have? We could make billions with such a thing."

"You already make billions," Dooley replied. "Why you're hiding it, I don't know. Perhaps you intend to colonize all of space in your own image. Whatever the reason may be, you know it, and I want to find out. Convince me, and, if it's a moral reason and for the good of humanity, I'll help you hide it. That's why I came to you first, instead of just releasing the information. You might have a good reason. Even though I can't imagine one."

Pencannon sighed. "Could you wait outside for a minute, Senator? I think I'd better discuss this with my board."

Dooley shook his head. "I don't think so," he said. "If I leave this room, I go straight back to Washington, and the crystals get released. I don't want to give you time to think up a good story. I'm tired of being bamboozled."

A thin man with gray hair and piercing blue eyes who was sitting to Dooley's left put his hands, palms down, on the table. "We'd better talk to this man," he said.

"I agree, Mr. Parker," Pencannon said. "Sit down, Senator, we'll tell you what's going on."

Dooley pulled the chair out and settled into it. "This better be good," he said.

"If nothing else, I think I can promise you that this is 'good,' Senator Dooley," Pencannon said. "But it is a complex story, and I must ask you to withhold judgment as to our motivations or the correctness of our actions until you have heard it all."

"Fair enough," Dooley said. "Shoot." He leaned back in his chair and laced his hands together under his chin.

Pencannon paused for a minute. "What you say is true," he said finally. "We do have a fleet of manned gashoppers—which is what we call them—using the interstitial drive to, ah, travel about the Universe. They are not actually faster-than-light; the interstitial drive propels these ships into another space-time continuum, where the vector relationship between the basic dimensions is other than it is here.

"This place—this alternate Universe—exists in a one-to-one relationship with our own, but it seems to be folded in ways that our own Universe is not, so it is possible to travel to distant places in our own

Universe by shortcutting through the other. The first experiments with the drive did kill anything living that was aboard the test ships, but we soon learned how to cure that. The result was the gashopper—a giant gasbag filled with certain rare gasses that, when ionized, protect the contents from most of the transition effects. A few manage to leak through, giving the passengers an interesting time, but not enough to kill anyone. Usually."

"All very interesting," Dooley said. "But why keep this to yourself? I can see that it would be hard to prevent the gashopper invention from being stolen when the thief has the whole Universe to run and hide in, but surely you'd maintain the bulk of the business. I'm sure you could get the Earth governments to give you all the protection they could."

"Ah, but this is more than a business problem, Senator," Pencannon said. "Our sociologists have told us that news of a deep-space drive, and the opportunity of going to distant Earth-like planets could start major rioting here on Earth. Particularly if that opportunity was not able to be exercised. Now, I admit that there is only a 15 percent probability of such rioting being very extensive, but, still, do we have the right to take such a chance? The board has decided not, Senator Dooley."

"But why could the opportunity not be exercised? In only a couple of years, we could have ships exploring all the nearer stars. In a decade we'd have fleets of ships going out in all directions. It would be the salvation of the human race."

"That is so," Pencannon said. "If we can solve the mathematics of transition, and astrogate the damn ships. As it is, what we're doing is throwing darts at a dart board the size of the Universe. It is seldom that we hit anything."

"What do you mean?"

"What Mr. Pencannon means," Parker said, leaning forward and slapping his palms on the table, "is that, although there appears to be a one-to-one mapping between this Universe and the interstitial Universe, we have yet to determine what that correspondence is or how it works. We send ships out"—he made a gesture with his left hand of sending a ship out—"and hope they'll arrive at something useful. But this is a big Universe, and the odds are not on our side."

"We have a fleet of some thirty gashoppers," Pencannon said, "which is all we can afford to run. Each of them goes out about four times a year, and we've been doing it for almost twenty years. Which means we've made almost two thousand exploratory trips. And what do we have to show for it? Four systems with a planet in the proper orbital position to support life. And we've lost one of those!"

"Lost?"

"Actually, it was stolen."

"It's complicated to explain," Parker interrupted. "When you program a ship's astrogation system to go someplace, it can return without problem. And it will go to the same place the next time. But another, seemingly identical gashopper, programmed in the same way, will end up somewhere else. At first we thought it was slight differences in mass, but the same gashopper, programmed the same way, always goes to the same places no matter how loaded, so it's something else. As a result, we have two gashoppers that go to one system—on entirely different astrogational settings, mind you—two other gashoppers that go to two other systems, and sixteen that keep finding naked stars or large areas of empty space."

"It sounds like an interesting problem," Dooley commented.

"A masterful understatement," Pencannon said. It creates some fascinating problems of its own. We live in the fear that sometime we'll have changed something on one of the gashoppers that goes to one of our colonized planets, and it won't go there anymore."

"About six years ago," Parker said, "someone stole one of our ships. It happened to be one that had found a stellar system. So, effectively, they stole the habitable planet, too."

"How did that happen?"

"We have a, ah, fink in the organization," Parker said. "He works for Griffin Universal, but his loyalties lie elsewhere."

"Do you know who it is?"

"We do now," Pencannon said with some satisfaction. "We just forced him to show his hand."

"How?"

"We let him think that one of our couriers had the information on how to astrogate the gashoppers."

"But you just told me that, effectively, you can't astrogate a gashopper."

"Ah, but *he* doesn't know that. So the organization he works for has just kidnapped the courier. Thus, we now know both the fink and his organization. A group called, believe it or not, Seekers of the True Mu."

"Mu?"

"Mu."

"What are you going to do about it?"

"Well, at first we're merely going to hope that they try to use the astrogation instructions they have just acquired. If so, their gashopper will go somewhere else and never find their way back to the stolen planet."

"Can they get back to Earth?"

"Oh yes. When they give up looking through the Universe, they can get back."

"What about the people marooned on the planet?"

"We'll find them again someday."

"What about the kidnapped courier?"

Parker shrugged. "Nice boy," he said. "I hope nothing too bad happens to him."

TWENTY-ONE

See the pretty things. Here and there, up and down, in and out. Spreading across the vastness of time-space-mind. Pretty things. Hard to keep them in focus all at once. The pretty things he saw, the pretty things he knew, the pretty things that were just—over there—sort of—stretching beyond. Did not have to be by a thing to see it. Did not have to see a thing to know of it. Things made waves, stretched images, reverberated through all space and all time. Their presence was knowable, was unavoidable. Pretty things to give pleasure; always there. But there was so much—so very much. Where was *he?*

Time and space were just different directions. Funny how he'd never noticed that before. Before? Which way was that?

Ugly things. In front, behind, beyond, beneath; studded through the Cosmos-that-was-all like the twitching bodies of insects caught in resin. Like the frozen bodies of insects caught in amber. Things that were nevermore. Things that spit. Things that hurt other things. Things that smiled and smiled, and yet were villains. Ugly things.

Mixed was the pretty with the ugly, the good with the bad, the clear with the murky; some things, the important things, stuck out above the mixture, like volcanic islands pierced the ocean surface and rose to new heights, their roots disappearing deep into the primal all. Were they important because they stuck out, or did they stick out because they were important? Something to examine, to decide. But where, in all this, where was *he*?

Funny how everything ended right over there. Just kind of broke off sharply. *Crack!* Sharp as an almond. Sharp as a tooth. Which way was that? What we call the future, it must be. Why was it cut off, then, so sharp? Did he have no future?

Where was he was one question. But there were others. Who was he? He considered that question. It was hard to focus on any one question. What was he? What was he that he should see so much, know so much?

Events fluxed and grew, and shrank and disappeared no—not so much disappeared, as had boundaries. Terminated at each end, one in the past and one in the future.

The event of his life terminated at both ends. But, he could see, his awareness extended beyond his life on both ends. But this sharp ending that was—that was—right over *there!*—this clifflike ending. This was a different sort. Not the end of his life. Not the end of time. Now that he could see through it, it was just a transition. An abrupt transition. A twist in time. But it twisted back on the other side.

Did these words have any meaning? Did he need words? Perhaps he could create his own. Twist the ones he was familiar with into new meanings. He would think about that for a while. But which while? They all coexisted, all the whiles.

* * *

A dose of bounce was a wonderful way to control someone, if all you wanted was control of his body. Peter's body walked, and ate, and drank, and did those things that a living body does, at the impulse of his autonomous nervous system and the direction of those around him. His mind, broken loose of its moorings in time by a PHD mist, tried to find a place to stand where he could survey that which was now revealed to him.

His captors, after dosing him and Escobaga with PHD, took them to a nearby private house and locked them in a neat, clean upstairs bedroom. Not that Peter would have noticed if they'd put him in a closet; his present circumstances meant little to him. Indeed, he couldn't have located the "present" on his timeline if his life depended on it.

Escobaga, whose drug of choice was alcohol, had no previous experience with bounce. He was having a totally different reaction. He was seeing pretty colors, and strange shapes, which had no apparent relationship to his mundane surroundings. Strange creatures from his id were explaining the innermost secrets of the Universe in terms he could almost understand.

In both cases the desired effect was achieved; neither of them was capable of desiring, much less effecting, an escape.

Downstairs, in the living room, their three captors, an older man, a quite young man, and the girl with the squeeze bottle, were carefully, with the aid of expensive electronic instruments, dissecting Peter's protect case. Eventually, as they were intended to, they discovered how to remove the false inner top and reveal the small, flat compartment within. In the small, flat compartment was a small, flat, metallized plastic strip.

"This is it!" the older one said, holding it aloft with a pair of nonmetallic tweezers and peering at it as though its secrets were printed in glowing letters on its surface. "Have we got a reader?"

"We should be careful, Dynast Blakesley," the girl said, running her fingers nervously through her long blond hair. "It might be programmed to decompose, or something, if we try to read it wrong."

"Wrongly," Blakesley corrected.

"Whatever. We don't want to gamber it up now that we've got it."

"Gamber?" Blakesley asked musingly. "Another new slang expression? I can never keep up."

"Don't try," the young man suggested. "Let's just take this somewhere where they have the equipment to read it safely."

"What about the two upstairs?" the girl asked.

"We can't let them go," Blakesley said. "Since we kidnapped them from our own museum, they're liable to figure out who did it."

"No more killing!" the girl said sharply.

"Now now, Maria. You know I did not approve of that. We'll take them out to Garrett Field, and ship them to the gashopper on the next one-gee. They can become honored citizens of New Mu."

"They won't like it," she predicted.

"They will," Dynast Blakesley assured her, "when they consider the alternatives."

TWENTY-TWO

The one-gee ships were rocket rams; with their scoops stretched out in front of them making them look like great backward shuttlecocks, they burned the wispy gasses of empty space and maintained a constant acceleration of ten meters per second per second. It is possible to build up a very impressive final velocity very quickly at a constant one-gee acceleration. Were it not for the "wall," the ships could hypothetically have reached 92 percent of the speed of light. The "wall," which was the upper practical limit to the velocity of a one-gee ship, was the point at which the energy at which the particles hit the scoop was greater than the structural strength of the ship. Instantly the ship disintegrated, and the space gasses brightened for a few moments.

But for the flip-flop trip to Pluto orbit, or anywhere in the Solar System, the "wall" remained beyond reach, and the trip was fast, safe, and comfortable.

Since the one-gee ships could not operate near a planet—the great kilometer-wide scoops couldn't have even held their shape in the outer fringes of Earth's atmosphere—there were no direct spaceports on Earth. Traveling off-planet involved a three-step process of taking a ferry with great air-gulping jet engines to a low-orbit station, changing to a transfer-orbital shuttle, and then waiting at one of the great high-orbit spaceports for your one-gee ship.

Garrett Field was the Southern California point of origin for this time-consuming process. From here the jet ferries left for low orbit with supplies and personnel, as well as the tourists bound for a week's vacation at one of the high-orbit spaceports. To here the craft returned, full of space-processed drugs and materials, and bored scientists and workers.

In the southeast corner of the field, where the nonscheduled lines were hangered, separated from the other properties by a few hundred meters of scrubland broken by one narrow taxiway, were the plastic domes of Bateman Casterwigg & Sons Charter and Rental Service.

It was here that Saralu Ngaxu had followed the three busloads of black children that had left the Higher Outreach Primary School that morning. She parked well outside the gate, amid a cluster of other cars, and watched the children unloaded from the busses and herded into the leftmost plastic dome by six white women who looked more like prison guards than schoolteachers. And standing in the shadow of the dome's large green doors were several black women, wearing uniform-looking gray dresses and white canvas shoes, who helped escort the children into the dome.

The plot, Saralu reflected, sickens. If these children were being brought here, it could only be because they were about to be shipped off-planet. To do what? She couldn't imagine. And who were the black women—prisoners, or willing tools of the people within?

A large hypled with six doors pulled through the gate and up to the dome. Five people got out and entered the green doors. Two of them appeared to Saralu to be drugged; they walked with a loose-limbed, shambling gate, and had to be told repeatedly what to do before they complied. It wasn't as though they were resisting, but more that they were not capable of paying attention. Saralu doubted whether they had gotten that way of their own free will. Another fact to add to her growing indictment of those who ran the Higher Outreach Primary School.

She had to get a look at the interior of that plastic dome. Which would have to wait until after dark. She took out a compact image amplifier and recorded views of different aspects of the compound for later study. The small green boxes mounted every two meters right inside the chain link fence, the sentry box at the entrance, the security cameras mounted on high poles in the four corners of the compound— all received careful attention. Saralu Ngaxu was a thorough, competent, thoughtful worker. Where angels feared to tread she went softly and very well-prepared.

It would be about four or five hours before it was dark enough for Saralu to try to make her way into the Bateman Casterwigg & Sons complex, a time she could well use for study and preparation. First, the purchase of some appropriate clothing and very specialized equipment, and then a light meal, and some time to think out what was happening, and what her best angle of attack would be. She had a list of her father's contacts in the area, and from her father's contacts one could buy *anything*.

At eleven o'clock that night, Saralu parked her car in the Triplanetary parking lot, on the scheduled commercial flight side of Garrett Field, and emerged from the driver's door in a pair of black sneakers and a black plastic garment that covered everything but her eyes. She took a backpack of the same material from the seat next to her and strapped it carefully into place low on her back, and then locked the door and trotted the two kilometers across the field to the southeast corner.

At the edge of the scrubland separating Bateman Casterwigg & Sons from the main taxiway, she dropped to her belly and started a low crawl between the clumps of desert brush toward her goal. When she was about a hundred meters away, she paused and turned on the valve of a small cylinder attached to her blacksuit. This fed liquid nitrogen along a web of capillaries right below the surface of the suit, and dropped the exterior temperature of the suit by about thirty degrees. Her image would now fade off any infrared receptors, which were programmed to react to objects hotter than their surroundings, not ones that were cooler.

Slowly, on elbows and knees, she creeped toward the fence. Was there a Doppler radar inside? She had seen no signs of it, and it would be a troublesome and illogical device to keep in use. Jackrabbits and mule deer would set it off if the discriminator were set too low, and if it were high enough to eliminate false positives, it might miss a few people. Still, those inside the fence were not necessarily logical, and

Saralu felt as though she were painted in fluorescent colors as she gingerly squirmed the last few meters to the fence.

The small green boxes mounted on short poles every two meters inside the fence line were proximity indicators. They would be set off when any large object came within a meter of one. But they were not invulnerable. The easiest way to put one out of commission was by freezing it. Saralu took a small cylinder out of her backpack and directed a fine stream of liquid oxygen at the nearest one. She counted to twenty, and then redirected the frigid stream to the next green box in line. Slowly she moved closer to the fence, dousing first one and then another of the proximity boxes with the liquid oxygen until the cylinder was empty. Now she was up to the fence.

She waited. Surely someone would have come to check by now if the cold treatment had not worked, or if an overalert sensor had spotted anything. She waited. Nobody came. Nothing moved inside the compound.

She slid the knapsack off her back and pulled it up toward her head until it was six centimeters away from her nose. Pulling the side vent open, she took out a probe and delicately touched it to the wire fence at several different places. The tiny marking diode flickered slightly at each touch as the inductance changed, but not enough to indicate any sort of current—either alarm or shocking—in the fence. She touched the probe to the fence post; still no reaction.

Slowly, cautiously, she stood up, testing each succeeding line of chain as she did. At about a meter off the ground, the probe suddenly blinked green as she touched one line. She fingered several micro-switches on the probe to get a range of readings, and then pulled it away and closely examined that line of chain link. It was carrying a low-voltage, high-frequency current, which meant that it was probably a very fine cable replacing the original wire. It served as a stress detector, and would signal when anyone cut the wire or climbed the fence. If the unit was sufficiently sophisticated, it would even give the perimeter location of the attempt.

Saralu took a small coil of wire from the backpack and tied one end to the fence two links below the alarm cable. Stretching it to its full meter-and-a-half length, she pulled it taut and fastened the other end to a similar link a meter and a half to the right. Then, with a small pair of wire cutters, she created a hole for herself directly below, where her inserted wire would take up the stress.

First her backpack went through the hole, and then she followed. Was that it—or was there some last-ditch defense which she had not yet detected? She pushed the strands of the wire fence back together and interlaced some short pieces of wire through the cut ends. It would come apart again at a touch, but the hole would not be evident except on close inspection. Very cautiously, she crawled forward. There was one television camera in view, but it was probably switched to infrared at night, and wouldn't pick her up. The absence of perimeter lighting showed that they were not depending on visual sightings.

When she reached the edge of the dome, she sat for a while, prepared to dash back through the hole in the fence if anyone appeared, or if floodlights suddenly went on, or attack dogs suddenly rounded the corner, or if there was any other hint that she had been discovered. But all remained silent. Perhaps, she thought, they were being subtle. But they somehow didn't seem like an overly subtle group, whoever they were.

She stood up and, closing the nitrogen valve, slowly peeled the skin-tight plastic suit off and removed the sneakers. She was now clad only in a bra, panties, and a wide plastic carrier stretched flat around her waist that held an assortment of possibly useful items. In the backpack was a gray dress and a pair of shoes like those she had observed on the black women in the doorway when the children entered. She stuffed the plastic suit and sneakers into the backpack, slipped her feet into the shoes, and pulled the gray dress over her head. Then she looked around for a place to conceal the backpack. There was a meter-square structure two meters high by the side of the building with two pair of double doors, above and below. The lower doors gave access to a large water valve, and she stuffed the backpack behind the black-painted water pipe that led to the valve, and reclosed the doors.

The door to the dome was closed, but not locked. She listened at the door for a minute, but all was silent inside. No guard? Was it possible? Cautiously, she pulled open the door.

There was a guard. He was in a small room to the left of the door, his feet propped up on the desk, his chair back on two legs, sound asleep. Saralu tiptoed by him.

The hall was long, and wide, and punctuated with many doors. But the doors had glass panels in the upper halves, and Saralu could see into the empty offices behind. A narrower corridor teed on to the end of the hall. Saralu peered down both ways, and saw nothing but corridor. She turned right.

The doors here had no glass panels. She paused at each one to listen, but heard nothing. A roomful of children—even sleeping—couldn't be that quiet. She went on.

At the end of the corridor was a door leading to a stairway. She entered it cautiously and went up one flight. The door was locked, but it was a simple lock. She picked it with a tool from her waistband and pulled it open.

The room was large, and the few widely spaced glow lamps made the walls recede into darkness so that it looked even larger. There were rows of neatly spaced stretched canvas army cots, that looked like Boer War surplus, filling the room. On each of the cots, under a tan army blanket, a black child was sleeping.

Pay dirt! Saralu thought. *But now what do I do about it?*

She walked down one of the aisles, looking at the sleeping children. There was no more knowledge to be gleaned from them. They were children; they were sleeping. They almost certainly knew no more about what was happening to them than she did.

A bright light suddenly flicked on. "Girl!" a harsh female voice called. "What are you doing in here?"

Saralu froze. Was there a right answer to that question? Slowly she turned around, keeping her body hunched over and her eyes to the ground, in a parody of the black women she had seen that afternoon.

"Stop fussing over those children and get back to bed!" the voice said. It belonged to a tall pasty-faced woman in a black dress who was standing by the far door. "You've got a busy day tomorrow."

"Yes'm," Saralu mumbled, wondering which way her bed was.

"Well, come on then," the woman said, going over to a door to her left and pulling it open. "Go back to bed now. You'll be getting up soon enough!"

"Yes'm," Saralu said, shuffling over to the open door and entering the bedroom beyond. There were a row of cots in there, with five young black women asleep in them, their clothing folded neatly on the floor by each cot. The pasty-faced white woman seemed unaware that there were not supposed to be six black women—or perhaps she couldn't count that high. Saralu did not inquire, but went to the nearest cot and lay down.

There would be a long day tomorrow. Of that she was sure.

TWENTY-THREE

The Deep Space Committee of the United States Senate was meeting in secret session. This was no longer as simple a thing to do as once it was. A secret session must be held in a room prepared to hold secrets, with copper wire mesh embedded in all four walls, the floor, and the ceiling to discourage electronic eavesdropping. A crew must come in immediately before the meeting with a rolling table full of special equipment to assure that these walls have not been penetrated by a wire as thick as a human hair, that might hold a peewee mike. Then all vibrating surfaces must be damped, so that a laser reader cannot focus on the window, or the outer wall, from some miles away, and read the aural secrets in its vibrations. All phones and computer terminals must be removed; the power plugs and light sockets inspected; the furniture checked for concealed recorders; the official recording apparatus inspected to make sure that it does not broadcast what it is recording; the clothing of all who enter inspected to make sure that it is not, without its wearer's knowledge, either transmitting or recording.

Then, when all are seated and ready to begin their secret session, electronic and sound generators must be turned on outside to blanket the transmission of any apparatus that has escaped the search. Which makes the surrounding offices, for three rooms in every direction, unusable for the duration, and the usual occupants of those offices very surly.

"Thank you all for attending this special meeting," Senator Dooley said when his fellow committee members had reached their seats and readjusted their clothing. He nodded to the committee stenographer, who leaned forward and flipped on his official recording device. "This meeting," Dooley said clearly, for the record, "the twenty-third of the session, and the third designated as secret, is now in session. Present are Senators Birsbee, Colt, Dumatt, McFee, Rotsler, and Unger, with myself, Senator Dooley, as chairman."

"What's the rush?" Senator Dumatt asked, smoothing down the front of her business smock. "And why the secrecy?"

"And why," Senator McFee added, "are we being besieged by bouncers? There are three in my office since yesterday, and two in Senator Colt's."

"I've got a pair myself," Senator Unger added, pouring himself a cup of coffee from the small urn at the end of the table. "It makes me feel important, but a little nervous. I remember Pollack."

"Pollack who?" Senator Bursbee asked.

"Representative Pollack, a Constructionist from Iowa. About sixteen or seventeen years ago a cluster of bouncers formed in his outer office, watching everything he did. There were seven or eight of them who would wander in and out, although I don't think there were ever more than two or three in the office at one time. He really figured he was big stuff, destined for greatness. These people who could see into the future were so interested in him. But it didn't work out that way."

"What happened?" Bursbee asked.

"His office manager was Dombee Santellosson."

"The Fast-Food Bomber?"

"That's him. Blew up the old House Chambers, taking fourteen of our country's elected Representatives with it, and his defense was that he was mentally deranged because he'd been eating so much fast food. Got twenty years. Was out in seven. But Pollack was never re-elected to public office. There's a moral in there somewhere, if you want to dig for it."

"The moral," Senator Dooley offered, "is never try to foretell the future. If you could, you'd dribble all over yourself like a bouncer, which would cost you votes."

"Let's get down to it," Senator Dumatt said. "I have to chair a Judiciary Committee meeting at four o'clock, and I don't dare be late, or they'll start without me. What's so important?"

Dooley snapped open his protect case and removed a sheaf of papers. "Here," he said, "pass these along."

"What is it?" Senator Unger asked, taking his sheet and passing the rest along.

"Draft form of new legislation I am proposing. It's, ah, subtly phrased, so I wanted to go over it with each of you before it appeared on your desk through the regular channels. It is not what it seems."

"It seems," Senator Dumatt observed, "to be a mass of inarticulate garbage. 'A Comprehensive Bill for the Regulation of Off-Earth Populations'? What off-Earth populations? The colonies are all under United Nations control. The United States has two space cities, and we already have legislation in place to control them. What does this change?"

"This is for new off-Earth colonies," Dooley said. "It assures that we —the United States—will regulate and govern them until such time as they choose to become independent and, if they wish, apply for United Nations membership on their own."

"Nobody is putting up new space cities," Unger said. "It would be pointless, since nobody wants to live in them."

"The, ah, colonies envisioned here are planetary," Dooley said.

"Planetary? That makes no sense. What planet?"

Senator Dooley referred to his notes. "Turn off that machine," he told the official stenographer. "We are going off the record."

The machine was switched off, and Dooley leaned forward. "There are very few secrets in this world today," he told his fellow senators. "We are about to share one of them."

TWENTY-FOUR

The fifty black children, escorted by two stern-looking white women and six black women in shapeless gray dresses, filed on board the orbital ferry two-by-two, looking peaceful and chemically disinterested. Perhaps there should only have been five of the gray-clad black women, but what's one servant more or less among so many?

After the children were stowed came the colonists, two hundred disciples of the True Mu, their faces scrubbed, not yet fully believing in their good fortune and the grand future that awaited them as they went to take their place in Muvian society in this Promised Land. A stern, uncompromising group they tried to be, secure in the Truth as revealed to them by their leader, Dynast Blakesley. But a look of doubt curled around the corner of some of their mouths, as it must have on many of those who, in previous generations, had given up all their worldly possessions for the promise of a new life in the hereafter. But when one is actually boarding the ship that will take one to the hereafter, one gains in confidence.

A hard-faced man named William Jesse Harker came on board by himself a half hour later and joined the passengers.

Shortly before takeoff, Peter Lyon and Michael Wong Escobaga were led on board by the blond girl, Maria, and her young male friend, and strapped into seats. They did not complain. They were there in body, certainly, but where their PHD-befuddled minds were was a subject of rhetorical conjecture. "When they come out of this," Maria remarked, "they'll thank us. See if they don't."

"In a way I envy them," the young man said. "They'll be citizens of the New Mu before we are. But we have our work here."

"It's an interesting moral question," Maria said, tightening Peter's seat belt for him. "If doing good for someone without his knowledge is particularly selfless and itchy-fine, then doing good for someone against his will must be even more itchy-special-fine."

"It isn't against his will," the youth remarked. "He doesn't have a will. He won't, either, until he comes down off the bounce. If he ever does."

"Well, it *would* be against his will, if he had one," Maria insisted. "Come on, let's go."

The orbiter took off and laborously climbed to a height of ten kilometers, where its giant rocket-jet engines could work efficiently. There, using the thin atmosphere for oxygen and lift, it built up speed and climbed the next fifteen kilometers, where the jets switched to internal oxygen supply and began functioning as full rocket engines. In twenty minutes it was docking with the orbiting space station.

For two days the colonists enjoyed themselves in the station's luxury hotel, playing weightless sports, while the one-gee ship was made ready. It took until the early hours of the second day for Saralu Ngaxu to make her way to one of the hotel's I.V.C. Telecom privacy booths and place a call to her daddy.

"Where the hell you been, daughter?" Daddy Exx demanded, "and why you dressed like that?"

"Don't leave out your verbs, Daddy," Saralu said. "It's an unnecessary affectation. And, besides, you'd better let me talk. I may be cut off."

Bill Exx nodded. "Go on, daughter," he said.

"I'm calling you from a space station. One of the Consolidated Hotels chain. It's hard to tell which—they all look alike—and I'm not in a position to ask. I've found the missing children—they're up here with me."

"What are they doing up there?"

"I think I have it figured out," Saralu said. "And I don't think you're going to believe it."

"I'll practice," Daddy Exx said. "Talk, daughter."

"The Higher Outreach Primary School is a creature of an organization that calls itself Seekers of the True Mu," Saralu said. The white students are all the children of members of the group. They get a standard education—or what passes for a standard education among these people. The black students are all dull-witted, compliant orphans, who are trained with a combination of drugs, mind-control techniques, and pain conditioning to obey those put in authority over them."

"What is all this in aid of, daughter?"

"I think I know," Saralu said. "I think these Seekers of the True Mu are starting a colony somewhere, and they want servants."

"A colony?"

"You got it, Daddy."

"A *space* colony? They're getting all these people to spend the rest of their lives in a metal cylinder? I'd like to meet their salesman. Hell, I'd like to hire their salesman."

"I don't think it's exactly a space colony, Daddy," Saralu said. "From what I heard, I think it's a colony on another planet."

"Now, where are they going to get another planet?" Daddy Exx demanded.

"Probably circling around some other star," Saralu told him.

"Well, I'll be a. . . . You sure about this?"

"Reasonably."

"Well, then, you stick with them, you hear? Find out where this other planet—this other star—is located, and how they manage to get there. I'll start working at this end."

"I intended to do just that, Daddy. We're doing this to rescue the orphans, right, Daddy?"

"Of course, daughter," Daddy Exx told her soothingly. "What else could I have in mind?"

"One never knows," she said. "I'll be in touch when I can."

"Listen," Daddy Exx said, "take care of yourself. Hear me?"

"I promise, Daddy," Saralu said. "You can bet on it."

She broke the connection and cautiously slid open the opaque plastic door to the privacy booth.

A tall blond man, wide as a barroom door and thick as granite, was leaning against the exterior door frame. He put his arm across the opening as Saralu got up to leave. "Hello, Miss Ngaxu," he said. "I've been looking for you. Good to see you again."

"I don't know you," Saralu said, trying to get around the man's hamlike arm.

"The name is Harker," he told her. "William Jesse Harker. I've been watching you for two years now. Watching you day after day—inventing excuses, making up stories. Just to watch you. When all the time there was nothing against you. But look at this—I've been right all the time. You are spying on us."

Saralu felt a twinge of fear. Who was this man, and what was he talking about? Could it be that he was, indeed, the hidden watcher that she had been aware of month after month for the past two years? Well, she couldn't just stand there looking frightened. "You're crazy!" she said, pushing at his arm. "Let me go or I'll call someone."

"Who you going to call?" he asked her. "You're not supposed to be here. You're supposed to be down on Level G, watching after them black children. And by rights you're not supposed to be there neither. You're not one of them Aunty Thomasinas. You're supposed to be at the orphanage, which is three hundred and fifty kilometers from here straight down, and that only twice a day."

"What do you want?" she asked, giving up trying to push at the immobile hamlike rod that was his arm.

A twisted smile crossed his face, making him look even uglier. "You," he said. "I've been wanting you for two years, and now I'm going to get me some."

Saralu stepped back and stared at the man. He was serious; she could see that. And her options were limited. "Here?" she asked.

He took her seriously, and considered for a second. "No," he said. "We'll go up to my room. I've got a first-class room. You'll like it."

Saralu shrugged. *Well, little girl,* she thought, *now your fair black body is in for it.* Almost meekly, she let him lead her away from the booth. An interesting problem: If she made a scene, she'd get caught and at best locked up and at worst killed. If she didn't, she was about to be raped. And he'd probably turn her in after that anyway, so she would have gained nothing for the trauma and indignity. Time for some quick—and constructive—thought.

They reached the door to Harker's room, and nothing had suggested itself to her. She couldn't overpower him; he outweighed her by easily fifty kilograms, and it looked like solid muscle. Perhaps during his throes of sexual excitement she could brain him with something. If there was anything useful near the bed. If he used the bed.

Harker fingered open the door and pushed her into the room in front of him. "Now," he said, slamming the door behind him, "you just—"

There was a dull thud. Harker's face suddenly went slack, and he fell to the floor. A tall, plump, balding man with a broad mustache, who had been concealed behind the door, put the metal pipe he was holding carefully down on Harker's chest. "A pleasure to meet you, Saralu," he said, turning to the girl and sticking his hand out to be shook. "My name is Michael Wong Escobaga."

She took the hand, her sense of unreality increasing. "Where did you come from?" she asked weakly, sitting down on the edge of the bed. "Do I know you?"

Escobaga pulled Harker's unconscious body over to the bed, and then rolled him under. "There," he said. "The room looks much neater now. No no, you don't know me; nor I you. A friend of mine, Peter Lyon by name, told me that you were going to be here sometime in the next couple of hours, and that you'd need my help. He couldn't come himself. He has trouble making coherent sentences, much less walking a straight line, so he sent me. I wonder if there's anything to drink in here."

"How did he know I was *going* to be in trouble? And what interest have you—or your friend Peter—in helping me?" Saralu shook her head. "This doesn't make any sense to me."

"I'm with you, lovely lady," Escobaga said, locating a bottle of Scotch in Harker's luggage and liberating it. "For you are a lovely lady, despite your current inappropriate garb. I'll tell you what little I know." He peered into the small bathroom and retrieved two plastic glasses. "Will you join me in a small libation to celebrate your deliverance?"

"Make it a large libation," Saralu suggested. "I hope no one else is as observant as you about the correctness of my dress."

"People see what they expect to see, or wish to see," Escobaga said, filling both glasses, and handing one to Saralu. "My story goes like this. My friend Peter and I were kidnapped by members of a group that calls itself the Seekers of the True Mu."

"They seem to do a lot of that," Saralu said.

"Yes? Well, they did it to us. They kept us quiet and, ah, complacent with a drug called bounce, which has very strange effects, but they are all internalized. One is no trouble to the outside world when one is on bounce."

"The stuff the bouncers take," Saralu said. "Those people who are supposed to be able to see into the future, but not do anything about it."

"The very," Escobaga agreed. "Well, after the first shot, which was an aerosol, they fed it to us orally. And I didn't like the taste of it, or something, because I spit mine out."

"They didn't see you?" Saralu asked.

"No," Escobaga told her. "I wasn't exactly all there at the time, but what I assume happened was that it took a minute or so for my brain to figure out that I didn't like this liquid they'd squirted into my mouth. So instead of initiating a swallow reflex, it initiated a spitting refex. By which time our jailers were looking elsewhere. I would like to take credit for outrageous cleverness, but it was entirely unconscious on my part, I assure you."

"And your friend?"

"He has taken the stuff before. I have a feeling that the doses he has had this time have pushed him over the edge. He looks a lot like a full-fledged bouncer to me."

"Well, I know they can see the future, or something, but I always heard that they couldn't communicate."

"He hasn't been doing any communicating until today," Escobaga said. "And he had to work real hard to get this out. It took about two hours, but he was intent and earnest, and he tried hard; so the least I could do was listen."

"What did he say?"

"He said that I'm to save you so that you can save us. And between us, all of us together, I think, we're going to save the world. Or possibly the Universe. I'm not sure about that last part."

"That doesn't make sense," Saralu said.

"Look at it this way," Escobaga told her. "If he hadn't been right about the first part, I wouldn't have been behind that door waiting for you. And your giant friend wouldn't be under the bed right now."

"You have a point," Saralu agreed. "How am I to go about saving you?"

"You are to return to your duties, whatever they are. We are shortly to be put aboard a faster-than-light ship for a journey to some distant star. . . . You don't seem surprised?"

"I had assumed as much," Saralu said.

"My, word does get around. Well, we will be locked in cabin twenty-three, on C Deck. Or so Peter says. At what my friend Peter describes as the moment of maximum crisis and confusion, you are to release us."

"That's kind of vague," Saralu said. "I hope I pick the right time."

"You will," Escobaga assured her. "Peter knows all. He can't communicate it very well, but he knows it. Don't worry about the bozo under the bed; he won't come to until we're long gone. I've got to go back to our room and lock myself in before they notice that I'm not there."

"Say," Saralu said, "if you can get loose now, why don't you just take the next shuttle back to Earth?"

"Peter said not to," Escobaga told her. "And one must trust one's friends. Especially when they can see the future. On the other hand, it's hard to tell what he really did say; I hope I'm right. See you in a week or so. Good luck."

"Sure," Saralu said. "You too."

TWENTY-FIVE

The gashopper *Ra*, with Captain Walweb at the con, blipped into interstitial space from somewhere inside the orbit of Uranus. Walweb felt the familiar nauseating sensation of the shift, and was then enveloped in a green viscous haze. Tiny invisible fingers seemed to be pushing at his skin from the inside.

"Sometimes," he muttered, "the pseudo-effects of interstitial space seem less pseudo—and more annoying—than others." He looked up to find the green face of the navigation officer hovering over him. It turned blue as he watched, as did the surrounding air. "Well, McAlister," he asked, trying to ignore the sick taste in his mouth, "what is it?"

Miz McAlister smiled at him. Her teeth appeared purple in the interstitial haze. "That disk you got seems to be real easy to use," she told him. "I'm setting the new coordinates now."

"Good," Walweb said. "Good. It's about time they came through with that navigation stuff. The excitement of interstitial space travel is quite enough without worrying whether we're going to end up inside a planet when we come out."

"But it's more than that!" McAlister said. "Don't you see? We're a real interstellar spaceship now, not just a ferry. We can go anywhere we want to. We can explore the Universe!"

"We can go to Mu," Walweb said firmly. "Later we can explore the Universe. First we can plot a course to somewhere within two days of the planet, where there are no solid objects. We have colonists and servants to deliver. We have *me* to deliver."

"No problem," McAlister assured him. "I can probably make it to within two hours." She went back to her own console and busied herself punching numbers onto the screen.

"Err on the side of safety," Walweb called to her. "My doctor told me to avoid excitement."

In a small locked cabin on C Deck, Peter Lyon and Michael Wong Escobaga lay on adjoining cots, facing each other. Neither of them spoke.

On G Deck, which was not partitioned into cabins, fifty black children and six black women stared stolidly into the green soup that their atmosphere had become. A hypnotic induction disk preaching obedience was being played constantly into their ears, but otherwise they were left alone.

For five days the gashopper twisted on through the starless void of the interstitial dimension, altering its course in smooth sweeps according to the new programming of its navigation board. Two hours and fifteen minutes past noon on the fifth day, the red line on the course screen intersected the blue dot that represented Mu, and Captain Walweb deflogged the drive. The squirmy purple atmosphere disappeared, and the itching in his elbows subsided. He felt the familiar nausea of emerging from the drive.

A minute later the main screen in the control room went on, and one-by-one the scanners surrounding the ship threw their visions of the outer Universe up for inspection.

"What the—" Captain Dilbert Walweb, Lord Commander of the Galactic Seas, Procurator of the Inner Circle of the Seekers of the True Mu, was struck dumb. Mu was nowhere in sight. Ragnorak was nowhere in sight. No star to be seen in any of the scanners was close enough to make a visible disk. He took a deep breath. This was the sort of emergency he was trained for, and the reason he wore the three gold starbursts on his collar. He felt even sicker.

Walweb considered the possibilities, and came to the only possible conclusion: If what the screen showed was accurate, then they were irretrievably lost in the vastness of the Universe. He swiveled around in his captain's chair and glared at the control room crew. "If this is one of you muckers playing some sort of twisted game," he said, "you're going to spend a long time chipping paint."

The giant main screen suddenly went blank. A thin piping music came from the ship's speakers. When the screen lit up again, the view of the distant Universe had been replaced by a great smiling cartoon head.

"Greetings," the head said, a visible twinkle in its right eye.

"What the hell is that?" Walweb demanded.

Tepping, the electronics officer, looked up. "I don't know where the image is coming from, Captain," he said, "but it's being carried on every screen in the ship."

"Oh, fine!" Walweb lowered his head until his nose was touching the panel in front of him, and then sat up again. "Lost in space, and cursed with an electronic poltergeist. I should never have left the Navy."

"Allow me to introduce myself," the cartoon head said, turning from side to side and nodding indiscriminately at the assembled crew and furniture. "I'm Smiley, your electronic friend and guide through the Universe."

Tepping pushed himself away from his console and scurried over to Captain Walweb. "I've tried pushing every button on that damned board," he whispered, "and I can't shut the image down. It's being piped to every screen on the ship; even the ones that are turned off are being overridden by the emergency information circuit! I'm getting a very uncomfortable feeling about this."

"What could be causing it, Tepping?" Walweb barked, with no attempt to modulate his voice. "You must have some idea. Nothing like this has ever happened before!"

"Keep your voice down, Captain," Tepping urged. "We don't want to start a panic."

"Maybe you don't," Walweb told him, moderating his voice slightly, "but I'm going to *lead* one if we don't get this straightened out pretty damn fast."

"I'll be keeping you company for the next little while," Smiley went on, leering at them from the screen, "to acquaint you with some of the more obscure facts of existence; like corporate retribution and revenge."

"That sounds like a threat," Walweb muttered. "I've never been threatened by a cartoon before, and I can't say I like it much!"

"The only thing I can figure," Tepping whispered, "is that that navigation disk you gave us fed this stuff into the main computer, along with a series of master command sequences, so we can't override it. In addition, of course, to dumping us somewhere in the middle of the Universe without a compass."

"Oh, so it's my fault, is it?" Walweb demanded irritably.

"No, sir. I didn't mean that. You had no idea, of course. But I think someone has played a horrible trick on us."

"The navigational information was phony. That seems clear." Walweb considered. "I understand that our two, ah, unwitting passengers were the source of that disk. However, considering their present state, questioning them would be a waste of time. Besides, as mere couriers, they certainly know nothing."

The smile on the cartoon face grew broader, and a wicked-looking set of teeth were revealed. "The secret you were looking for does not exist," it announced. "There is no way known to navigate in interstitial space. By resetting the controls, you merely go somewhere else—at random."

"I was right," the electronics officer said glumly. "A very uncomfortable feeling."

"You may consider yourselves a sort-of controlled experiment," the toothy Smiley face said. "Perhaps, under the pressure of imminent doom, one of you will discover a way to navigate interstitial space. And perhaps not. But it certainly seems worth a try, doesn't it? After all—consider the alternatives."

"How do you think the passengers are taking this?" Tepping whispered to Walweb.

"Perhaps we can convince them that it's all a joke," Walweb suggested. "Although Seekers are not noted for their sense of humor."

In the cabin on C Deck, Peter Lyon sat up on his cot. "It is almost time," he said.

Escobaga, who was lying on his cot watching the cartoon figure on the tiny room screen, said, "Good-o," and swung his feet over the side of his cot, pushing himself to a sitting position. "Time for what?"

"Time for me to take over this ship."

"To take over. . . . Say, young friend, you are suddenly speaking rationally and clearly, and I'm impressed; but the totality of the idea you express still seems, if I may, a mite crazy. How are we to take over this ship?"

"It will not require doing," Peter said. "It will be done."

"How come you're speaking so clearly?" Escobaga asked. "Did the bounce wear off?"

"On the contrary," Peter said. "I am as high as I ever was. Higher. I see you through all of time, Michael Wong Escobaga. I see your beginning, and I see your end."

"Splendid!" Escobaga said. "You'll be great fun at parties. If you're still bouncing, my all-seeing friend, then why aren't you mumbling inanities and dribbling into your beard?"

"I don't have a beard."

"Silly me!"

"It's a synergistic effect," Peter explained, turning to Escobaga and staring at him. There was a deep look in Peter's eyes that Escobaga found strangely disconcerting. "I was completely under the drug; I had become a bouncer, until the ship blipped into interstitial space. Then, all at once, the fog cleared. It was like my mind had been knocked loose of its moorings by the PHD, and reoriented by the new view of interstitial space, and sort of clicked back into place. I can't explain it better than that, not without working on it. The effects of the interstitial drive and the chemical action of bounce work together to create something new: a new sort of vision. I could sense this, in a vague way, before we went onto the interstitial drive, but the actual occurrence was a great shock. I was blind and halt, Michael Escobaga; and now I can function, I can speak rationally in all time that I traverse—and I see the Universe!"

"That's nice," Escobaga said cautiously. "What does it look like?"

"Nobody on bounce has ever been in interstitial space before," Peter said. "But they knew! They all knew! This is what's waiting for all of them! They tried to tell me, but I had no idea what they were talking about."

"A familiar sensation," Escobaga said. "What are we talking about?"

Peter stood up and stretched. "Do you know where we are now?" he asked.

"Lost in space," Escobaga replied. "Without a paddle."

"I know where we are," Peter told him. "I know where everything is. This—accident—of taking a bouncer along on an interstitial trip has solved the problem of navigating in interstitial space. I can do it. Any bouncer could. And the trip will cure them. They can see the lines in space, like the lines in time, and travel along them."

"I take it back," Escobaga said. "You are mumbling inanities. Lucky for you you have no beard."

There was a noise at the door, and it slid open. A tall beautiful black woman wearing only a belted black leotard stood in the doorway. "If this isn't crisis and confusion, then I've never seen one," she said. "These locks pick easy." She replaced a small tool into a flat pouch, and stuck it back on the belt around her waist. "You must be Peter Lyon."

"Saralu Ngaxu," Peter said. "It is an honor to meet you. Come, let us help each other."

"Ah, why the brevity of clothing?" Escobaga asked Saralu. "Not that I mind, you understand."

"If I'm out of my area, they'll grab me anyway. It doesn't matter what I'm wearing," Saralu told him. "And I was tired of those slave clothes. Besides, they've got other things to worry about now than what happened to my gray dress."

"You go up to the bridge and find the captain," Peter told Escobaga. "Tell him I will be there shortly to save the ship."

"He'll have us both locked up again," Escobaga predicted.

"Not necessarily," Peter said. "He won't be pleased, but I think I can make him go along—by the force of public pressure. I have to do a few things first—with Saralu's help—and we have a good chance of making it home."

"I thought you could see the future," Saralu said.

"I can," Peter told her. "But it is indeterminate. The possibility of free will, and just random chance, can alter possibilities. The timeline that I am on, and that I see, is not the only possible one. But entering any of the others would, at this time, involve my death, so I favor this one."

"What of the alternative that would involve your death?" Saralu asked. "What would that mean for the rest of us?"

"What I see is the destruction of the ship," Peter said. "My death is your death."

"A consummation most devoutly to be avoided," Escobaga said.

"I can empathize with that." Saralu said. "What of the children?"

"If we are successful, they will go back home. Which, I believe, is an orphanage in South Africa."

"Then let's get to it," Saralu said.

A minor sort of chaos had descended upon the ship. The human animal, never wholly rational at the best of times, may become positively erratic when faced with an unfamiliar danger. A disciplined crew under a firm captain might have held things together, but the gashopper *Ra* had neither.

When Peter and Saralu reached the main passenger lounge, they found it full of would-be Muvian settlers trying to make sense of what was happening. The room had divided into six major shouting matches, with individual Seekers moving from the fringe of one group to the next, trying to hear something they could understand. Many were standing in front of the room's large screen, watching the cartoon face articulate its threatening inanities. A fistfight that had broken out in one corner of the room was being watched with interest by one clot of people, who did nothing to stop it.

"There certainly are a lot of Seekers," Saralu commented, as they stood by the door unnoticed.

"There's one born every minute," Peter said. "Attract their attention."

"How do you propose I should do that?" Saralu asked.

"Go stand in the middle of the room."

Saralu shook her head. "My daddy warned me not to get involved with no sweet-talking white man," she said. "But do I listen?" With seven quick strides she was in the midst of the chaos—and there she stood, legs wide, arms akimbo, defiantly staring about the room.

At first she was hardly noticed, and then she was largely ignored. Most of the settlers had not been informed of the subservient status of blacks in their new society, and so the presence of a tall, dominant, angry, beautiful black woman standing amidst them struck them as unusual, but not wonderful. And they were in no mood to deal with the merely unusual.

Some few of them, however, were filled with wonder. They wondered what in the name of the Elder Gods she was doing there—and how a black woman who looked like *that* had gotten aboard this ship in the first place.

Singly, they acted. One beefy cabin steward accosted her. "What the hell are *you* doing here?" he inquired. "Get back to your quarters!"

Saralu didn't believe in wasting energy, or fighting fair. She floored him with one punch to the windpipe.

The second approached more cautiously. "You did this!" he yelled at her. "You messed up the drive so we'd get lost in space!"

Saralu didn't argue with him. She merely rabbit-punched him in the solar plexus, and then chopped him across the back of the neck as he doubled over. He landed on his nose, and paid no further attention to the proceedings.

Peter, in the meantime, was going from group to group and muttering, "See that black woman over there? Listen to her—she'll save us!"

After about ten minutes of this, the room grew silent. Even the fight died of inertia as everyone turned to watch Saralu, staring curiously at the tall black woman, as though they expected fire to emerge from her nostrils.

"Listen here," Saralu said softly. "Listen here," making them crane their necks and cup their ears to hear what she said. Make them want to hear you first—make them work for it—and they'll respect what you say.

When the silence had grown complete, she raised her voice. "You got yourselves into this," she said. "Stranded in the depths of space, with no way back."

"What did we do?" one man demanded. "We're just trying to colonize a new planet."

"The fates are not kind," Saralu said. "You followed the wrong leaders, and you followed them blindly, and for that you should be destroyed. But there are innocents on this ship, and we shall try to defy fate—and there is one among you who can do that!"

Most of the people in the room had no idea what she was talking about, but it didn't matter. It sounded as pretentious as the "truths" they had been taught as Seekers—and offered a way out. They listened.

After Saralu had softened them up, Peter joined her in the middle of the room. "In a few moments comes the first crisis point," he murmured to her. "And upon small and subtle shifts do our lives, and the fate of this ship, depend." Then he turned to the group of settlers, who were beginning to mutter among themselves. "Hello," he said. "My name is Peter, and I can take you home."

The ship's security officer and three of his burly yeomen came into the room after Peter had been talking for less than a minute. They paused at the scene before them, and the security officer pointed an accusing finger. "What the hell is *she* doing here?" he demanded. "Get her out of here and back down to G Deck! That guy in the blue tunic too; he don't belong here. We got enough troubles!" The yeomen started across the room, pushing people aside.

"If he moves us," Peter told the crowd, "then I will be powerless to help you. It's your decision."

"How do we know you can find your way back?" someone in the crowd yelled. "That Smiley face said we're lost for good!"

There was a murmur of agreement, and a ripple of faces turning to each other, and then back to Peter for his reply.

"Oh, fine!" Saralu said. "What a time for a Seeker to begin to doubt."

"Stop those men," Peter said, pointing to the approaching yeomen, "and I'll tell you."

There was a moment's indecision. "You people keep out of the way," the security officer yelled. "You don't want to get into trouble!"

"You know any worse trouble than we're in right now?" one of the colonists called.

"Yeah," another agreed. "You guys just stay right there until this guy finishes talking. We want to hear him."

The yeomen tried to keep moving forward, but the crowd gathered around them and, with much muttering and growling, stopped them cold.

"We are past the first crisis," Peter told Saralu in an undertone. "If they hadn't been stopped, we would have been locked up, and the situation would have rapidly deteriorated. Then some fool would have destroyed the ship's air supply three days from now."

"Get on with it," Saralu told him. "They'll get restless."

"Now," Peter told her, "comes the interesting part." He turned to the group surrounding him and raised his voice. "Here is what they didn't tell you," he said. "This gashopper does not belong to the Seekers; it was stolen from Griffin Universal."

"What were *they* doing with it?" someone yelled.

"So what?" called a large man across the room.

Peter decided to answer the second question. "So the Seekers don't know how to run it properly. That's how we got into this mess. They stole what they thought was a navigation disk from Griffin, but it was a co-opt. It co-opted the controls, stuck that cartoon face on the screens, and sent us here."

"What can you do about it?" the large man called. Peter silently blessed him.

"I can get us home. Not to Mu, because I don't know where it is;

but back to Earth. And, within a year the secret of the gashoppers is going to be revealed, and we'll find Mu again, and you'll be able to go on to Mu, or wherever else you like. If we live through this, it will open up the Universe."

"How do we know you're telling the truth?" a short woman with a small child clutched to her breast yelled out.

Peter smiled. "Try me," he said. "If I'm lying, there's no place I can hide from you."

"Why do you need us?" the large man asked.

"I need the weight of your—argument—to convince the captain to let me navigate the ship," Peter told him. "The captain doesn't want to go home. He's not going to be loved by the authorities."

"Well," the large man said, "let's do it."

He spoke for the crowd.

TWENTY-SIX

Saralu Ngaxu's helicopter dropped into the inner courtyard of her parent's house in Dastubi Watti. "Hello, daughter," Daddy Exx said as she strode into the living room. "Where you been?"

"Somewhere in the middle of the Universe," she told him.

He nodded. "Nice to have you back. How are those kids you were so worried about?"

"The last fifty will be back at the orphanage by the end of next week," she told him. "And then we're going hunting for a planet called Mu, and get the rest of them back. And if I were you, I'd start making friends with all the bouncers I could find, because they're going to be very useful people in the near future."

"It sounds like you've been busy, daughter. Don't make your daddy ask a lot of questions—tell me where you been and what you been doing."

And she did.

R07

＊　＊　＊

Shirley Vermont answered her doorbell to find Peter Lyon standing on the stoop. "Well!" she said, "and where have you been, not even calling a girl for two months?"

"Across the Universe and back again," he told her, taking her hand.

"Nice of you to come over after a trip like that, I suppose," Shirley said, trying to frown at him. "And what do you want from me?"

"Two brown-haired children—a boy and a girl—and a happy but eventful life together in some very strange places," he said, kissing her.

She pulled away. "What makes you so sure?"

Peter smiled. "Trust me on this one," he said. "Come, take a walk with me, and I'll tell you about it."

"You have a strange look in your eyes," she told him.

"That," he said, "is part of the story."